"We're going to do everything we can to find her."

He would work his fingers to the bone, exhausting every last clue until she was home.

Belle bit her luscious lower lip as if to keep it from trembling. "I never realized the danger she was in. She was scared, but many children are scared in the clinic. I wish..."

So forlorn and upset. How could one fake sincerity? He'd dealt with many criminals over the years and considered himself a good judge of when someone lied and when they didn't. Belle North wasn't affecting tears to impress him.

Kyle forgot about himself and his overwhelming need to work this case. Her shoulders were round and soft beneath his fingers as he put his hands on her to give her comfort. His gut twisted at the vulnerability etched on her worried face, the fear in her eyes mirroring his own.

For a moment they were not agent and doctor, but simply two human beings connected by a missing child.

* * *

If you're on Twitter, tell us what you think of Harlequin Romantic Suspense! #harlequinromsuspense

Dear Reader,

Have you ever planned a road map for your life only to find yourself lost and not knowing where you should end up?

That's the dilemma facing Dr. Belle North, heroine of *Rescue from Darkness*. She knows she wants to be a doctor, but family pressure nudges her toward a specialty that isn't in her heart.

What is in her heart is a strong sense of justice and working with children. So when a child gets kidnapped and all signs point to the clinic operated by her family, Belle suddenly finds her internal GPS taking her down a road she never anticipated—working with Special Agent Kyle Anderson.

Kyle doesn't like doctors. Not one bit. Not since his beloved daughter died in the care of a pediatrician. Yet to do the right thing and find the missing girl, he has to team up with Belle. Like Belle, Kyle had planned a road map for his life but suddenly found himself without a compass.

In working together to rescue the child before it's too late, Belle and Kyle will find themselves adjusting their previous trajectories and finding new directions. They will realize that life, for all of its twists and turns, is precious and worth every step of the journey.

I hope you enjoy *Rescue from Darkness*.

Happy reading!

Bonnie Vanak

RESCUE FROM DARKNESS

Bonnie Vanak

HARLEQUIN
ROMANTIC
SUSPENSE

Recycling programs
for this product may
not exist in your area.

ISBN-13: 978-1-335-62663-9

Rescue from Darkness

Copyright © 2020 by Bonnie Vanak

All rights reserved. No part of this book may be used or reproduced in
any manner whatsoever without written permission except in the case of
brief quotations embodied in critical articles and reviews.

This is a work of fiction. Names, characters, places and incidents
are either the product of the author's imagination or are used fictitiously.
Any resemblance to actual persons, living or dead, businesses,
companies, events or locales is entirely coincidental.

This edition published by arrangement with Harlequin Books S.A.

For questions and comments about the quality of this book,
please contact us at CustomerService@Harlequin.com.

Harlequin Enterprises ULC
22 Adelaide St. West, 40th Floor
Toronto, Ontario M5H 4E3, Canada
www.Harlequin.com

Printed in U.S.A.

New York Times and *USA TODAY* bestselling author **Bonnie Vanak** is passionate about romance novels and telling stories. A former newspaper reporter, she worked as a journalist for a large international charity for several years, traveling to countries such as Haiti to report on the sufferings of the poor. Bonnie lives in Florida with her husband, Frank, and is a member of Romance Writers of America. She loves to hear from readers. She can be reached through her website, bonnievanak.com.

Books by Bonnie Vanak

Harlequin Romantic Suspense

Rescue from Darkness

The Coltons of Red Ridge

His Forgotten Colton Fiancée

SOS Agency

Navy SEAL Seduction
Shielded by the Cowboy SEAL
Navy SEAL Protector

Harlequin Nocturne

Phoenix Force

The Shadow Wolf
The Covert Wolf
Phantom Wolf
Demon Wolf

The Empath
Enemy Lover
Immortal Wolf

Visit the Author Profile page at Harlequin.com.

This book is dedicated to our beloved Holly, who has given us so much love and taught us the value of fighting the good fight.

Chapter 1

It was over, and he silently breathed a sigh of relief no one was hurt or killed in the shootout. Now he had to deal with the tough part—talking to the kid.

He'd rather interrogate the bastard who started shooting up everyone. Easier job.

Not that he didn't want to kill the SOB. In his book, terrorizing a child deserved more than handcuffs and a prison cell. But he was a professional and, long ago, learned to control his emotions in the field.

FBI special agent Kyle Anderson holstered his SIG Sauer. Hands on hips, he surveyed the scene at Glades International Airport. What a mess. Shocked civilians peering outside the terminal windows, terrified travelers clutching their luggage as local law enforcement kept everything in control.

The smell of gunpowder, jet fuel and something slick and coppery invaded his nostrils. He strode over to the five-year-old victim. The boy had been snatched from a playground by the suspect, a known felon who suddenly decided to audition for Father of the Year. Towheaded, brown eyes wide, the child sat on the curb, guarded by two zealous police officers standing nearby.

Kyle watched his partner escort the boy's absentee father

to a waiting vehicle. As the patrol car growled away, the boy burst into sobs.

His heart twisted as he sat down next to the terrified child. He loved and hated this part of the job. Children were like glass, and glass shattered.

He preferred taking down hardened criminals. They never screwed with his emotions.

"You're safe now, Michael," he soothed. "No one's going to hurt you. Your mom will be here any minute. We called her."

Trite speech. Meaningless when it came to reassurance. The boy kept crying. Of course the kid didn't believe him. Who would?

Kyle gave an awkward pat to the boy's shoulder, wishing he could calm him. Hell, the child had witnessed a gun battle and the man who was supposed to be his protector, his dad, fire an AK-47. Bullet holes peppered the walls of the parking garage, and several car-door windows were shattered.

He couldn't imagine what this kind of violence did to a small child. Michael should be playing peewee soccer or glued to a tablet video game. Not huddling in the backseat of a car, hands to his ears, terrified he'd die.

Not for the first time, another child's face came to mind. Brutally, he thrust the memory away. Now was not the time to think of Kasey.

Both he and his partner were members of the Bureau's Child Abduction Rapid Deployment Team, sent in to retrieve missing children. They'd gotten a break with Michael when a passenger recognized the car's license plate from the Amber Alert flashing on the airport parking lot marquee.

"Michael, I know you're scared, but I need you to think. Was there anyone else with your dad when he took you from the playground?"

No answer but sobs.

Okay, this was so not going well. Kyle gathered all his patience. Not that he had much, but this was a terrified little boy and he deserved more than getting grilled about his not-so-terrific father.

From his trouser pocket, he pulled out the silver dollar he always carried. Kyle held it up. "Want to see a magic trick? I can make money disappear. Without even going shopping."

At his wink, Michael stopped crying, stared at his hand. Rolling the coin between his fingers, he moved quickly, sliding it into his other hand.

Michael watched, tears still trickling down his cheeks. But his eyes were wide with apparent fascination.

"Where did it go?" He frowned. "I know. You have it."

"I don't have it," the boy told him.

Kyle reached behind Michael's ear, pretended to pluck the coin from behind his ear. Michael started to sob and scream again.

Damn. The trick always worked to pacify frightened children in the past.

Maybe you lost your touch.

Maybe you never had it to lose.

The silver dollar clinked to the concrete as he reached out to soothe the terrified boy. "It's okay," he crooned. "You're safe."

Over his shoulder the smell of floral perfume cut through the stench of fear and gunpowder. It was such a welcome scent that he inhaled deeply, grateful for the reprieve from violence and trauma.

"Hi, Michael," a sultry feminine voice said.

Thank the good Lord a relative finally got here.

But let's not jump to conclusions.

"Who are you?" he demanded, craning his head. Sunlight in his eyes, he couldn't make out the newcomer's features.

Instead of answering, the woman thrust out a box of cherry juice. "Here, sweetie. Drink this—it will help you."

Kyle grabbed the juice box before Michael could. "Who are you?"

"The officers asked me to look after him," she said calmly.

"It's okay, Agent Anderson," one of the cops guarding Michael assured. "I can vouch for Belle. She was at the airport, so I asked her to help with the kid. She's volunteered for us before."

"Volunteer, huh?" he grunted, picking up his coin and pocketing it. "Doing what? Delivering drinks?"

Her expression smoothed out. "I chair the policeman's benefit ball in Estancia Pointe every season."

Figured. A rich woman who thought she had the right to stroll onto his crime scene just because she knew how to run some fancy gala.

Kyle unwrapped the plastic straw, thrust it into the foil opening and gave it to Michael, who sucked hard. A little color had returned to his face.

He turned, noticed the woman's white lab coat, the blue stitching. Dr. Belle North. A doctor. Terrific. Last thing he needed right now was a rich medical doctor who thought she could save the day.

His earlier bad mood returned. "He doesn't need a doctor. The EMTs said he's not injured."

Belle North didn't even look at him but focused on Michael. "Some wounds are worse on the inside, Agent…"

"FBI special agent Kyle Anderson."

"He's traumatized."

"And you think a juice box can cure that, Dr. Phil?"

Now she did look up as she straightened. Tall, willowy, she was lovely, in an upper-class, polished way.

He liked his women petite, dark-haired and ordinary.

Hell, who was he fooling? He hadn't been in a relationship in years. He was thirty-one years old and career came first.

The job came first. Always. The job never let him down or abandoned him.

"The name is Dr. North, Agent. He's probably shocky and needs some sugar. Not to mention a quiet place away from all these guns and uniforms."

"It's a crime scene," he said tersely. "He's a witness. We need to determine if there was an accomplice working with the suspect."

"Can't you ask him later, when his mother gets here?" Dr. North sat next to Michael, rubbed his back. The boy rested against her, staring at Kyle's right arm.

Ignoring her, Kyle squatted by Michael. "Michael, did you see anyone else with your dad when he told you to get into the car? Did your dad talk to anyone on the phone?"

The boy shook his head, pointed to Kyle's sleeve. "You have a boo-boo."

Stinging pain laced his skin as he removed his jacket, saw the bright red blood oozing on his upper right arm. Kyle examined the wound with a rueful look. "Ruined another suit," he muttered. "Terrific."

Guess someone did get hit after all. No wonder the poor kid had freaked out when he reached behind his ear. The coppery scent of blood swam in his nostrils. With all his concentration homed on the shooting and bringing down the suspect without harming the child, he'd never felt the bullet graze. Already he could feel the descent from the adrenaline rush. It would be a tough one this time.

"I can treat that," Dr. North offered.

Mouth flattened, he shook his head. "It's nothing."

"If infection sets in, it won't be 'nothing.'"

"I'll pour some whiskey on it when I get home. After I file my report."

She rolled her eyes. "Such a cowboy. Perhaps you should

stop by a craft store for a needle and thread to sew it up yourself."

He considered. "Naw. Office supply store. Staples work better."

Her pretty mouth quirked, as if she struggled to suppress a smile.

Bet she'd be even prettier when she did smile. Right. He wasn't here to flirt, especially not with anyone from the medical profession. He'd take out his own appendix with a Swiss Army knife before setting foot in a hospital again.

"Michael, you're certain your father didn't have any friends or anyone else he talked to when you were in the car with him? Or name a place where he wanted to take you? Do you remember anything at all?"

Kyle added gently, "Take your time."

He beckoned to Roarke, his partner. The FBI agent joined Kyle and listened attentively.

The boy's brow wrinkled as he finished his juice. "He said something about Steve's house. Steve has a boat and me and Steve would go fishing in the Guf of Nexico while Daddy went to Phoenix."

Gulf of Mexico. "Check it out," he told Roarke. "Stephen Tyles is a former cell mate of Andre's, has a trailer in Key Largo."

"If Irma didn't destroy it," his partner noted, referring to the hurricane that devastated many Keys properties.

Kyle stood, grating his teeth as pain gripped him. They had a massive crime scene to investigate, and witnesses to interview. Not to mention he itched to take down Tyles, a petty drug dealer who wouldn't hesitate to sell his own mother, let alone someone else's child.

He'd bet his annual salary that Andre planned to sell his son to Tyles for quick cash, and the fishing trip Michael took would be a boat ride out of the country.

A police officer brought over a distraught woman, who ran and hugged Michael. Finally, the mother.

He started to get up, approach her when Dr. North stepped in front of him. "Let them be for a few minutes. He needs his mother, not interrogation. And you need treatment. You're bleeding."

Scowling, he shook off her hand. "Go find someone else to practice your voodoo on."

Soon as he muttered the words, Kyle felt a pang of regret. She was only trying to help.

Yeah, and what happened the last time a doctor tried to help? Not going there again.

"I don't practice voodoo, but in your case, I'd make an exception." She gave him a singularly sweet smile.

Roarke grinned. "Ignore him, Doc. He gets in a bad mood when someone shoots him. Like a cranky bear with a bad tooth."

"I've found duct tape helps cure difficult patients. Applied to the mouth, it works wonders," she said, her smile more a display of pearly white teeth.

Despite his irritation and the burning pain lancing his arm, Kyle felt a flash of pure male interest. Doctor or not, she stirred the ashes of a long-dead fire.

At least he'd thought that particular fire was dead.

"You're pretty when you grit your teeth like that," he told her. "Did you learn that in finishing school?"

Her smile slipped. "The only culture you have, Agent Anderson, is in a petri dish filled with bacteria."

Touché. He grinned, wanting to laugh, but his arm was screaming by now.

"Come on, Mr. Grumpy. Let's dress that arm before you bleed all over the front seat of my nice new SUV." Roarke steered him toward the waiting ambulance.

He stole a peek over his shoulder at Belle North. She glanced at him, looked away.

Then glanced back at him again.

Pretty, smart and compassionate woman.

Too bad she was a doctor.

What did he care? He'd never see her again.

Not if he could help it.

Chapter 2

He bit her finger. Hard. Some days, she wondered if it was worth sacrificing her free time.

And then other times, she'd receive a shy smile, a quiet "thanks, Doc," and the rewards of working with children were all clear.

Belle North glanced down at the shih tzu dog curled up on a fat brown pillow. "Some job you're doing. You're supposed to calm the kids down."

The dog lifted his head, wagged his tail.

Belle studied the tiny teeth marks on her injured index finger. "At least we know that patient didn't need dental work."

Shrugging, she ripped the disposable paper off the exam table and poked her head into the hallway. "I'm ready for the next one!"

Twenty children and adults already seen, and she hadn't had time for more than a few sips of coffee. The winter season had arrived in South Florida, and with the cooler temperatures swept in the annual influx of transients and migrant workers.

All patients at the Harold Donald Free Clinic.

Belle washed her hands and eyed the pint-size patient who walked into the room. Big eyes, dark hair and a miasma of fear so thick her heart sank. Mom was the same, looking around with the mistrust Belle had seen on many of her patients.

The father walked into the room with them, his gaze dark and stone-cold.

A slight shiver raced down her spine. Most times the mothers, not the fathers, accompanied the children. Unlike most of her clients, he looked different.

On instinct, she memorized the man. Pockmarked face, thin mouth, dressed in well-pressed dark trousers and a starched white shirt. A battered ball cap with a tractor-company logo hid much of his brown hair.

Belle scanned the paperwork every parent had to fill out. Anna Rodriguez, age six. She recognized the address on the form as a local homeless shelter. No allergies to dogs, which is why they brought Anna in here instead of letting Dr. George see her.

She gestured to the dog. "Come here."

Time for her pet to work her magic. Kids and dogs were like ice cream and cake. They went together.

The dog ambled toward the new patient, who eyed him with the same mistrust she eyed Belle. Anna was small, with olive skin, clear forest green eyes tipped with long black lashes, a sweep of inky black hair and high cheekbones. Model-worthy, except she wore tattered clothing that bore faint stains. Despite the clothing, she looked healthy and well-fed. She squeezed a battered brown teddy bear, hugging it tight.

The father frowned, looking around. "Where's Dr. Patterson? We saw him last time."

"He had a family emergency and had to leave suddenly. I'm taking his patients."

Belle frowned. She'd asked the nurse to pull charts on all the patients, but Anna did not have one. "If she's been here before, she should have a medical record with us."

The father didn't meet her gaze. "That's your problem if you lost her records."

Maybe her records were misplaced. Crouching down to eye level, Belle patted her pet.

"Anna, come here. You can pet him. His name is Boo." Anna did not move.

Usually when her pint-size patients played with Boo, Belle would take out her stethoscope and use it to show the child. For many it was their first visit to a doctor. But Anna was stiff and showed no interest in the dog.

Belle kept patting the dog. The man snorted. "Will this take long? I have to get back to work."

She knew how to deal with distrusting and impatient people. Bella offered her brightest smile and gestured to the chairs near the exam table. "Please, have a seat, Mr. Rodriguez. I promise to take good care of your daughter."

"Oh no, he isn't my father," Anna blurted out.

At the man's glare, Anna went quiet. He sat in the chair, and folded his arms, the mother beside him. Anna still trembled.

Belle took her stethoscope and showed it to Anna. "This is my instrument for examining your heart. Would you like to listen?"

Still the child did not move, nor smile.

The mother touched her daughter's arm and spoke in rapid Spanish. "It's all right, *mi corazón*. Let the doctor examine you and we'll go home. Remember?"

Anna gave a jerky nod.

Belle sat on the floor, petting her dog. "Poor Boo. He was hoping you'd like him. He's a special pup with a special name."

Anna took a tentative step forward. "Like in *boo-boo*?"

"Yup. That's where he got his name. He was a stray found living in a ditch. Hold out your hand and let him smell you."

Boo sniffed and then licked the small palm Anna held out. Finally she smiled.

"It tickles!"

The man grunted. "Dogs have germs. What kind of doctor are you? Are you even a real doctor?"

Anna's smile dropped. She squeezed her toy harder. One thumb went into her mouth as she nibbled on the edge of a fingernail.

"I just completed my pediatric internship last year, Mr.... Rodriguez?" Belle gave him a pointed look. "Are you the child's guardian?"

The woman said nothing, but he gave her a level look. "I'm a friend. Rosa doesn't speak much English, so she asked me to come here with Anna."

"I'll need your name for our files."

"Smith," he shot back. "John Smith."

Right. And I'm Pocahontas.

Best if she could get him out of the room. Sometimes macho men responded better to other men instead of a woman doctor. And she wanted to make sure Anna wasn't a victim of child abuse because the child was clearly fearful. Belle had set up a special procedure for that process.

Step one: get the parents out of the room. Including the "friend."

"Excuse me a moment." Belle opened the door, saw the physician's assistant in the hallway. "Dr. George, can you come in here for a moment?"

When the PA entered, she gestured to Smith and Rosa. "Can you go over the allergy form with Ms. Rodriguez and her friend, Mr. Smith, who helps interpret?"

Fortunately, George didn't need any additional hints. "I apologize. Our receptionist forgot to give you the extra paperwork. Can you please come back into the waiting room fill it out? It won't take long, but it is complicated and I may have to help you," George told Rosa and her friend.

The form was long and tedious to fill out. And quite distracting.

"Why? Why didn't she tell me there would be more papers?" Smith asked, frowning.

"Routine paperwork about Anna's medical history," George assured him.

"I already filled that out." The man scowled.

"It will only take a minute. It's to make sure the child receives the best care, and the doctor doesn't prescribe medications that might make Anna sick in case of an allergic reaction," George assured him.

The man glanced at Anna and smiled, but it didn't meet his eyes. "Come on, Rosa," he said in Spanish.

The woman immediately stood and went to him. Smith looked at Anna. "Your mama and I will be right back."

Step two: address the patient's physical concerns.

When they left, Belle lifted her onto the exam table. An odd odor clung to her clothing. Her nose wrinkled. The child's clothing was wrinkled and slightly dirty, and also carried an earthy scent.

"Anna, can I have your teddy bear? I promise you'll get him back right away."

"No." Anna hugged the toy harder. "No, don't take Andy Bear away!"

"It's okay," she crooned. "But I need you to lower him from your chest so I can hear your heart."

Anna shook her head. As Belle moved the stethoscope's disc past the bear to put on Anna's chest, the child whimpered.

"That's a pretty ribbon Andy Bear has," she told Anna, moving the stethoscope away. "Did the bear come with it?"

"No." Anna shook her head hard and clutched the bear. "Mama cut it off an old dress for me."

Well, she had other methods of reassuring her patients. Belle took a paper cup filled with crayons and a sketch pad. "Why don't you draw me a photo of Boo while I listen to your heart?"

As the girl worked on her drawing, Belle listened to her heart and lungs. A few times Anna coughed. Then she had Anna remove her shirt and inspected her for signs of abuse.

"Anna, has anyone ever hurt you or touched you there?" Belle made a gesture to the girl's privates.

Anna looked puzzled. "No."

"Because it's okay to tell me. I'm a doctor and I want to help you."

More confused looks. "No."

To her immense relief, she found no signs of bruises or abuse on Anna's body. She asked more questions and became satisfied the girl was simply scared. Kids were fearful in the clinic, especially if it was their first time visiting a doctor.

Part of her work was also diagnosing a child's living conditions. With Smith, impatient to return to work and distrustful of doctors, she would not get real answers. The mother had been quiet.

Judging from the dampness of Anna's clothing, she wondered if they slept outside.

"Did you have breakfast today, Anna?"

"Yes. We have burritos with frijoles and cheese and eggs."

Well, at least she was eating. "That's delicious. I like scrambled eggs and bacon, but I need to stick to oatmeal and fruit." Belle patted her thin waistline. "What's your favorite food?"

Expecting her to name something cultural, or as simple as peanut butter and jelly, she was surprised to hear Anna blurt out, "Beef tenderloin with chipotle sauce."

Belle laughed. "Were you watching a food show?"

Her nose wrinkled. "We don't have television."

"Oh. So you've actually had medallions of beef?" Belle felt Anna's pulse, and then her throat.

"Yes. It was really good."

What a curious little girl. But her past didn't concern Belle as much as Anna's present. "Anna, is Mr. Smith really a family friend?"

The girl glanced up at her. "He and my mama... Mama really likes him."

"Has he ever tried to hurt or touch you?" she asked.

More confused looks. "No."

Belle listened to Anna's lungs again to make sure they were clear.

"How did your clothes get dirty?" she asked.

Maybe the child was neglected and not abused.

"I was playing outside and then we had to come here right away." The child sniffled.

Belle went to the counter to get a tongue depressor. When she turned back, Anna handed her a folded square of paper. "I tried to draw Boo," she whispered. "Don't look at it until you're home. Put it on your refrigerator."

Smiling, Belle pocketed the drawing in her white lab coat.

"Have you been living outside, Anna? It's okay to tell me," she said gently.

The girl stared at the floor. "We were in a trailer, but had to leave. Mama was too scared to go to the shelter. We rented a tent at a park. Mama said we'll have a new home soon with John, but it won't be like anyplace we've lived because we'll move around a lot, which makes Mama happy. She doesn't like staying in one place. John wants to marry Mama. But we have to wait for him to get money."

That explained the man's attitude. She'd seen it before in proud men who hid their shame behind anger and arrogance.

She smiled. "That's nice. What kind of house would you like to live in, Anna?"

"A nice one, where I can have my own bedroom. Maybe a swing in the backyard and a garden where Mama can grow peppers." Anna stroked the bear's head.

Belle felt the child's lymph nodes. Slightly swollen. She glanced at her medical history. Missing the childhood immunizations needed for enrollment in public school.

"Anna, where do you go to school? Around here?" She was old enough for kindergarten.

Anna nibbled on the edge of a thumbnail. "Mama says I can go to school when John takes us to our new home."

Belle fished in the jar on the counter and handed Anna a lollipop. "I give all my brave patients lollipops. Do you like cherry? They're low sugar, but yummy."

Anna nodded and unwrapped the treat, then sucked on it.

A knock came at the door.

George entered, looking apologetic, followed by Rosa and John Smith. Smith had coffee in his hands.

"Sorry to interrupt, Doctor. She's finished with the paperwork."

"Good. So am I. Dr. George, I'll need two prescriptions, please." She told him what they were. Belle couldn't write prescriptions since she hadn't completed her medical residency and lacked a medical license.

Smith sneered. "And you call yourself a doctor?"

Belle forced a smile. Such a disagreeable man. Part of her wanted to try to hold him here, follow through on the nagging feeling he gave her. But patients still crowded the waiting room and they were shorthanded today.

"Anna is fine. Slight cough, upper respiratory infection. Nothing major," Belle reassured the mother. "Dr. George is writing you a prescription for antibiotics and cough syrup."

New emotion flickered in the woman's eyes. Same kind she'd seen before—shame. No money to pay the high-priced pharmacy. No need to alert everyone in the waiting room that these people couldn't afford medicine.

As the PA handed Belle the scripts, she gave them to Rosa. "Let's step outside for a moment." She offered a reassuring smile. "I could use some fresh air."

She walked outside the front door with Anna and her mother. Smith had already gone to the car and started it. Belle scribbled the scripts, adding a special smile face to indicate she'd foot the bill, and handed them over to Anna's mother.

"Take these to Skipper's Pharmacy down the street. The medicine is good, but the prices are even better. You won't pay."

Belle started to tell her about the blood work and making a follow-up appointment when a car horn blared.

"Let's go," Smith yelled out the open car window.

With a chorus of "thanks" and "bye, Boo," the mother and daughter rushed away and climbed into the car. Belle waved as they drove off.

On impulse, she scribbled down the license plate number of the rusting brown sedan. The bumper sagged to one side. She didn't like Smith, but Anna clearly showed no signs of abuse. Or even neglect. Later, she'd call Rosa's cell phone.

After returning to the exam room, she pushed a strand of long blond hair out of her face. Fifth prescription she'd subsidized today, but she didn't care.

She glanced at Boo. "You didn't need that Harry Winston diamond collar. You're not that kind of dog."

Boo wagged his tail.

If her patients could bring themselves to trust her and find a way to the free clinic, she could find a way to give them the medicine the children needed. The clinic was the only free clinic helping low income patients in the area.

The exam table had duct tape across the cracked leather, but it sufficed. Maybe the paint was dull and the floor scuffed, but Belle had brightened the room with cartoon paintings and the ceiling was blue, studded with pink clouds and unicorns.

It helped to have something pretty and bright for the kids to look at when they had to lie back so she could examine them.

After examining five more patients, she took a break. This kind of work made her forget all about self-care, but nothing she could ever buy for herself equaled the pleasure felt at the end of a long day of seeing patients and knowing she helped them heal.

Briefly she wondered about the FBI agent she'd met the other day. So handsome and striking, but growly.

Bullet wounds would do that to you. I wonder what he's like when he's not in pain?

Dismissing the man, because who had time to think about men, she sipped her water. Belle started making mental notes about supplies when the door opened.

Her good mood evaporated. She turned away.

"What happened to all your good manners, Clint? Did knocking go out of style?"

Her older brother snorted. "I'm in charge of the foundation that funds this place. I don't need to knock."

What a dork. Arrogant, entitled.

Seeing Boo, he squatted down and rubbed the dog's ears. "Hey, buddy."

Boo's tail thumped the ground as Clint looked around. "Do you need anything?"

Her heart softened. "We could use more tongue depressors and gloves."

Clint sat on the exam table, his polished leather wing tips glinting in the overhead fluorescent light. "I meant lunch. It's after two."

Stomach grumbling, she shook her head. "Thanks. I'll eat later."

"Belle, Belle, the self-sacrificing martyr. Well, I suppose when you get a cardiology residency, you won't have time to eat, either." His nose wrinkled. "But at least then you'll be making money."

Belle clenched her fingers around her stethoscope. Each time Clint visited, she felt the familiar poke of guilt for failing to live up to the family standard.

As if only making money counted.

And why wouldn't it? Her family legacy might as well have dollar signs on their coat of arms. Great-Grandfather was an oil baron and all the Norths after him had impressive résumés that did their families proud.

I'm the black sheep. Tempted to open her mouth and bleat at Clint, she instead pointed to the door. "Out. I'm seeing patients."

Clint jumped off the table. "You should get married and have a family of your own to make Mother happy."

"You mean get her off your case because she hasn't seen progeny from you?" Belle asked sweetly.

Clint frowned, knitting his dark gold brows together. "I'm focusing on my career. Too busy to have a relationship. When was the last time you even had a date?"

"And what about my career?" Belle inhaled a calming breath.

"You're the girl, Belle. Mother lives for the day she can plan your wedding."

Silly thing to live for. "She lives for all the charities she helps. That's her life. Not mine."

He glanced around the room. "If you worked full-time with Dr. Sanders, you'd be too busy to waste your time here."

She had a job, working three days a week at a cardiology practice owned by her father's golf buddy.

But the clinic gave her the most joy.

Her family had founded the clinic, and it operated out

of the family's foundation. Donating to charity was acceptable and expected.

Getting up close and personal to the very people they helped? Her family still shook their heads over her decision.

Eight months ago she graduated medical school but resisted family pressure on getting her cardiac surgery match. Belle struck a compromise. Gap year. She'd work part-time for a well-established cardiac surgeon and apply for the next cardiology match. In exchange her parents would leave her alone to live her life without restrictions for twelve months.

She'd failed to tell them she'd also applied for a pediatric match in Washington, DC, at the same time she'd applied for the cardiology match in Boston.

Surgery wasn't getting up close and personal, but it was prestigious. Yet she didn't want to hide behind a mask in an operating room.

She wanted to be involved.

She wanted to please her parents.

"It's called helping people, Clint. Not wasting time."

He took out his phone. "What other supplies do you need?"

She rattled off a long list. He scribbled them down on his cell, then pocketed the phone.

"Mother is expecting you tonight for dinner. Don't disappoint her again like last weekend." Hand on the doorknob, he turned. "And there's two men from the FBI in the waiting room. That's why I came in here to see you."

Unease trickled down her spine. "For what?"

"Something about missing kids." Clint frowned. "The special agent in charge called the foundation and I told them to stop by."

"What missing kids?" she demanded. "Why didn't I hear about this before?"

Clint's gaze flicked to the ground. "It has nothing to do

with the clinic. Some kids vanished and they've been here in the past. Feds are checking all angles. That's all."

She wasn't in the mood for investigators to poke around the facility, ask questions and scare away patients. After Clint's lecture, she only wanted to get on with her workload and then head home with Boo. A chilled glass of chardonnay, a good book and maybe takeout Chinese food.

But the thought of children vanishing after they'd visited here bothered her more. "I didn't hear anything about missing children."

Clint refused to meet her gaze. "It hasn't been on the news. Guess they've kept it quiet."

With all the Amber Alerts these days? "Tell them to come in right now to my office."

She'd rather deal with this and send them on their way than have her patients upset with the agents lingering in the lobby.

When the two agents entered the postage stamp–sized room, she did a double take. Boo, sitting on his pillow under the window, wagged his tail.

"You again?" Belle felt a stir of female interest and pure professional dismay.

"Me again." Unsmiling, he regarded her.

She recognized them both immediately from the airport encounter.

The other agent looked amused as he nodded at her. "Nice to see you again, Dr. North. I'm special agent Roarke Calhoun and this is my partner, special agent Kyle Anderson."

Calhoun had dark hair and green eyes that held intelligence. He had an alertness about him, and his straight posture and formality indicated ex-military.

He gave her an admiring glance. It didn't irritate her because she was used to men staring at her. With her long blond hair and brown eyes, she'd often been asked why she didn't model.

Special agent Kyle Anderson studied her as if he'd never seen a woman before, sweeping his ice-blue gaze up and down her body in a caress that wasn't sexual, but quite intentional. His inky black hair was clipped short. An intriguing streak of gray shot through a hank of hair hanging over his forehead. He had raw edges that sent her pulse skittering and swiped away her breath. Anderson exuded pure masculinity and he was handsome enough to make her feel feminine and aware.

Make her forget she was a professional physician. *Enough. Deal with them and send them away.*

Unlike Roarke, Kyle Anderson didn't smile. But his deep voice and brute masculinity made her own palms damp. It had been a long time since a man made her sit up and pay attention. After the urbane, polished men who'd filled her social calendar and her circle, he was refreshingly...

Direct. Belle suspected FBI agent Kyle Anderson harbored no guile, and no patience for games, either.

"How can I help you?" she asked.

She hadn't meant to make her tone so sharp, but Anderson's scrutiny rattled her composure.

Anderson studied her with his cool gaze. "A child is missing. And we believe she is connected to this clinic."

Chapter 3

A missing child, one of the worst nightmares for any parent. Surely it could not have happened here. But she would help in any way she could.

"Would you like to sit?" Belle indicated the two chairs squeezed into a corner near her desk. Roarke thanked her, but remained standing.

Anderson shook his head. "I'm not here for a social call." His gaze narrowed. "Especially not with a doctor. I don't like them."

Terrific. An FBI agent with an attitude. Belle lifted her chin. "I don't like federal agents coming in here and disrupting my clinic."

For a moment they faced off like two Western gunslingers. Belle's heart skipped a beat. Instinct warned this was a dangerous man. The ruthless type who would stop at nothing to get what he wanted. Good thing he was an FBI agent and not a hired killer.

Agent Calhoun cleared his throat and broke the tension.

"We've traced the girl's last known visits to your clinic, Dr. North," Calhoun said in a mild voice. "Do you have security cameras?"

She nodded. "But they're outside only."

"We'll need to see your tapes. Who funds this operation?" Kyle demanded.

Belle bristled. "You already know the answer, otherwise, you'd never have called my family's foundation. My family owns and operates this clinic."

"Your brother, Clint, was helpful. But you're the person we need to talk with because you're here more frequently." Calhoun was more approachable than the scowling Anderson. Still, she remained wary.

"Dr. North, how long have you worked here?" Calhoun asked.

"I've volunteered here Wednesday through Friday for eight months. Today I'm filling in for the chief physician who normally works on Saturdays, the busiest day of the week. We're closed Sunday." Belle pushed a hand through her hair, putting her ponytail in disarray. "Please tell me what's going on. How did this happen?"

The two agents exchanged glances. "Have you noticed anything unusual in the past month? Children followed by strangers?" Roarke asked.

"No." She noted the troubled glances they gave each other. "I need to know exactly what happened. If you don't give me details, I can't help you."

The news they shared made her stomach clench with worry. A child who'd visited the clinic had vanished right after she'd left. She was fourteen years old.

Belle pulled up computer records, the sour taste of worry making her feel ill. What if the girl wasn't alive anymore? She knew the power of Amber Alerts and the system, but still, not all the children reported as missing were found alive. "I can't give out medical information on the children..."

"HIPAA rules don't apply to minors," Anderson cut in.

She frowned. "My rules do."

"We'll need to see your files," Anderson countered, bracing his palms on her desk.

She ignored him, her pulse beating fast from his nearness. "I can tell you if this girl visited here and how long she stayed and when she left. We keep extensive records on all patients."

"Back off, Kyle," Roarke told him. "Whatever information you can give us will help, Dr. North."

Belle clicked through her computer. Part of the updating she'd done was making digital files, and giving the nurses laptops to log data. "Why am I only hearing about this now?"

More exchanged glances. "The girl was only reported missing a few hours ago. Her parents were out of town and left her older brother in charge. He was too busy partying to notice his sister was gone."

Fingers hovering over the keyboard, she waited. "Name?"

"Sandra Dixon. She vanished after leaving here the other day. Never made it home." Anderson locked gazes with her.

Belle frowned as she clicked through the records. "That name isn't here."

"It wouldn't be. Wasn't the name she used when she visited. We don't know what her alias was." Anderson scrubbed a hand over the slight bristles on his jaw.

After he showed her a photo, it clicked. She looked up the information. "Eva Brown. Obviously, I knew she was here under another name. She said she had a cough. She only wanted to talk."

"About what?" Anderson asked. Lordy, that scowl would frighten away a grizzly bear, but she wouldn't let him browbeat her. Not when children's lives were at stake.

"Eva—Sandra wanted to know how long a woman could survive with breast cancer." Belle felt a lump at her throat, forced herself to speak evenly. Poor Sandra, scared out of her wits and needing answers.

"She was terrified of dying. I did an ultrasound myself and assured her she was fine. Then she confessed her mother was recently diagnosed with breast cancer. Her parents had gone out of town to consult with a top-notch oncologist." Belle opened her desk drawer and handed Anderson a brochure. "I gave her this information to look over, told her to go home and talk with her mom when her parents returned, and tell her mother how worried she was."

"Sandra never made it home," Calhoun said.

Anderson studied her as if she were responsible. "Did you let her walk out of here alone?"

That accusatory tone annoyed her. "She came with a friend. An older girl."

Anderson flipped out a notebook, scribbled something. "We'll need her name. Most stranger abductions start with contact with the child close to home. In this case, we think the first contact was here at the clinic."

"Although most girls who are taken are younger than ten," Roarke mused, "we're checking out every possibility."

It didn't make sense. Sandra was a teenager.

"Is there anyone here who knows the missing girl?" Roarke asked.

"Cathy knows Sandra. She's ten and her sister is the one who drove Sandra after she left."

She called the young girl inside, assuring her mother she needed to speak to her alone and she would be right back.

When Cathy walked inside, the girl quivered.

Anderson squatted down to eye level. "What's wrong, honey?"

The soft pitch of his voice, the gentle manner as he laid a hand on the girl's shoulder, contrasted to the scowl he'd given Belle. He handed the girl a tissue to wipe away her tears.

Anderson glanced at Boo. "What's your dog's name?"

After Belle told him, Anderson held out a hand. "C'mere, Boo. Meet Cathy."

Tail wagging, Boo loped over. Anderson scratched behind

the dog's ears and Boo's tail whipped through the air. Clearly the agent had a way with dogs and kids.

Just not her.

Cathy petted Boo and Anderson joined in, talking in a low, soothing voice to the dog and the child. After a couple of minutes the girl stopped crying.

Anderson patted her hand. "Cathy, we need your help. We need to find Sandra. She could be in trouble and we need to help her. Her folks are worried sick that bad people took her."

Cathy's lower lip trembled. Belle squatted down. "Honey, if you know where she is, please tell us. I promise it will be okay."

The approving nod Anderson gave her as he glanced at Belle shouldn't have made her heart beat harder, but it did. Why should she care about impressing this man? The children mattered. Not him.

"I know where Sandra is," the girl confessed. "She ran away and she's staying in the shed in our yard."

Roarke pulled out his cell phone. "I'll notify the cops and her parents."

As Roarke walked out of the office with Cathy, Anderson lingered. Belle sighed. "That's great news."

Anderson kept studying her. "I'll still need that security footage."

"Why? She was found." Unease crawled through her. The federal agent stared at her as if she'd been the one to nudge Sandra into running away from home.

"Protocol. Want to make sure everything here is legal. You treat a lot of patients." He gave her a pointed look. "Unless you want the medical board in here to go over all your files, Dr. North."

"No." Belle brushed back a lock of hair. "We have nothing to hide."

She headed into the storage room, where Clint had set

up the monitors for the outside cameras. Belle clicked on the password to access the playback feed.

As she did, the tape played cars leaving, passing by on the busy street. "It's hard to make out details."

He watched the screen with intensity. She had a bad feeling about this. "Someone complained about us."

Anderson didn't tear his gaze from the screen. "Yes. We received two anonymous complaints about this clinic."

"About what?" Bristling, she folded her arms. "We have the highest quality of medical care in this clinic, all for low cost. If patients truly can't pay, they get their care for free. Without us, patients would be forced to go without or head to the ER."

"I'm not at liberty to say."

She wished Mike Patterson were here. Dr. Patterson was the chief medical officer who ran the clinic and dealt with all the legalities. Belle felt out of her league.

She shut off the monitor and faced him.

"If you're prohibited from telling me, then how could I help you find out? Maybe you'd better leave."

Anderson straightened. "I could return with a subpoena."

"Or you could tell me what you're looking for and I can help you."

He seemed to consider. "The complaints were regarding a suspicious man in the parking lot after hours."

Doubts filled her. "We lock the gates each night. This is a questionable area of town. But isn't that a matter for the local police?"

"Long as I'm here, I said I would look into it. Especially since there was a kidnapping associated with this clinic. Now, I need to look at that security footage, Doc."

Belle knew the man lied, but she turned the tape and monitor on again. Later, she'd have a chat with her brother.

Anderson leaned close to the monitor, his arm brushing hers. She drew in a deep breath. *Steady now.*

He pointed to camera two. "See that? Same cars."

The agent clicked through to the previous night, and then the next. "It's all the same footage. Different dates, same footage."

Mouth dry, she stared at the screen. "That makes no sense."

"Someone tampered with the footage, put it on a loop to make it look the same to hide something. Who has access to this room?"

"Everyone on staff. And the cleaning crew. They come in after we close, but they're never left alone. Usually one of us is working late."

Anderson glanced at her. "Who has the code to the cameras?"

"Myself, my brother, Clint, and Tony, our security man. But he's only here during the day. Dr. Patterson as well, the head of the clinic."

Anderson frowned at the screen. "They were covering something."

"It could be the same person who stole medication last month. We did have a theft." She drew in a breath. "We keep everything locked up, but two vials of drugs weren't accounted for when we did inventory."

"What drugs?"

"Propofol."

Anderson's gaze narrowed. "You keep that here? It's used for general anesthesia. This is a clinic."

Belle lifted her chin. "It's also used for outpatient surgeries once a month. We have a limited quantity of the drug. But the surgeries are only conducted once a month, so we didn't discover it missing until we had one scheduled."

He made a note. "I'll need a list of every person who

accessed this room, and I'm confiscating your security footage. I'll also need to talk to everyone on staff."

Hesitating, she stared at the footage. It deeply troubled her to think something was wrong at this clinic. Clint needed to know what happened.

"Dr. North?" Anderson gestured to the security monitor. "I can get a search warrant. But I'd like to think you want to help."

Belle drew in a breath. "Use my office to question them. I'll have our assistant come in and help you dismantle the recorder. I need to get back to my patients."

She returned to her caseload, which was thankfully much smaller. Then again she suspected the federal agents had scared away some of the clients.

In the middle of the next exam, a knock came on the door. Belle excused herself to the mother and her son, and stepped outside. Agent Anderson paced the hallway.

"I'll also need the phone number and address of this Dr. Patterson."

"He's on a family emergency. A funeral. Can't this wait until he returns?"

Anderson gave her a pointed look. "No."

Belle took out her phone, told him the information. "Is that all?"

"For now."

She gnawed on her lower lip. "Tell me the truth, Agent Anderson. It wasn't a suspicious person in the parking lot you're searching for. What's really going on?"

He turned around, folded his arms across his chest. "All right. There've been three cases of missing children connected to this clinic. All turned up at their parents' houses alive two days after the abductions. Most recent was ten days ago. Nancy Hernandez. The last place she was seen before her abduction was this clinic. Her mother said she brought her here for a chest cold."

Nausea roiled in her stomach. "Is she…still missing?"

Please don't tell me she was found dead.

"No. The mother said she turned up two days later on the front lawn. Someone dumped her there, alive but drugged. The mother was afraid to go to the police. It wasn't until Nancy told an aunt what happened that the family did finally contact the local police."

"I'll look her up on the system."

"You can look all of them up on the system," he shot back.

Hard to argue with that.

They returned to her office, but the database was slow today. As he read off the names, Belle pulled the paper chart instead from the bank of filing cabinets in the cramped room where they kept medical records. The first two girls were here for routine exams and regular patients. Nothing stood out.

Nancy was a new patient.

"Here. Nancy Hernandez. Age six, dark hair, green eyes. I have all her vitals. Dr. Patterson examined her, prescribed antibiotics."

"No follow-up visit?"

"None. She was here January 23." Belle dreaded the answer, but had to ask. "What was in Nancy's system when she was found?"

"Propofol."

Oh dear. The dots connected; she knew this didn't look good, even if they were innocent. "Do you think the theft and Nancy's disappearance are connected?"

"It could be the start of a child-trafficking ring."

Belle set the file down, her nausea increasing. "One centered on this clinic? Are children who are abducted usually okay?"

The grimness on his face didn't reassure her. "Most children are found alive."

"And the others?"

"You don't want to know." Anderson took out his cell phone, glanced at it.

"But Nancy was found alive and at her parents' house."

"It could be because she was too young for their purposes. Or that she was too ill. She had to be hospitalized."

That chest cold might have turned into pneumonia if the child was exposed to the elements. "Is Nancy going to be all right? Did she suffer…any other trauma?"

Anderson rubbed his jaw. "No. No bruises or sexual molestation. She was released yesterday. Says she doesn't remember anything, just a needle prick. Her mother is afraid to let her out of her sight."

Poor girl. But at least she was alive. "Of course we'll help in any way possible."

"Huh. That's not what your Dr. Patterson said when detectives questioned him after Nancy's mother reported the crime."

Belle bristled. "Dr. Patterson was in the midst of a family crisis. His uncle was dying from cancer and he was trying to wrap up his cases and file insurance claims."

Agent Anderson gave her a long, thoughtful look. "You always get so defensive, Doc?"

"Damn right I do."

Then his expression hardened. "Your clinic is suspect, Dr. North. I'm watching you. I'm leaving, but I'll be back."

She scowled. "Don't let the door hit you in the butt, cowboy."

The slightest smile quirked his full mouth. "That's agent to you."

The remark and that smile took her off guard. Belle pushed a hand through her bangs.

"Well, fine, Agent Cowboy."

Another quirk of his full mouth. Then the serious look was back, as if he regretted showing a human face. But wow, for a moment, that smile turned him into a man she wanted to know better.

Good thing he'd stopped smiling.

He removed a card from his back pocket. "If you see or hear or even smell anything suspicious, anything, call me. I mean it. Anything."

As he handed her the card, their fingers touched and her nerve endings tingled. Such chemistry. Belle's heart pounded harder from that brief contact. Anderson looked rattled, as if it affected him, as well. The spicy scent of his cologne wound around her, and she found herself staring at his blue-and-white-checked tie. The whimsical pattern contrasted with the hardened image he presented.

Yet he'd been so gentle, almost tender, with Cathy.

Dismissing Anderson from her mind soon as he walked away, Belle returned to work.

By the time she got home later that day, exhaustion claimed her. Yet if she skipped dinner with her family, she'd never hear the end of it. Belle kicked off her shoes and sat on the sofa. Boo jumped up beside her, wagging his tail.

She closed her eyes for a moment.

When she woke, it was well after nine that evening. Cringing, Belle checked her messages. Five voice mails.

Belle called her mother to apologize, but Shirley Vandermeer North had none of it.

"We waited to have dinner for an hour, Belle. The least you could do was to call and let me know you decided to avoid me." That crisp, condemning tone made her wince, feel all of five years old again.

"I worked a long day, Mom, and I fell asleep. Sorry."

"You need to stop working there, Belle. Stop going to the clinic. If you would only…"

Belle tuned her out, letting her drone on and on. She held the phone up to Boo. "Here, you want to listen to her for a while?" she whispered.

Boo whined. Belle sighed, set the phone down on the sofa. After ten minutes she picked it up.

Her mother still droned on. Nothing stopped Shirley Vandermeer North from her favorite pastime—lecturing her only daughter.

"I will be expecting you for my monthly tea tomorrow at four o'clock sharp. Mindy Worthington and Natalie Haven will be there. They wish to say hello to you."

Her mother's favorite society friends always eyeballed her for volunteering for their numerous charity committees. Saying "hello" was a signal the ladies wanted her help.

I'll be damned if I stop working at the clinic to sell tickets for a raffle or attend another drab charity ball.

"I'm going to bed, Mother. I'll see you tomorrow at four."

She hung up.

Belle slept deeply that night, and when dawn streaked fingers of rose and lavender across the gray sky, she rose to take her usual jog. She ran, showered and then dressed, grabbing her doctor's coat to take to the cleaner's.

Suddenly she remembered the tightly folded paper in her pocket. Anna had insisted she take it home and put it on her refrigerator.

Belle opened the paper, expecting to see a childish rendering of a brown dog.

But under the drawing of Boo, the words penned in red crayon sent her heart rate soaring. The paper fluttered to the floor as she stumbled backward.

HE SAYS HE WILL KILL MAMA IF I DON'T GO WITH HIM. HELP US. PLEASE.

Chapter 4

He hated waking up in a strange bed. Hated that horrid feeling of confusion, not knowing where he was before his gray matter clicked in.

Hated running out of hot water during his shower, too.

And not having any regular coffee didn't make it better.

Life could be worse. Had been worse. He'd learned to deal.

Clad only in gray sweatpants, Kyle padded around the kitchen in his bare feet. He finally found a half-opened can of instant decaf, added it to a cup of microwaved hot water. Then he took the case file on Nancy Hernandez and went out onto the lanai.

Dawn had broken over the horizon, streaking the sky with color. A hint of humidity lingered in the air, enough to balance the cool breeze. Another glorious day in South Florida, and he had no clue why someone had abducted Nancy Hernandez and then dumped her like a sack of trash on her family's lawn.

He didn't want to work this case. It scrambled his emotions, made everything in his finally well-ordered world go haywire.

No choice. Children's lives were at stake and he'd made a promise to always save the ones who could be saved.

Florida was different from the catatonic pace of the field

office in the Midwest, where he'd worked for the past year. Even though it was early February, the snow piled hip deep in front of his apartment, he didn't want to come here. Hell, he'd had enough of living in Florida after his personal life went to hell.

But his supervisor ordered him back to Florida two months ago. He was good at tracking down missing children and he was needed on the East Coast.

If the abduction of Nancy Hernandez proved a puzzle, then the abduction of two other girls her age was downright troubling.

Both girls were last seen visiting the clinic. Both had walked there, since it was in their neighborhood. Their mothers had been distracted near the clinic by a man who stopped in his car to ask for directions in Spanish. They had walked to the corner, a bare few feet away, to point out the road to the man, who'd then driven away. When the mothers turned around, the girls were gone.

Whoever did this had to be working as a team, and the team had either watched the clinic or the team worked there.

The other two girls, unlike Nancy, were healthy, but for the copious amounts of Propofol in their bloodstreams. Kyle worried that the next kid to suffer the same fate might have a reaction, and end up dead.

Who was taking little girls and why? Were they part of a child-pornography ring? The Bureau had checked constantly, but nothing showed up.

Yet.

Kyle stared at the photos of the three girls, silently thankful they were all found alive, if not that they were filled with terror over their experience. All of them had dark hair, blue or green eyes and they were between five and six.

Whoever had kidnapped these girls did so for a reason. The low-income areas where they lived were frequently targets for crime, but not something this bizarre.

Was a local gang looking to steal young girls for a pornography operation?

Or worse?

Flipping through the file brought no new answers. The local cops had set up a missing-persons hotline for people to leave anonymous tips in either English and Spanish. No leads there yet.

He sipped his coffee, staring at the palm trees in the backyard. The pool pump hummed, another reminder he was far from the Midwest.

Someone who worked at the clinic had to have known the kids, had to have known the parents and lured them away. *What about that pretty blonde doctor?*

Dr. Belle North. Tall and shapely, with warm brown eyes and a sweet expression, when she talked with children. With him? Colder than the Arctic. The man in him responded to her warm laugh, her gentle manner with the children and that sexy wiggle to her hips when she walked.

The calculating FBI agent in him saw a person of interest in the only thread tying this case together. The Harold Donald Free Clinic had to be the contact place for the abductions.

But the sexy and alluring Dr. North was the first woman to truly capture his jaded interest in three years. Roarke had commented on it at the office.

"Pretty doc, huh? Even Mr. Grumpy Pants here thought so," he'd teased.

Kyle didn't mind, only because Roarke knew how the accident had mauled his spirit. Roarke had been there the day they lowered Caroline into her grave, and later when he'd buried little Kasey...

Don't go there.

He studied the photos of the clinic's exterior, entry and exit points. He tapped the file folder, lost in thought when his cell rang. Kyle glanced at the number.

Dr. Belle North.

Pulse racing, he answered. "Anderson."

Kyle listened, his palm growing clammy. "Give me your address."

He hung up soon as she finished. Dressing took five minutes and then he climbed into his department-issued black SUV.

Half an hour later, Kyle pulled into the driveway of a modest single-story home with tropical plants flanking the yard. No gated community, no cookie-cutter houses like he'd come to expect in other neighborhoods. It was the kind of neighborhood he liked, but one that didn't fit the high pay grade of a working physician.

Kyle was nearly at the front door when it opened, revealing a worried Dr. North clad in a sleeveless peacock blue dress, elegant blue high heels and stockings that clung to her shapely legs. He couldn't help an admiring second look.

"Nice dress. Church?" he asked.

Her pretty mouth quirked. "Brunch with friends."

Then the worry lines returned. "Please, come in."

He respected the fact she looked fresh, awake and lovely at this hour on a Sunday. He usually looked bleary-eyed and moved like a zombie until coffee fueled his system.

More surprises inside the house. She led him into a living room with a blue sofa that had a small tear in one cushion, and the Berber carpet was old and worn. No pictures on the white walls, but seashells adorned several baskets set about the room. Boo slept on a dog bed in front of a fireplace that hadn't been cleaned. A vase of daisies sat on an antique table near the picture window.

Belle sat on the powder blue armchair while he sank down onto the sofa. "It's temporary. I'm renting until I leave for a residency match. Whenever I can get one."

He could appreciate temporary. "The note?"

Biting her lower lip, she snapped on latex gloves lying

on an end table and then handed the drawing to him. "I'm sorry I got fingerprints on it from previously."

A small smile quirked his mouth. "No problem. You always have gloves in the house?"

"I am a doctor. Well, MD. I have the title but not the license until I complete my residency." She studied him with those incredible dark eyes, such a contrast to her pale skin and fair hair. "Would you like a pair?"

He dug out disposable gloves from his jacket pocket. "Brought my own."

Her smile did something to him, twisted him into knots. Kyle looked at the drawing. Large block letters, written in haste with a shaky hand. Poor kid probably was terrified.

Yet filled with courage. It took bravery to do this.

A soft sigh filled the air. Belle. So absorbed in the drawing, he'd almost forgotten she was there. But yet it was impossible to fully forget, for her presence was a lingering sweet fragrance.

Kyle became aware of the fresh, subtle scent of her perfume. Not overbearing or cloying, but delicate. So feminine. He felt like a big bear with giant paws compared to the slightness of her slender fingers.

"I'll send this to the lab, see if they can pull any other prints off it," he told her.

"Save the effort. The only two people handling the drawing were myself and Anna."

Damn. He'd hoped for more evidence. "Who was with her in the room when you examined her?"

"Family friend who claimed he was there to interpret." Belle frowned. "He said his name was John Smith. I sent him and the mother out of the room with a distraction so I could perform a thorough exam."

Belle's troubled gaze met his. "Anna was quite nervous, so I wanted to rule out abuse."

This was news. Kyle leaned forward. "Was there any?"

"No. She showed no psychological signs of it, either, when I questioned her. The friend was brusque, but that's not unusual. We get a few macho men who are embarrassed to use the clinic's low-cost services."

She snapped off the gloves and set them on the table. "I wish I had detained him. If only I knew!"

"It wasn't your fault," he said quietly. "There was probably nothing you could have done."

"I feel like I could have done more."

"What does Anna look like?" He dreaded and knew the answer already.

"She's six years old, dark hair, green eyes. Thin, about thirty-nine inches tall, weighs thirty-seven pounds."

All the other girls who'd been abducted were in the same age, height and weight range.

"I did write down his license plate."

"The license provided on the paperwork?" Most likely false.

Belle shook her head. "The one I saw on the car. Just to be safe, I jotted down the number after I gave Anna's mom the prescriptions she needed. I sent them to Skipper's Pharmacy. I have an arrangement to give certain patients free meds."

Kyle stopped scribbling on his notepad. "You have the full plate number?"

At her nod, he felt a wave of relief. First real break they'd had in the case. "I could kiss you for that."

Her cheeks pinked to a delicate flush as she handed him the paper. Clearing his throat, he jotted down more notes.

That was much more than he could have hoped for. He called the local police department they'd been working with to have them run the plate.

The news was disappointing, but expected. He thumbed off the phone. "Stolen."

Still, they could trace it, see if any security cameras in the area picked up the truck's movements.

Belle rose. "I made a fresh pot of coffee. Would you like a cup?"

Kyle glanced up. "You're a lifesaver. All I had in the house was decaf."

"Horrors. Sounds like a torture chamber."

He grinned. "No cream, two sugars."

By the time she returned with two mugs of steaming coffee, he'd analyzed the drawing. Kyle sipped his coffee, thanked her and pointed to the rendering on the paper.

"Smart girl. She drew the dog, but not how you'd expect. Most kids draw objects and include things from their ordinary world—mothers, fathers, siblings, friends. Their house. Two-story or one-story. Stuff they're familiar with—even their school, teachers. This doesn't look like a typical home. See those bushes and the water and that triangle with the number eight?"

Joining him on the sofa, Belle peered at the drawing. The close proximity of her made him fully aware of the scent of her perfume, the softness of her skin as her bare arm brushed his. She pointed to the triangle. "Does it mean something? What's the number eight? A symbol?"

"Maybe. What was her appearance like? Tell me whatever you can about her."

"I thought she'd been abused because she seemed scared and her father was gruff. Her appearance struck me as homeless."

"The man who said he was a family friend?"

Belle sighed. "Anna told me he was much more and planned to marry Rosa, her mother. Do you think he is the one who abducted her?"

"Could be. Or maybe he was selling her to someone." Kyle squinted at the triangle. "Homeless, huh? Probably a tent. Had you ever seen this John Smith before in the clinic?"

"No, but remember, I don't normally work on Saturdays. And John Smith said they last saw Dr. Patterson."

He'd tried contacting the doctor, but all calls went to voice mail. Not odd if the man was out of town for a family funeral.

Still, it didn't cast Dr. Patterson in a good light.

He tried to remember which local parks offered camping. "Camping on a permanent basis is one step above sleeping on the street. In the season, it's much cheaper than a hotel, although with all the tourists visiting here in the winter, reservations are hard to find at the more desirable locations."

"For recreational vehicles, yes. But tents…" Belle set down her mug on the coffee table before them. She reached into the pocket of her lab coat. Using a latex glove, she handed him a slip of paper. "This fell out of my pocket after I dug out the drawing. I wasn't certain if it was important."

Kyle silently swore. The receipt, for seven days at a campsite at a local park, was critical. "Why didn't you tell me about this on the phone or when I first walked in the door?"

Every moment was critical in finding a missing person.

Her mouth thinned. "I didn't know. I wasn't certain it belonged to Anna, or if it was something else. I send my lab coats out for cleaning and someone could have slipped it in there by mistake."

"I'll be the judge of that." He softened his tone. "She could be miles from here by now. But this gives us a starting point."

Kyle downed his coffee. He called Roarke, relaying what Belle had found.

The news his partner relayed made his stomach clench.

"Someone left a message in Spanish on the missing-persons hotline. Female, voice sounded in her twenties. Said she recognized John Smith yesterday at the clinic and had seen him at a local playground, alone, last month staring at all the kids. She thought he was INS, got spooked and told the other mothers to grab their children and leave," Roarke told him.

He gave the address of Hideaway Park. "Meet me there."

After hanging up, Kyle slipped the receipt and the drawing into a large plastic baggie and zipped it. "Thank you for your help," he told Belle.

As he headed out the door, she followed, locking up and saying goodbye to her dog. Belle clutched a garage-door opener. "I'm going with you."

"I don't think so." Kyle opened his car door.

"You can't stop me."

Stubborn civilians. He gave her a stare that had known criminals quaking in their cheap shoes. "No."

"You don't know what she looks like. Or what her mother looks like." She frowned. "Or this John Smith."

More than likely he was not. Much as he hated admitting it, he needed her to ID Anna.

"Your brunch?"

"Already canceled." Her smile held a note of triumph.

Kyle clenched and unclenched his fingers after closing his car door. "Okay. But you're staying in the car after we get there. Deal?"

"Yes. Only if you don't need my help." Belle pressed the garage-door opener. "We can take separate cars."

The garage door slipped upward, revealing a new red Corvette sitting inside, shiny and sparkling. Whoa. Sweet. Kyle's jaw dropped. "Well, damn."

Belle sighed. "Graduation present from my parents. And a bribe to nudge me into a residency in cardiology."

"I got a pocketknife when I graduated."

For a few precious seconds, he remained lost in thought,

staring at the car. Seventeen again, a sweet cherry-red convertible, when life was great and all he needed was the open road ahead of him. Reckless and filled with confidence, the times when he didn't have an up close and personal acquaintance with the horrors people could inflict on innocent children. The times before he knew the anguish of watching his wife's body lowered into a cold grave, the sleepless nights spent at Kasey's bedside, praying for a miracle doctors failed to deliver...

Kyle shook himself out of the past. "You know where the park is?"

Belle gave him a look that all but said, *Seriously?*

"Don't speed in that thing," he warned.

"I'm a doctor." She gave another smug smile. "I can always use that as an excuse."

"Yeah, and I don't want to have to bail your cute butt out of jail."

Inside, he nearly groaned. Did he actually call her bottom "cute"?

Far from looking insulted, the faintest smile touched her pink-glossed lips. "Okay, Agent Cowboy."

Minutes later, he was behind the steering wheel, zipping down the road toward the park as Belle followed. Her car looked as if it drove like a dream.

Even if they headed into a nightmare.

Please let Anna be there—let everything be okay.

The silent mantra had been played over and over in his head countless times in the past. Most times, the kids were okay.

He hoped Anna was a drama queen craving attention, and all they'd find was an annoyed mama and a little girl looking guilty for causing such a stir.

When he reached the area, the campgrounds had only a few people. A family cooked breakfast on the charcoal grill, and a father and son fished in the lake bordering the campsite.

At tent number eight, he parked. The space was empty. Kyle had a bad feeling about this. He went to Belle, who rolled down her window.

"Stay in your car and let me check things out first," he told her.

Near the back of the tent, he paused and squatted down, staring at a darkened patch of grass. Kyle became aware of footsteps crunching on the undergrowth, and the delicate scent of perfume.

"I told you to stay in the car," he snapped.

"And I told you I would, unless you needed my help." Belle sucked in a breath. "That's blood."

He withdrew his pistol and followed the faint trail to the lake bank.

Partly hidden by saw palmetto bushes and scrub, a woman lay half-submerged in the lake. He hurried toward the prone figure, praying he wasn't too late. As he reached the body, Belle gasped.

"That's Rosa! Anna's mother." She whipped her head around. "Where's Anna?"

Deep in his gut, Kyle knew the truth.

Anna Rodriguez was gone, and now they had another missing girl to find.

Chapter 5

All her medical training kicked in as Agent Anderson hauled Rosa's body out of the water. As he called 911, Belle searched the woman's pale face and blue lips. Not breathing. She checked for a pulse.

Nothing.

"Help me," she urged him. "Do you know CPR?"

Without answering, Kyle straddled Rosa's body and began chest compressions. Belle let him. He was far stronger and could keep trying far longer than she could. "Fifteen compressions, then two breaths," she ordered.

Belle tipped back the woman's mouth as Kyle counted. Dark bruises ringed her neck. At fifteen, he stopped and she pinched Rosa's nose and breathed into her mouth.

Nothing.

"Again," she snapped.

They repeated the process.

They had no idea how long Rosa had been submerged, or had gone without oxygen. Yet every bone in her body urged her to try and keep trying.

Please live. Don't die on me.

Her body and brain went on automatic as she kept trying. Seeing Agent Anderson grew tired, Belle nudged him aside.

"Switch places."

CPR was hard, tiring work and yet she kept at it. A person could live ten minutes without oxygen. At least the compressions would give Rosa a fighting chance as the heart was forced to pump blood through her body.

Muscles burned and ached. As she began the fifth round of pushing on Rosa's chest, she felt a helpless sense of unreality.

"I don't know if we can save her," Belle told him.

Expression tight, he shook his head. "No! Keep at it! I'm not losing her!"

Sirens whined in the near distance. A group had gathered nearby. They were circling them, like vultures, the curious park visitors who gaped at them. Belle's anxiety rose. "Need space. Give us room," she told them.

A cool, hard stare at the crowd and Agent Anderson snapped out an order in his deep, authoritative voice. "Get back now."

Bystanders stepped away. A park ranger drove up in an all-terrain vehicle and jumped out. "What can I do?" the ranger asked.

"Take over compressions," Anderson ordered.

Belle didn't argue. Her muscles ached and she lacked the strength of the more robust ranger. Instead, she stayed close, listening for breath sounds.

Rosa gagged. Rushing to her side, Belle gently turned Rosa's head to one side as the woman began to vomit out water and mucus.

"Anna," the woman said, moaning.

Rosa fell into unconsciousness once more as the ambulance pulled up. Agent Anderson snapped at the crowd to clear out as the emergency medical technicians raced forward.

Numb, Belle recited the case history. Female, approximately twenty-five years old, mouth full of water...

Bruises on her neck, indicating her attacker first tried to strangle Rosa.

As the medics worked on Rosa, relief filled her. She had a pulse and was breathing. *I did it.*

Belle glanced at Agent Anderson. *No, we did it.*

His gaze softened at her. "Come on. You look a little shocky." He pointed to the ATV. "Mind if we borrow it?"

They rode in the ATV a short distance to the park office, which had a vending machine. Kyle bought her a can of cola and they rode back.

"Thank you, Agent Anderson."

"Kyle," he told her. "My name is Kyle."

Belle drank the soda, the caffeine and sugar shooting through her system and clearing her mind. His big presence felt oddly comforting. Like a sentry standing guard, protecting her from the police now dispersing the crowd and clearing the scene.

The ambulance whined as they carted Rosa away.

"What are her chances?" he asked.

"Depends. She'll need a hundred percent O_2 and blood-gas analysis. If they can manage the hypoxemia and acidosis, she has a fighting chance. We don't know how long she was out, so they'll probably intubate her in the ambulance to keep her breathing."

Kyle's brow wrinkled. "Acidosis?"

"Buildup of carbon monoxide in her bloodstream. Hypoxemia is low O_2 in the blood."

"So questioning her is out for the moment."

Belle lowered the soda can from her mouth. "We just saved her life and you want to question the woman right now?"

Cold, callous. Yet she understood his attitude. Professionalism was needed when one worked. Otherwise, the work couldn't get done. She'd been taught as a doctor to turn off emotions while working with patients.

It was a skill set she had yet to master.

"We know Anna is missing. Rosa is the last one to see

her alive. She can help fill in the missing pieces." A muscle twitched in his strong jawline. "The difference between an hour and two hours could mean the difference between finding Anna dead. After one day, eighty percent of the missing children turn up dead."

Belle shuddered. Saving lives was in her blood. The thought of discovering Anna dead in a ditch somewhere, imagining how she had cried out for her mother...

"I don't know how you can do this kind of work," she muttered.

Kyle took the soda can from her hand, drank deeply. He wiped his mouth with the back of one hand and returned the can to her. "You just do it."

Her mouth hovered over where he had drunk, the spot warm from his lips. Belle imagined his mouth and the hot pressure of it on hers...

Scowling, she set the can down on the ATV's dashboard. "You can't question Rosa. I'm telling you, even if she gains consciousness again, she won't be able to talk."

"Leave that to me when the time comes."

Ticktock. The clock was running. If they didn't find the girl in twenty-four hours, her chances of remaining alive dwindled.

No emotions. No guilt, anger or fear that he was going to lose another one, just like he'd lost Kasey. Cold, hard professionalism kicked in as the local police cordoned off the crime scene. If Dr. Belle had taken his pulse, she'd have been stunned to see his heart rate rise above sixty.

Roadblocks had been set up and deputies searched each car that left the park, and every car for a vicinity of five miles. Park rangers were working on identifying everyone in the area. Interviewing them about anyone they might have seen, cars that were in the campground, how Rosa and her daughter acted while they were here.

Kyle needed a list of everyone who'd been in this park from the day Rosa and her daughter arrived. Delivery people. Construction workers. Other campers. Motive was important. If the kidnapper grabbed her as part of a child-trafficking operation, she could have been tossed into a van and headed for the state line to be smuggled out.

Crime-scene techs were working the scene. The local sheriff's office had mobilized and brought in every available deputy. In most cases, he worked closely with local law enforcement, letting them take the lead because they knew the area and could prove immensely useful. Forensic evidence could give them clues of the struggle that had ensued, and the suspect's identity.

Kyle hoped Anna might have run off and hidden if she witnessed the violence against her mother. But his gut, which always proved him right, warned otherwise.

They had a witness who could tell them everything... if she were conscious. The deputy sent to the hospital to check on Rosa had reported back the woman was as Belle indicated—intubated and in a coma.

Maybe he should have gone to the hospital. But he tried to avoid them unless absolutely necessary. The antiseptic smell of bleach combined with bodily fluids...the anguish on faces of waiting relatives coiled his guts into a knot. Never thought he'd be the one waiting on a hard chair, tensing each time the door swung open and a nurse came out to inform relatives of a status update.

He scanned the crowd. Deputies were taking names, questioning possible witnesses. Someone had to have seen something.

"A police sketch artist is on her way for you to give a description of the man who brought Rosa and Anna to the clinic. We'll feed it into the local, state and federal databases," he told Belle.

After mobilizing the local authorities and setting up a

command post, he and Roarke had begun coordinating the investigation.

Belle had already given a description of Anna so they could put out an Amber Alert. Kyle pulled Belle over to a nearby picnic table and sat her down.

"You're the only other person besides Rosa who interacted with Anna and this John Smith. I want to know everything about this man. How did he act? Did he have any scars, tattoos, identifying marks? What was he wearing?"

Kyle jotted down details as Belle closed her eyes and rattled them off. Height about five feet, seven inches. Brown eyes.

Belle frowned. "Neatly dressed, with a white button-down business shirt, jeans. His shoes were scuffed but looked like faux leather. Laced up. Dirty blond hair, and I mean dark as well as greasy, beneath a ball cap with some kind of tractor logo."

"International Harvester?"

Belle closed her eyes. "John Deere."

"Detailed," he murmured.

"I have a photographic memory." Her carnation-pink mouth lifted briefly before her lower lip wobbled again. "Helped get me through medical school."

Or did she state details to throw suspicion off herself and the clinic? Kyle couldn't be certain.

"Anything else? Did he say anything about where they were headed? Did Anna tell you? Sometimes kids going on a trip are so excited they'll talk nonstop about it."

"No. She only mentioned they were moving soon as John Smith came into some money."

Belle pressed two fingers to her temples. "Can you get anything on the car he was driving? Even if it was stolen?"

"It's on the Amber Alert and the sheriff's office issued a BOLO, but chances are this Smith guy will ditch it or switch plates. At least it's a lead."

"BOLO?"

"Be on the lookout."

"What next?" Anxiety tightened Belle's pretty face as she watched techs scour the area and leave markers indicating possible forensic evidence.

"They'll look for hairs, fibers, fluids, anything that might lead us to the kidnapper's identity."

"You already know that. It was John Smith, the man who said he was their friend and took them both to the clinic."

"We have to rule out everything," he told her. "And everyone. We'll use the map to ID registered sex offenders in the area."

Blood drained from her face. "Sex offenders, here?"

Kyle's guts coiled tight. "Park's a few miles away from a retirement community."

Belle frowned. "I've heard of STDs being prevalent among the elderly because believe it or not, they have a lot of sex, but sex offenders?"

"Many are prohibited from living without a thousand feet of a school, day care, park or any other place frequented by children. They seek out age-restricted retirement communities, especially if they have a parent or grandparent already living there."

She gave a delicate shudder. "I never imagined that."

Dr. Belle North wouldn't, of course. In her sensible high heels and blue sleeveless dress, a string of expensive pearls around her slender throat, she appeared more at-home at a social tea.

Not a crime scene.

She seemed fragile and vulnerable, and he resisted the temptation to offer comfort. Those big brown eyes looked at him like a wounded deer.

She's still a suspect, he reminded himself. No matter how sweet she appeared. Belle North was one of the last people to see Anna Rodriguez. Kyle caught the delicate scent of her perfume again and breathed deep. She was a beautiful lily in a bed of ragged weeds.

A portly deputy approached, iPad in hand.

"No matches on the LPR software, Agent Anderson," the deputy told him. "We get stolen vehicles, robbery suspects shooting through stoplights all the time and our cameras pick up their license plates. Except for this morning. Seems like everyone around here is at church."

Except the kidnapper. Kyle rubbed a hand over the bristles on his chin, remembering he'd skipped shaving this morning to rush over here with Belle.

"We have one witness who claims to have seen Rosa and her daughter this morning around sunrise," the deputy added. "Name's Carl Tucker."

Kyle dug a notebook out of his back pocket and walked over to a pimply-faced teenager who stared at his sneakers as if they held the secrets of the universe. Belle trailed behind him. A delicate fragrance of some kind of flowers clung to her. For a moment he wanted to turn, inhale her scent. Take Belle into his arms and bury his face into her hair.

She was an eye-catching distraction. Not good.

"Special agent Kyle Anderson, FBI. What did you see?" Carl didn't lift his gaze. "Am I in trouble?"

Frowning, he glanced at the deputy, who held up a small baggie. "It's not oregano from his mama's kitchen," the deputy drawled.

Out of the corner of his eye, he saw Belle's mouth twitch in amusement.

"I'm not interested in your recreational drug use. If you saw something this morning, tell me. There's a little girl missing and her mother's in the hospital," Kyle told him.

The young man paled. Gulped. "Okay, okay." He finally looked up, jammed his hands into his jeans pockets. "I was by the lake, me and my girlfriend, and I saw them by the water. It was maybe around seven o'clock. Looked weird."

"What did you see?"

"Arguing. This woman and a little girl. I could hear her all the way across the lake." His eyes squinted. "Kid was pulling on the woman's arm. I think she said something about *vamonos*."

Spanish for *let's go*. Anna knew the dangers they faced, and was trying to convince her mother.

He made a notation. "And?"

The teen scanned the room nervously. "We heard some screams. I don't know. I got nervous and we left that area, walked closer to the back of the park. Didn't want anyone finding out we had, uh, you know."

"This?" Disgusted, he shook the baggie. "You sure you didn't see anything else? Anyone else?"

"No." The kid looked hopeful. "Can I go now?"

"No." Kyle nodded to the deputy. "Keep him here until his parents show up."

"Aw, man," the teen protested.

"On second thought, don't call his parents. Give him some time. Maybe he'll remember something else."

Kyle walked away, frustration mounting.

He went to the roped-off crime scene to scan the area. Belle followed, her dark eyes wide and troubled. "Is there any chance she's lost in the park? Maybe she ran off when her mama got hurt?"

"The deputies will search every square inch. Will take some time." He paused, and added gently, "They're calling in the dive team now."

Paling, she swallowed hard. "To see if she's dead."

"Not necessarily. It's a forensic dive team…" His voice trailed off. Who was he kidding?

"I see," she mumbled, turning as pale as her freshwater pearls. "Of course. Autolysis comes first, immediately after death. Bloat doesn't come until enzymes begin producing gases, and then bacteria and skin deterioration, stage two of decomp, which wouldn't happen for twelve hours after death…"

"You can stop reciting what happens during decomp, Doc. I'm familiar with the process."

"Sorry… I always recite facts when I'm nervous…"

Recognizing her shock and a desperate attempt to compensate, Kyle took her elbow and steered her to a picnic table. "Easy," he murmured gently. "We always work on the presumption she's alive. Prepare for the worst—hope for the best."

Unable to help himself, he touched her shoulder. Belle North remained a suspect, but with every passing moment, doubts filled him. He'd dealt with many people in his eight-year career with the feds, from the innocent to the pond-dwelling scum.

Her distress wasn't fake. It was real.

"I wish I would have called the police yesterday," she murmured, rubbing her temple. "I could have prevented this."

"Maybe. Maybe not. Maybe Smith would have moved sooner and Rosa would have died. You can't blame yourself. You did what you were supposed to do."

Belle bit her lower lip.

He hated leaving her alone, but there was protocol to follow. "Stay here. I'll be back soon."

Roarke was consulting with detectives from the local sheriff's office. His partner glanced up. "I called the hospital. Rosa Rodriguez is still unconscious. She's in critical condition. She may pull through. Or not. In any case, she's not in any shape for questioning."

Worst fears confirmed, he shoved back the growing panic that flowered every time he was called to investigate a missing-child case. No real leads, and despite the swarms of deputies combing the area for clues, the road-blocks, it didn't look promising.

Walking away from the detectives, Roarke led him over to a shady tree. "You okay? This isn't like the last one."

A rough nod. Their last case had been grueling, investigating a six-year-old who'd gone missing from her neighborhood in rural Iowa. The missing girl had been towheaded, with a wide smile that was a close match to his daughter's.

They'd found her alive, thanks to the forensic evidence and a lead Kyle had doggedly followed, despite the local cops insisting it was a dead end.

He took the coffee Roarke offered, gulped it down. "Fine."

Roarke's gaze shot over to the table where Belle sat. "Nice-looking doctor. She has the eyes for you."

Startled, he nearly dropped the cup. "Right."

"Right. Anyone can see how she looks at you, Kyle. The sparks between you could ignite a woodpile."

"She's a suspect."

"Under suspicion, but not a suspect," Roarke murmured. "Go for it."

He snorted. "I'm not going for anything. We have a job to do."

"A job you hide behind."

Stomach clenching, he glared at his friend. "Since when is hard work frowned upon in this unit?"

"Since the day the chief told you to ease off and take a break, which you never did." Roarke paused, his green gaze kind. "You can't mourn Caroline forever. Get a life, buddy. Find a woman to date—hell, when was the last time you had sex?"

"Last month when you set me up with that blind date," he said dryly.

"I'm not talking about one-night stands. I mean a real

relationship. Someone to come home to at night, someone to hold, someone worth fighting for. This job will turn you into a robot if you don't."

"It's not Caroline." He drained the now-cold coffee. Hell, he'd mourned his wife's death, but they'd been on the verge of divorcing. Guilt drove him, not grief.

"It's not your fault," Roarke said gently. "You couldn't have saved Kasey."

His baby girl. Only two years old. Every day he saw her sweet face, those tousled curls, and heard her excited babble as a fresh discovery entered her world.

"Maybe. Maybe not." He tossed the cup into a nearby trash can. "News crews here yet?"

Roarke's face tightened. His partner understood. No more personal business would be discussed at this time. "Not yet. Media specialist is working up a press release right now."

He snorted again. "How long does it take to write a release about a missing child? Pressure the chief. Sooner the media releases the information to the public, the greater Anna's chances are."

His partner nodded. "The USERT divers are on their way from Miami."

Standard response in a missing-child case around water. Skilled divers from the Underwater Search Evidence Response Team would comb the lake for any evidence relating to Anna's disappearance and Rosa's attack. For a moment he was grateful this crime happened here in urban South Florida. Rural cases proved more challenging and it took time to haul in experts and equipment.

But in rural areas it was harder to hide a child. Here?

The possibilities were endless.

Chapter 6

Two sheriff's office boats skimmed over the water, their outboards roaring as deputies searched the murky lake. An angry whop whop whop drew his attention skyward. The sheriff's office helicopter flew over the lake, stirring small waves. Kyle nodded at the machine. "Infrared?"

"Yeah. Both boats have sophisticated sonar, too. If Anna's in the lake, they'll find her." Roarke's mouth tightened. "Chances are, that bastard who drove her to the clinic took her."

"Let's hope we don't find her here. She'll still have a fighting chance."

Kyle returned to the canopy where Belle sat, watching the hive of activity around her. It must look like organized chaos to a civilian, but everyone remained focused on the job.

Finding Anna.

"You okay?" he asked, touching her arm. Her skin was soft, like warm velvet. A bite of unwanted desire nipped him.

Focus. Now's not the time to think of your own needs.

And yeah, he had needs. He was a guy, and Belle's soft skin made him think of hot summer nights tangling together, sweat slicking their naked bodies...

Focus.

"I guess. I've been racking my brain about her and all the details I can recall about her medical examination. Do you really think she's alive?"

She bit her luscious lower lip again. Kyle nodded. "Always work on the belief she is. Got any ideas?"

"Can I see where they slept? Maybe there's something there that will give me insight as to her condition and why she came into the clinic with the infection."

Putting a hand on the small of her back, he guided her toward the yellow canvas tent where Anna had stayed with her mother. Belle seemed petite and fragile, elegant in this rough-and-tumble area. With her excellent bone structure, breeding and classic beauty, she was more suited for luxurious afternoons lounging on a yacht. One of her heels sank into the dirt and she tripped.

He caught her elbow, feeling soft skin beneath his calloused fingertips, and prevented a nasty spill. Belle gazed up at him and for a moment, he forgot the ugliness around them.

All he knew was Belle, her wide brown eyes, sunlight glinting in her silky blond hair, her glossy lips parted as she stared up at him.

Then she murmured a "thank you" and shattered the moment.

Kyle nodded brusquely. "Don't recommend heels here."

"I didn't dress for a day at the park. My mother says a lady should always wear heels." Belle's cute nose wrinkled. "I suppose I disappointed her with med school because I had to wear flats or risk spraining my ankle running from class to class. She once bemoaned the fact I showed up to dinner in sandals. I thought I would give her a heart attack when I told her they were from a thrift store."

Jamming his hands into the pockets of his trousers, he considered the tips of his own leather shoes, the once-polished tips now scuffed and dirty. With Belle's slender legs, she made anything on her feet look good.

At the tent, crime-scene tape ringed the perimeter. A crime-scene investigator greeted him.

"The mother's clothing is all here, in two garbage bags. Guess they couldn't afford suitcases."

He steeled himself. "The girl's clothing?"

The man's expression tightened. "We found several articles of clothing fitting a five- or six-year-old. If someone snatched her, they took only the girl."

"Or she could be at the bottom of the lake," another technician added.

An inward gasp of breath from Belle. Kyle glared at the overeager tech. "Stop wasting time and get back to work. I want a full sweep of that tent. Hair, fibers, everything. If someone so much as sneezed inside, I want to know."

The tech gulped. "Yes, sir."

"Wait."

They turned to Belle, who was staring at the tent. "Did you find a battered brown teddy bear with a purple-and-pink bow around its neck?"

"No," the older tech answered. "We swept it clean, too."

"Then she's still alive. She has to be alive. Anna wouldn't go anywhere without that bear. I tried to take it from her in the clinic and she protested. The kidnapper must have taken it when he grabbed her."

Another hopeful sign. Kyle scribbled a note in his pad. "Add that to the child's description," he instructed the deputy. "A toy that distinctive will help identify her."

By now bands of volunteers combed through the park's extensive grounds to search for the missing Anna. Kyle harbored no hopes she'd be found here. His gut warned she'd been snatched and Smith fled in a car or another vehicle.

Belle stared at the canvas tent and frowned. "They're sure this is the tent where Rosa and Anna slept?"

"It's not conclusive until we ID their belongings and match either their prints or DNA, but this is the one the ranger said they paid for."

Ducking beneath the crime-scene tape, she went to the piles of clothing deputies had sorted out. A crime-scene tech started to protest, but Kyle shook his head.

Her frown deepened as she dug through the pile and then picked up a child's sweater and corduroy trousers.

"Anna suffered from a mild respiratory infection that could have been from sleeping outdoors in damp conditions. Yet it hasn't rained in two weeks. This tent is well ventilated and the hardwood floor keeps it off the ground. Her clothing was mussed and dirty. She said she was playing outside, but wouldn't her mother dress her in better clothing instead of what Anna had worn?"

Kyle saw her point. "She wasn't sleeping here, but for some reason, they returned here this morning. Perhaps to retrieve their belongings. Whoever did this may have already kept the mother and child in another location."

He turned to the park ranger in charge of the campground. "Do you keep records of every vehicle that drives in and out of the campground?"

The man shook his head. "We don't have enough staff for that. We do record the license plate of the vehicle of each camper that registers. Rosa Rodriguez paid through the end of February. Plate has the same number you gave us. Brown four-door sedan."

The old car Belle had seen John Smith driving at the clinic. But if the car was parked here, someone must have seen it.

A short time later, after interviewing a couple who'd been camping for the past two weeks, Kyle had his answer.

Beneath the tent set up at the command post, he stirred a cold cup of coffee. Belle sipped tea. Red lipstick stained the foam cup. A perfect outline of her perfect mouth. For a fleeting moment, he let himself imagine that perfect mouth pressed against his as he took her into his arms.

She was not his type. Too polished and pretty. With her finishing-school looks and breeding, Belle was as far removed from his childhood in New York as a Palm Beach poodle was to a street-smart mutt.

But Belle North was attractive and he was beginning to like her. His gaze strayed to her bottom. Nice and rounded. The doctor fired him up for some reason, made him well aware he was a red-blooded man.

Not a stone-cold agent who kept to himself.

"She was never here. Not until this morning," he mused.

Yet this John Smith had driven them to the clinic, and where had they gone from there? Back to Smith's house? If they stayed with him, why was Anna in such bad shape?

Neighbors would talk if a single man brought home a woman and a young child. People gossiped.

"Is there anything else you recall about Anna that could help us track down where she stayed? Her clothing was dirty. How did it smell?" he asked.

Belle closed her eyes again. Damn, he wished she wouldn't do that. So distracting, as if she got ready for him to kiss her and kiss her hard.

"Earthy," she murmured. "Like a child smells when they've been playing in the mud. But something else, as well. Not dirt..."

Those lovely brown eyes flew open. "Like the fertilizer the gardener puts around my mother's rosebushes."

The cup dropped from Kyle's hand, spilling dark liquid on ground. He turned to the nearest deputy. "Any nurseries or garden centers within five miles of the park?"

"Palm City Growers, but they're never open. They're right next door, a block north of here."

"Who owns it?"

The deputy shrugged, but a park ranger standing nearby

spoke up. "Orlen Ryan. He's older than the dirt itself. His son pays the taxes on the land and the building. They used to sell palm trees, but old Orlen hasn't been around in forever. Sweet, but stubborn old guy who refused to sell to the city when they wanted to expand the park."

"Any employees?"

"Maybe one or two who drop by to take care of the trees. Place is a dump, but code enforcement never bothers with Orlen since he used to be mayor a long time ago."

"I'll check it out. If the unsub is there, I don't want him spooked by patrol cars," Kyle told the deputy, who gave him directions.

"Look for a sign that says Trees for Sale by the roadside. There'll be a driveway next to it," the deputy advised.

Belle looked bewildered. "Why would Rosa and Anna stay in a nursery instead of here?"

Kyle didn't answer, but headed for his car, talking on his cell phone to Roarke and informing him of the new development. Belle trailed behind. "I'm coming with you."

"No, you're not," he growled. "This is an official investigation."

Truth was he didn't want her tagging along in case of trouble. All his male protective instincts flared around her. Instincts he hadn't remembered in years. Belle had a way of winding past his tough defenses and professionalism.

"And Anna is my official patient. If she happens to be there, in need of medical attention, I am a doctor," she pointed out.

As he reached his vehicle, Belle slid into the front passenger seat, her dress hiking up to reveal a creamy expanse of thigh. Grunting, Kyle got behind the wheel. The doctor shared his dogged determination and sense of responsibility. Had to admire that, even as it frustrated him.

He drove north on the busy roadway and found the sign. A clearing in the front was cluttered with a small yellow tractor, rusty farming equipment and several potted plants badly in need of watering. As he turned into a one-lane dirt road flanked by tall palms, black olive trees and brush, an itch began at the base of his spine.

They were onto something. That itch always heralded a hot lead. They sorely needed a big break in this case if they were to find Anna alive.

Deep inside, he suspected Dr. Belle North was far more involved than he wanted to admit.

Chapter 7

A few yards from the road's entrance, a sagging but locked chain-link gate prohibited entry.

Kyle parked the car and then rummaged in the trunk for a pair of bolt cutters. After snapping the lock, he replaced the bolt cutters. Kyle withdrew his sidearm and shot Belle a warning glance.

"Stay here."

To his relief, she remained in the car. Kyle opened the gate and used the trees as cover as he approached the building the deputy had mentioned.

The one-lane road ended at a dirt parking lot, overgrown with weeds. A gray one-story building was half-hidden by brush and palm trees. Trash littered the grounds, from old plastic potting containers to empty bags of fertilizer, rusty shovels and digging forks.

Two battered pickup trucks sat off to the side, along with a white panel truck on cinder blocks. A blue tarp covered another vehicle, showing balding tires and part of a rear bumper that sagged to one side.

The door to the building was open when he tried it. He checked inside, clearing each room. Nothing.

SIG Sauer steady in his hand, he circled around the perimeter. Nothing. In back of the building were four long rows of straggly palm trees in sagging pots, stretching for at least a hundred yards. A tangle of weeds and brush grew against the chain-link fence. But the grass and weeds had been trampled, wearing a path to another building in back.

Kyle followed the path, circled around the shed. Nothing. The lone window had been blacked out. The door sagged on its hinges and remained locked, but unlike the padlock out front, this one was shiny and new.

Why put a new lock on an old building, unless you had something to hide?

He called Roarke and told them to send the crime-scene techs.

By the time he returned to the entrance, several patrol cars had already pulled into the circular drive. Police milled about, searching for clues. The place crawled with uniforms.

In her blue sleeveless dress, Belle stood out like a pearl in a sea of green. Holstering his weapon, he strode over to scold her for leaving the car when he noticed her expression.

Eyes huge in her face, she stared with avid interest at the vehicles parked near the fence. Her long, slender fingers trembled as she pointed to the blue tarp.

"That's the car," she whispered. "I remember the rear bumper was halfway off."

Belle raced forward, fumbled with the tarp.

"Help me," she told him, fumbling with the mud-stained plastic.

Together they yanked it off the car. Dirt stained Belle's expensive blue dress and muddied her hands. She bent over and peered inside.

The car was empty. But rust stained the steering wheel and there were small stains on the seat.

A cry erupted from Belle's throat. Kyle's own hands trembled as he donned latex gloves and then retrieved a small stuffed teddy bear from the backseat.

A bear with a purple-and-pink ribbon around its neck. One eye was missing.

A child's toy. Looked similar to the one he'd given Kasey for her second birthday.

Kasey had adored her teddy. She'd clutched it in a death grip, babbled her incomprehensible toddlerspeak.

"Kiss Teddy," she'd demanded, holding the toy up for his inspection.

Teddy had never left Kasey's side. Not when she ate dinner in her high chair, or played in the living room all those nights he worked late and seldom came home before dawn, not when Caroline strapped her into the car seat and they drove to run errands or visit the playground...

Except that last night, when Caroline's temper snapped and she'd tossed a pair of suitcases into the trunk, bundled a sleeping Kasey into her bumblebee jacket and sped away from the house...

Teddy had been in Kasey's nursery when he returned to the empty house. Teddy went into his hands, and then into his car.

Into the hospital room, where machines blipped and clicked and whirled, his daughter's eyes had closed against the fluorescent lights overhead. Such pretty, long lashes. Such a big, ugly bandage on her little head. He'd taken Teddy and gently slid it under his baby girl's arm.

"Kiss Teddy for Dada," he'd whispered, stroking Kasey's cheek. "C'mon, baby girl. Kiss Teddy."

"Agent Anderson?" Belle's voice broke through his thoughts. "Kyle?"

Her soft, sultry voice held a tremulous note. He shook himself free of the past. He had a child to find.

A child he could save.

Not like his daughter.

Kyle motioned to a nearby tech, who bagged the bear. He dug into his trouser pocket for the coin always there and drew it out.

Stupid habit, but running the coin through his fingers felt comforting. Was there such as thing as a lucky silver dollar?

How about an unlucky one?

"Are you all right?" Belle asked.

For a moment, he'd forgotten she was there. Belle North, doctor. What a racket. Profession that made money and claimed to save lives.

They didn't save his daughter's life.

"Fine." *Focus, damn it.* "Is that Anna's bear?"

Belle nodded, visibly shaken, but doing her best to appear calm and in control.

"She has to still be alive," she said, her gaze riveted to the toy as the tech carried it off. "She must be."

He wasn't the only person determined to save the child. Belle seemed woebegone, her huge eyes pleading with him for reassurance.

So different from the doctors he'd dealt with in the past. Concerned. Patient, not brisk and impersonal.

Reassurance? He couldn't offer any. All he could do was the job. The job was everything now. Fingers tightening on the silver dollar, he spoke in an even tone.

"We're going to do everything we can to find her." They would find her. With half the force on this case, scores of volunteers, Anna would be found.

He would work his fingers to the bone, exhausting every last clue until she was home.

She bit her luscious lower lip as if to keep it from trembling. "I never realized the danger she was in. She was scared, but many children are scared in the clinic. I wish…"

So forlorn and upset. How could one fake sincerity? He'd dealt with many criminals over the years and considered himself a good judge of when someone lied or they did not. Belle North wasn't affecting tears to impress him.

He replaced the coin in his pocket. Kyle forgot about himself, and his overwhelming need to work this case. Her shoulders were round and soft beneath his fingers as he put his hands on her to give her comfort. His guts twisted at the vulnerability etched on her worried face, the fear in her eyes mirroring his own.

For a moment they were not agent and doctor, but simply two human beings connected by a missing child.

"Don't blame yourself. You're not a seasoned professional trained to spot potential kidnappers."

"No excuse," she muttered. "I should have known. Maybe if I had called earlier, I could have stopped him from taking her. If Anna is…"

Belle fell silent, her words clear.

"She's not," he said fiercely. "We have to work on the assumption she's not."

She sagged against his arms. Uncaring of the uniforms buzzing around them, Kyle held her, rubbing her back. Belle smelled wonderful and clean and fresh, her slender body soft in his arms. He offered what little comfort he could, taking comfort himself in the simple act of reassurance.

A gentle cough from one of the deputies interrupted him.

"Agent Anderson, the owner's son is here."

Kyle pulled away from Belle as if she were an open fire. Not good to fraternize with a possible suspect. No matter how many tears she shed or how sincere she appeared.

The owner's son wasn't impressive. Middle-aged, with a slight paunch oozing over his leather belt, the man introduced himself as Clive Ryan. Ryan looked bewildered at the flurry of uniforms combing through the weeds. Two K-9 units pulled up. The dogs would find Anna's scent, if she had been here.

Or if her body was…

Kyle didn't waste words. "The shed in the back. When was it last used?"

The man frowned. "Months ago, maybe. Roof leaks.

Keep nagging Dad to let me tear it down, but he doesn't like change."

"Who else has access to the front gate and the office?"

"Myself, my sister and our cousin. We take turns watering the plants, but mostly we're too busy with our jobs and our families."

"Anyone else? Caretakers? Clients, friends of your father's?"

Ryan frowned. "Not that I recall. 'Cept Jesse."

Interest flared. "Jesse? Employee?"

"Friend of my cousin's. Said he could clean up the office, all those old records. Place is a fire hazard. I've warned Pops..."

"Last name?"

Ryan squinted. "Douglas. Or Dugin. Can't remember. We don't have any money to pay him, so he offered to trade by cleaning up the back. Scrap metal's worth a lot in the recycling businesses down the street."

So was silence. Away from nosy neighbors or other businesses, hidden from view, the nursery offered a perfect hiding place.

"What about the shed?" Kyle asked.

A frown from Ryan. "My dad built it as a spare office, but it's run-down. Jesse asked about the place, if I wanted him to clean it up. I told him, yeah, just don't touch the mulch and fertilizer. He hired a crew, ah, two weeks ago and they hauled a lot of stuff out. Got the bill a few days ago."

Loud, excited barking warned the dogs had caught a scent. Kyle motioned to Belle.

"Come with me. If by chance they've found her, she'll need a familiar face."

Anna wouldn't be in the old shed, but he had to say something to assure her.

Reassure himself, as well.

Two dogs pawed at the door. "Open it," he tersely instructed a deputy.

Lock snapped, the door creaked inward.

They stepped inside. Dark, dank, smelling of old cedar and fertilizer. Flipping the switch, they found the answer.

Rotting bags of mulch and fertilizer were stacked against one wall. But it was the opposite wall that gripped Kyle's attention.

Two roll-away cots with colorful blankets were tucked against it. A counter held a microwave, bottles of water and empty food wrappers. He picked one up with gloved fingers. Burritos.

New mini fridge under a table...he opened it. Stuffed with food. Smith hadn't intended for Rosa and Anna to starve. In fact, if the building weren't leaking, it might even be comfortable.

Two large suitcases stood in the corner. He opened one, found it filled with clothing.

Kyle investigated the hallway and opened a door, leading to a cramped but clean bathroom and a tiny shower.

"Who else has access to this place?" Kyle demanded of Ryan.

The man looked around with a bewildered expression. "No one. I told you, only Jesse. He said he was going to clean it out."

This Jesse had done more than clean out the building.

Jesse/John must have banked on no one else being around and decided to move Anna and her mother this morning.

Crime-scene investigators entered the shed and began their work.

"This is a terrible place to bring a child, even if he made provisions for them." Belle shuddered as she looked at the blacked-out window, the walls seeping with dampness. "Why here?"

"Hidden, away from prying eyes, unlike the park, which is popular, especially with campers during the winter season."

No one manned the park entrance stations during the week. Fees were charged only on weekends. John Smith, aka Jesse must have sneaked Rosa and Anna out during the week and brought them here. Promised them a real home of their own, and marriage to Rosa.

Unemployed and desperate, Rosa had agreed to remain hidden. Men like Jesse knew how to manipulate women to get to their kids. Knew how to weave webs of lies to keep their victims quiet and complacent.

But then Rosa must have insisted on returning to their tent to collect their belongings. That was when Smith decided to kill her and abduct Anna.

At least they had a break in the case. They had a name, which could be traced.

A few moments later, he had answers, as well. A state database turned up a Jesse Dugin. Outside the shed, Kyle showed Belle the photo that popped up on his cell phone.

Her breath hitched. "His hair is lighter, but yes, that looks like the man who brought in Rosa and Anna to the clinic."

Jesse Dugin had been convicted of petty larceny and burglary, out on parole for two years. He held a job as a driver for a small roofing company that did repairs.

Kyle suspected the vehicle Dugin drove was an unmarked white panel van, perfect for ferrying around roofing tiles, ladders, tar…and little girls.

Still, Dugin had made a huge leap from small crimes to the federal crime of kidnapping. Why? Money, most likely.

They had a lead, which sprouted tentacles of other leads. And plenty of work to follow them.

All the while the minutes slipped away. If Dugin was connected to a child-trafficking ring suspected of taking the other girl from the clinic, they needed to track him down now.

Roarke stepped forward. "Local law enforcement's holding a press conference in fifteen, Kyle. They want us there at the park."

"You handle it. I'll be there shortly."

Jesse Dugin, it turned out, also used to drive the occasional delivery, according to the sloppy paperwork detectives found in the office. He used a white panel van registered to the nursery.

Kyle frowned at Ryan. "Where's the van?"

Ryan shrugged. "I guess Jesse took it. Pop let him use it as his regular transportation."

"Pop" had enabled a hardened felon to take over the business and do whatever he pleased. "Ever hear of background checks? They're a wonderful thing," he asked.

Sarcasm dripped from his voice, but Ryan looked oblivious. "Pop has a kind heart. He saw Jesse was down on his luck, so he gave him a job."

And a place to hide out and temporarily hide a terrified child and her mother until he could kill Rosa and abduct Anna. Thankfully Dugin's plan failed when it came to Rosa. Kyle checked his phone for messages from the hospital. He'd alerted them to text with any changes in Rosa's condition.

He gave Dugin a dismissive glance. "Tell your father we're shutting this place down until further notice."

A crime-scene tech called him from the bathroom. When he entered, the man held up an empty vial and syringe.

Propofol.

"There's a few vials just like this in the trash," the tech told him. "He must have drugged Anna before taking her."

A few vials used on a child weighing less than forty-five pounds? Kyle examined the syringes. "I want each of these tested for DNA against the samples we received from the other girls who were reported kidnapped from this area in the last two months."

When he exited the bathroom, a deputy came over, tablet in hand.

"We checked everywhere and there's no record of an Anna Rodriguez or a Rosa Rodriguez living together. There was a Rosa Marie Alvarez and Anna Alvarez living in the Palmetto Pines trailer park in Hollywood. That was in December. They left in January."

"It has to be them. If they're in hiding from someone or the law, they'd change their last name. Get those flyers with the mother and daughter circulated, start knocking on doors," Kyle ordered.

"There's a team there now. We'll also have volunteers canvass the area. If Anna has been there with her mother, we'll find out."

Getting the neighbors involved was important. Mobilizing the community meant it would be harder for Smith to hide Anna.

But Kyle suspected Smith was far away. Which meant... He turned to the deputy. "Ask the neighbors what kind of car was seen last at this Rosa Alvarez's trailer."

He returned to Belle, who sat on one of the cots, hands clasped in her lap. "Is there anything else you can recall about your examination or conversation with Anna?"

She closed her eyes. "Yes. Something odd. Her mother spoke little English, but Anna was fluent. She lives in a Spanish-speaking household. Where did she learn a word like *tenderloin*?"

Kyle scribbled notes in his pad. "We checked out the last place Rosa, or whom we believe was Rosa, lived. It's a trailer park with mainly Spanish-speaking residents. Kids, yeah, maybe she hung out with children who were bilingual."

"It wasn't the fact she spoke English, but her vocabulary. She said her favorite food was beef in chipotle sauce."

His pen stopped. Now, that was truly bizarre. "Gourmet food for a kid who's lived in a trailer park and a tent? What else did Anna say? Anything about where she ate this food?"

"No." Belle bit her lower lip. "I wish I'd asked."

"Could be an upscale restaurant her mother worked for. Or a caterer. It'll be difficult to trace, especially if they employed her under the table and paid cash."

She looked around the shed and took a deep breath. "I think Anna made herself cough so she could come to the clinic and give me that note. She was trying to save herself and her mother and I failed her."

Despite her seemingly inward strength, she looked frail. Then she looked at him, frowned.

"Is there anything else I can do here?"

"No." He signaled for a deputy. "I'll have an officer drive you back to your car. We'll search your clinic later, but right now we need to follow up on any fresh leads."

"Of course," she murmured. She handed him a cream-colored business card, her family name elegantly engraved on the front. "I'll be at my parents' house at four o'clock."

Kyle tapped the card on the edge of his jacket, watching her walk out of the shed.

He liked her.

Too bad.

Belle North was still a suspect and would remain one until cleared.

Chapter 8

Emotionally and physically exhausted, Belle dragged herself back to the house to shower and change for her mother's tea that afternoon.

Socializing with her mother's wealthy friends was the last thing she needed, but she'd receive nothing but lectures if she skipped it. Belle stripped off the now-filthy blue dress, letting it drop to the rug, and stared at herself in the mirror.

Dirt smudged her chin and jawline, and her mascara had run, making her resemble a raccoon. No, a raccoon with pearls.

She thought about tossing on a pair of old jeans and a Harvard sweatshirt for tea. Maybe mother wouldn't criticize her appearance if she wore her alma mater's logo.

Belle laughed humorlessly. Her mother would expect her shining and well dressed, makeup perfect, hair coiffed.

Special agent Kyle Anderson hadn't cared that she resembled a drowned raccoon. No, he'd offered her a clean handkerchief to wipe away her tears.

She recognized in him the same tenacity others said she'd exhibited in school and with patients. Belle refused to give up.

So did special agent Anderson. The thought cheered her. With his dedication, Anna had a chance at being found.

Humming as she showered, she washed her hair, thinking of the hunky agent with the burning blue gaze. He'd been intense and focused on the search and investigation. Kyle possessed a ruthless streak that promised results and punishment for those who hurt innocents.

I bet he's like that in bed as well...all that intensity and concentration centered on his partner. She shivered delicately. *Not that I'll find out. He isn't interested in me.*

Romantically speaking, Kyle was far out of her league in both experience and skills as a lover. Her résumé might impress medical professionals, but it had come at the cost of sacrificing her personal life. In college, she'd had a boyfriend for nearly two years. The sex had been average. When he headed off to law school, it was almost a relief to wave goodbye so she could concentrate on her studies and accelerate through undergraduate school.

There was nothing average about Kyle Anderson.

Less than an hour later, she arrived at her parents' oceanfront mansion for tea. Belle politely greeted the guests after the maid ushered her into the living room. She glanced at the priceless oil paintings and artwork, the wide glass windows showing the Atlantic Ocean's turquoise waters, the glass tile that tastefully complemented the powder blue walls.

Belle perched on the edge of a chair, suddenly wishing she was anywhere but here. She focused on her mother's friends.

Mindy Worthington was a genteel and elegant woman in her late sixties whose pet project was tracing back her family lineage to the Mayflower. She was a member of the Daughters of the American Revolution and came from very old money.

Natalie Haven was younger, in her midfifties and had ascended the social ranks so quickly, it made the blue-haired ladies' heads spin. Estancia Pointe was known for its wealth, privilege and social snobbery. Yet with her Southern charm, deep pockets and social connections, Natalie had overcome the traditional prejudice against "new money."

Mindy chaired the prestigious North Ball each February in Estancia Pointe, while Natalie sat on the silent-auction committee. Proceeds from the gala benefited the North Family Foundation.

Great cause—helping underprivileged children with scholarships and funding for the clinic. Belle wholeheartedly supported it.

But she tired of the pretense and the artifice. Working in the clinic had given her an idea of the real world and the difference she could make.

A difference other than picking floral arrangements for a charity ball.

Silver platter on her outstretched palms, the maid brought in the tea service, setting it on the coffee table. Mrs. North poured, chatting about the latest coverage in the papers of the committee tea.

Pursing her thin lips, Mindy shook her head as she accepted a cup. "That photographer was terrible. He made me look awful in that lighting. I was simply appalled he chose to photograph me with that brash Stacy Keens. I insisted on photoshopping her out."

Hiding a smile, Belle stared at her tea. "I thought Stacy was a dedicated volunteer. Hasn't she contributed significant amounts to the foundation?"

Mindy's chipmunk gaze turned bright. "She's a poor replacement for you, Belle. If you had reconsidered and chaired the silent-auction committee…"

"I did last year," she pointed out. "I will be at the gala, but work at the clinic consumes my time."

"The clinic." Mindy made a face. "A wonderful cause for your family, but must you rub shoulders with those people?"

The society matriarch gave a delicate shudder. "Those diseases they must carry…"

"I'm a doctor." Belle struggled to clamp down her temper. "I became a doctor to help treat disease and help people. They get sick same as you and I do, Mrs. Worthington."

Just as your son did. Evan, Mindy's only child, was Belle's age and had completed his chemotherapy after being diagnosed with cancer.

Her own mother smoothly switched the subject. "Mindy, dear, if the pictures the photographer took aren't to your satisfaction, there's still time to find another photographer."

"That would be for the best." Mindy sighed. "The photograph of me showed all my crow's-feet. And he thought that suitable for the society page? In color?"

Belle sipped her tea. Bland, weak. She added another lump of sugar, just for taste. Natalie peered over the top of her cup. "Belle, are you looking forward to getting a cardiology match for your residency in Boston? Your mother has talked of nothing else."

Her smile slipped a little. "It's a wonderful opportunity."

Not that I'm really certain it's for me. But what else am I going to do? My friends say if I get matched it's the chance of a lifetime.

"Of course, if she found the right man, Belle could be convinced to forgo moving to Boston."

Belle narrowed her gaze at her mother. "Perhaps I'd be convinced to forgo it for other reasons than a man."

"Belle…"

Mindy gave her a knowing look. "You remember my son, Evan? He's a full partner now at Ludwig & Sterns."

Who could forget him? Short, arrogant, horse-faced and preoccupied with his investment career. He'd pouted like a child when she'd beaten him at tennis when they were teenagers and once tried looking up her dress. Evan had confessed a teenage crush on her. She had felt bad when he'd been diagnosed with cancer, but it hadn't changed his personality for the better.

"He's back home now, Belle. Why don't you two have dinner tomorrow night? I know he'd love to see you again."

I have to wash my hair. Or weed the garden. Maybe even do my taxes.

The buzzer at the front gate rang. Saved by the bell. She set down her teacup in the saucer with a hard clink.

The maid stood at the living room entrance. "Mrs. North, there's an FBI agent here to see Miss Belle."

"Please open the gate and send him in," Belle told her.

Her mother's guests exchanged puzzled looks, while her mother's jaw tightened so much Belle feared her teeth would crack.

Minutes later. Belle jumped to her feet as Kyle Anderson strode forward. "Good afternoon. Sorry to interrupt your party, Dr. North," he said in his deep voice. "I'm headed over to the clinic and need the security code to get inside."

In his dark gray suit, blue tie mussed and day beard scruffing his cheeks, Kyle had a no-nonsense air. His vibrant, quiet masculinity sharply contrasted with the fussiness of the tea, the ladies in their pretty designer dresses and the lace doilies on the table.

The women in the room were deeply concerned about photoshopping their photos in the society pages.

Kyle was deeply concerned about finding Anna and saving her life.

Belle gestured to the room and made introductions.

"A real FBI agent." Mindy simpered. "Are you in trouble, Belle?"

"She's aiding an official investigation." Kyle didn't smile. "A child is missing."

Belle's mother put a hand to her chest. "Oh dear. That's terrible! And how is our clinic involved?"

"The girl was visiting the clinic. It's standard procedure, Mom. I promised special agent Anderson our full cooperation."

"Of course. Anything we can do to help." Belle's mother looked distressed.

"Did you find anything else at the shed?" she asked.

He glanced at the other women. "No. Everything was wiped clean. The suspect was a pro. Even the car didn't have prints. We're hoping to find something at the clinic. Do I have your permission to search it?"

He eyed her. "We could obtain a search warrant, but it would go faster if we had your permission to enter and search the premises."

"Of course. I'll go with you. I'll leave my car here and take an Uber back."

Belle's mother clenched her hands. "How old is the child?"

"She's six."

Mrs. North's mouth wobbled. "Poor baby. Please, Agent Anderson, let us know what you need."

"Thank you, ma'am."

"I mean it, agent. Anything we can do to help find her. Our family's resources are at your disposal."

Belle blinked. That was kind of her mother. Then again, her mother was known for her altruism.

"Is the FBI offering a reward?" her mother asked.

"Yes, it's twenty thousand dollars."

"Good. If no one comes forth with information in the next day, let myself or my husband know and we will double the amount. Anonymously, of course."

While her mother's generous gesture had her friends cooing with approval, it only sharpened Kyle's gaze. Belle silently cursed. Did her mother realize it made the family only look even more suspicious?

"Thank you, ma'am." He turned to Belle. "I'll need the security code to disarm the alarm system and the keys. If you'll give them to me, I'll be on my way and you can return to your guests."

"They're not my guests." Belle smoothed her dress. "I'll go with you. We'll need to stop off at my house. The keys are there. And you'll need the passwords to the computers, as well."

Mrs. North blinked, "Honey, can't you get one of the staff to do that?"

"It's Sunday, Mom. Their day off. The clinic is closed Sundays and Mondays." She turned to the two other women. "My apologies, ladies. It was lovely to see you again."

"Belle." Mrs. North's voice trembled. "You promised me you'd attend tea."

Shooting her mother a defiant look, she picked up her cup and drained it. China clattered as she set the cup down. "There. I've had tea. There's a child's life at stake. I should think that's more important than discussing society-page photos."

Her stomach in knots, she stormed outside. Kyle held the door open for her, his mouth twitching in apparent humor.

"Rough day at the mansion?" he quipped.

She took a deep breath. "I've never done that before."

He opened the passenger door of his sedan. "Have tea?"

"Told off my mother." She slid inside.

Kyle whistled. "Takes a lot of courage to stand up to family."

She ran a hand through her coiffed hair, ruining it. "Not courage. More like foolhardiness. My mother will never let me forget this. Maybe I should leave the country."

As his dark eyebrows raised, she added, "That's a joke."

"Uh-uh. Let me know if you want me to investigate her. Put a little heat on her. Did she ever participate in any radical protests in her wild youth?"

"My mother, wild? That's like saying Jackie O was at Woodstock."

His wicked grin charmed her. "You never know about people. Are there photos you can use to blackmail her? Maybe she was caught shoplifting at a big-box store?"

Giving a breathless laugh, she shook her head. "My mother? She's more into her society appearances and charity work than breaking the law. She would no more frequent a discount store than she'd show up in public without makeup. But if you could loan me some duct tape for her mouth…preferably something in a nice pattern that wouldn't clash with the furniture…"

A deep, hearty chuckle rumbled from his chest. Belle liked that sound. It reminded her that FBI Special agent Kyle Anderson was a real person.

As he started the car, he gave her a solemn look. "Thanks for your help."

"It's not a big deal. Afternoon tea is no longer my comfort zone." She ran a finger over her black clutch purse. "In a way, it never was, but I kept trying. She is my mother. Have you ever tried pleasing someone and no matter how hard you work at it, you'll never succeed at making them happy?"

For a moment he said nothing, only stared at the roadway and the elegant royal palm trees lining it. "Yes," he finally told her. "My wife."

Darn. Disappointment arrowed through her. Of course he wasn't single. Weren't all the good ones taken already? "You're married?"

"Was. She died."

Belle felt a pang of sympathy. "Oh. That's so tragic. Disease?"

Kyle shot her a sideways glance. "No. Car crash. We had problems. My job doesn't exactly make me a candidate for Attentive Husband of the Year."

"No. I can imagine it doesn't."

He turned onto the ramp for the freeway. "You're an

interesting person, Belle North. Most people would gush and say they were sorry for my loss."

"I am sorry for her death. And that she died so tragically. I'm just not good at meaningless platitudes." She stared at her hands, remembering her mother's disapproval at the ragged nails, how she badly needed a manicure. "Medicine has taught me that there are times for offering sincere condolences, such as when you lose a patient. But I wish there was something more I could say other than *I'm sorry.*"

Approval flashed on his face. "So do I. When you've had to tell a parent, time and again, that you're sorry for the loss of their child, it becomes almost meaningless."

"Yet you have to say something, express some kind of regret. At least that's how I feel about it. What do you say to them?"

His chest rose and fell. "Usually I leave the condolences to my partner. Then I tell them, *I'm sorry I couldn't do more to help your child in time. I tried my best, but it wasn't enough. I promise you that we will do everything we can to give you justice.*"

"I like that," she decided. "It sounds like you are taking personal responsibility for each case."

"I do," he said quietly.

Such a heavy burden to bear. She studied his rumpled suit, the smear of grease on his trousers. Agent Anderson wasn't afraid of hard work.

Neither was she.

"Do you ever have any fun? I mean, other than by hand-cuffing the bad guys?"

He gave another hearty chuckle. "Now you sound like my partner. I get downtime for errands and stuff like that."

"I meant other than grocery shopping and laundry." She rolled her eyes. "Take a vacation, indulge in sports."

"There's the sweetest little fishing spot near my apartment," he murmured.

She rubbed her hands together. "Oh, baby, now you're talking. Bass boat? Or do you have an inboard?"

"Outboard twenty-foot runabout I share with a friend. Haven't taken her out in a long time."

"Why? Don't you like boating?"

"No time. I'm usually working."

She wondered what made him so uptight. "I love boating. If you live in Florida, it's a wonderful way to relax. You should try it."

Kyle glanced at her. "My boat is small. Nothing like your family yacht."

"My family yacht is a sailboat. I learned how to sail before I learned how to talk."

Belle directed him to her house from the freeway. He turned onto the main road leading to her house. "Must have been hard to learn to talk anyway, with that silver spoon in your mouth."

Bristling, she started to retort when she caught a slight grin. Teasing her. Fine. Two could play at this.

"My silver spoon happened to be gold. Monogrammed."

"I suppose your diapers were all monogrammed, as well."

Belle sputtered. "Excuse me? What about you, Agent Cowboy, if we're talking diapers. Or did you run wild and naked as a baby?"

"I save the running wild and naked for now. Lots more fun."

Heat crawled up her neck. *I bet it is more fun.*

Kyle Anderson could be fun as well if he lost some of that tension riding him. The man needed to relax.

Following her directions, Kyle pulled into her driveway.

Belle dashed inside, grabbed the keys and gave a quick pat to a sleeping Boo.

Back in the SUV, she turned the keys over in her hand. Against her better judgment, she had started to like Agent

Anderson. The purely feminine part of her that felt the attraction sizzling between them felt compelled to draw him out. Peel off a layer to find the man beneath the gruff exterior and the rigid dedication to the job.

"Have you ever sailed?" she asked.

Seemingly lost in thought, Kyle stroked the steering wheel. Her fascinated gaze tracked the moves. He had nice hands, long, subtle fingers. What would they feel like stroking her naked skin?

A flush ignited her face. Hopefully he wouldn't notice.

"Yeah. Buddy of mine has a sailboat moored in Miami."

"Sailing takes skill, but there's nothing like the challenge of heading into the wind, the breeze on your face, nothing but you and the open sea."

He drew in a deep breath, released it. As if he, too, felt the sexual tension sizzling between them in the close confines of his vehicle.

Then a smile touched his mouth. A dangerous smile.

He continued, "Of course, you haven't had real fun until you've sailed naked. That's the challenge. The wind in your face and your hair, and the rudder hitting you in parts unknown. Bet your mother would enjoy something like that."

Belle dissolved into laughter at the thought of her genteel mother even trying to skinny dip. When she finally ceased, she saw they had pulled up to the clinic.

Dozens of black-and-white patrol cars parked in the lot. Not only patrol cars, but vans with satellite dishes, men and women milling about, television cameras in hand. Even with the windows rolled up in the SUV, she could hear the cacophony.

Her laugh died on a gasp. "I guess the sheriff's office finally got that press release out."

Kyle pulled into a space. "This isn't going to be easy, Belle. You don't have to do it. You may wish you stayed at that tea."

"It's my family's clinic. You need someone from the family there as you search it."

"Yeah, it's best that you're here. You ready for this?"

He had deliberately distracted her with small talk earlier. Clever. She put her hand on his jacket sleeve.

"Thank you for getting my mind off my own problems."

Kyle stared down at her hand. "No thanks needed. You were tense. Thought you could use a diversion."

Then he squeezed it tight. "Let's do this."

As she stepped out of the SUV, reporters bolted over. Microphones were thrust into her face, and the loud shout of questions made her head spin.

"Are you the owner of this clinic?" one yelled.

"Do you represent the North family, who does own it?" asked another.

"No comment," she said clearly.

Hand on the small of her back, Kyle guided her through the crush, his big body shouldering aside the throng.

Her hand was remarkably steady as she unlocked the front security gate, and then the door. Kyle helped, holding the door open. He motioned to a deputy.

"Keep all of them out." He gestured to the media, "Tell them any official statements will be forthcoming from your department. The FBI is offering a twenty-thousand-dollar reward for information that leads us to Anna Rodriguez, also known as Anna Alvarez. The man we're looking to question was wearing dark sneakers or shoes, white shirt, jeans and a gray jacket."

"Yes, sir."

Nerves slightly rattled, she disarmed the security system, glad Kyle took charge of the chaos outside. Two other agents, including Agent Calhoun, entered the clinic, along with a slew of crime-scene investigators from the sheriff's department.

Belle only hoped they could find something that would

lead them to Anna. Far as she knew, the clinic was spotless and their reputation sterling. But perhaps some DNA or fingerprints might help.

"Walk me through exactly where they sat, what room they were in," Kyle instructed.

His presence was soothing, his manner professional. Belle pointed to the rows of chairs in the waiting room. "You can try dusting for prints there, but I honestly can't tell you where they sat. You'll have better luck in the exam room."

She opened Exam Room 2. "There were plenty of patients after Anna, and we always clean up after each one."

Kyle looked around. "Including the doorknobs?"

"No."

"We'll dust that. Just in case. Did Smith touch anything else?"

"He filled out the paperwork for Anna. I don't suppose you can lift prints off paper."

"You'd be surprised what our lab can do."

Snapping on a pair of sterile gloves, Belle went to the cramped office where they kept paper files on all the patients. But as she searched, unease gripped her. Meticulous as the receptionist was, the file should be here…

"Find anything?" a deep voice inquired.

"Oh!" Belle whirled, almost tripped.

Hands on her arms, Kyle steadied her. "Easy."

"You're very quiet. I didn't realize you came in. Or that you were right behind me." Heart racing, she swallowed hard. Having him this close, the heat of his palms on her cool skin, was highly arousing.

Her libido didn't care about a missing child. Normal biological reaction to a handsome, masculine guy with authority.

"I tend to do that to people." Mouth twisted in a crooked

smile, he pointed to the filing cabinet. "Let me guess. File's gone."

She nodded, shoving a hand through her hair. "I could check and see if it's misfiled, but…"

"Is there anything else Dugin touched?"

"Not that I recall. He may have had a cup of coffee. We offer free coffee."

"When does your dumpster get picked up?"

"Tomorrow. It's in the back, locked behind a gate to prevent anyone from the neighborhood dumping there, or raiding it." She handed him the thick ring of keys.

He handed them off to two investigators who'd trailed them into the exam room. Two additional ones began scouring the room.

"I'll be in my office," she told him. "I'm going to search for Anna's digital file. It should be there. Let me know if you need anything."

Once inside the tiny office she shared with George and Dr. Patterson, she opened the top drawer of her desk. Every day before leaving the clinic, she made notations in a leather-bound journal about her caseload.

Last night before leaving, she'd made certain to record her observations about Anna.

The journal was missing. Belle frowned. Someone inside the clinic definitely wanted to eradicate any trace of Anna's visit.

The computer offered no digital footprint, either. Anna's file was gone.

It was as if she'd never been here.

I bet the cleaning crew threw out everything and wiped down every single surface. It will be a miracle if they can lift any usable fingerprints.

Maybe she'd left the journal in another drawer. She searched but found nothing. The bottom drawer contained a sloppy assortment of papers, prescription pads, pens and empty pill bottles.

"George, Dr. Patterson, you both need to be tidier," she murmured, digging through the mess.

Her fingers hit an indentation at the drawer's bottom. Curious, she lifted it, wondering what lay beneath.

Oh no. This wasn't good. Even if it was innocent, it looked pretty bad. Belle ran to find Kyle.

When he came into the office, she silently pointed to the false bottom.

Kyle opened the thermal lunch tote and unzipped it. He plucked out a thick stack of one-hundred-dollar bills and thumbed through them with his gloved fingers.

"Whose desk is this?" he asked.

"I share it with Dr. Patterson and George. But that's Tony's lunchbox." Her heart sank as she realized the importance of what she'd found. "Our security man."

Kyle handed the tote over to a crime-scene tech. "Get this to the lab ASAP."

Belle licked her dry lips. "Do you think he did it and this is his payment?"

"Maybe. But the fact that someone tampered with your security footage and now we found this doesn't look good for him. We'll bring him in for questioning." Kyle's expression hardened. "If he's been stealing drugs from you, chances are he may have been forced into other illegal things here."

Such as kidnapping little girls. Belle nodded.

"Whatever you need from us, we'll provide it for you."

But deep inside, she knew it wasn't looking good for them. And every minute that passed with Anna missing, her chances of being found alive grew slimmer.

Chapter 9

Dead ends. Nothing but dead ends.

Dugin was no closer to being found than before.

After finally tracking him down Monday morning, police brought in Tony, the clinic's security guard, to the station. Now he sat in an interrogation room as detectives peppered him with questions. Questioning Tony Fontaine looked to be a dead end. The security man insisted he'd hidden the money because he withdrew it from the bank, planning on taking a cruise for his anniversary. George had told him about the false-bottom drawer and Tony stashed the cash the day Anna went missing, planning on giving it to the travel agency.

Bank records confirmed the withdrawal.

At the local police station on Monday, Kyle and Roarke watched the taped interrogation from the security camera.

"Well, this is a waste of time," Roarke muttered.

Kyle said nothing, his mind analyzing the recent events. "Wait. Maybe we'll get something on the clinic's security footage."

But Tony admitted the machine was broken and the clinic lacked the budget to fix it.

"Miss Belle, she's so good to all of us. But we're behind on budget. So instead of telling her about the system being broke, I had a friend try to fix it. He ended up looping it over and over. Everyone in this community respects the clinic," Tony insisted to the questioning detective. "They need this service. If we keep overspending, the foundation will have to shut it down."

Too many threads were connected to this clinic. The sheriff's office had questioned all the clinic's employees, except one.

"Well?" Roarke asked.

He studied his cell phone. "Anna's been missing one day. All the other girls were returned to their families forty-eight hours later. This isn't the same victimology. Her mother was assaulted, unlike the other girls, whose family members were left unhurt. If Dugin did this, why didn't he attack the other girls' families?"

"Because it wasn't necessary," Roarke mused.

"Maybe. It could be that Anna's mother got in the way and he didn't want a witness. Still, this case bothers me. The MO is different. All the girls had green eyes and dark hair, but Dugin had Anna and her mother living in a secure location for at least a week. Why go through all that trouble? Why not simply take Anna and leave? Hiding someone for a week isn't easy."

"Unless you want to be hidden," Roarke said, his gaze sharp.

His partner had firsthand experience with that. Kyle never questioned his history, but knew Roarke had a reason for leaving the military and working for the FBI. He was a newer recruit, with sharp instincts and an even sharper intellect.

"Okay, let's say Rosa's on the run from the law. Or someone. We don't yet have a DNA hit on her, so we have no idea of her real identity. Everyone in the trailer park where she's thought to be have lived said she was quiet and nervous. Then she gets kicked out for not paying bills and comes north, homeless, with her kid, desperate…"

"Where she meets Dugin, who promises to be her savior. Where did they meet and how? The clinic?"

The security guard might know. He was a link in a long chain. "Let's do this," Kyle told Roarke.

Kyle knocked on the door, and entered, closing it behind him. He introduced himself and then stared at Tony as he spread out the flyers with Anna's face and Rosa's.

"Have you ever seen this woman or her daughter at the Harold Donald Clinic before?" he asked.

Tony frowned. "I might have. There's a lot of people who pass through. I just hang outside and in the lobby."

"Tell me about Dr. Michael Patterson, the man in charge of the clinic. What does he do?" Kyle told him.

Tony licked his lips. "Everything. He was hired by Mr. Clint to run the place. He's a good doctor, works every Saturday, too."

"He oversees ordering medication, including Propofol? Did you know five vials were missing in the last two weeks and not reported to the authorities?" Roarke asked.

Sweat trickled down the big man's temples. "One of the nurses told me, but when I reported it to Dr. Patterson, he said he would conduct his own investigation."

Right. Meaning, not do a damn thing.

"Where is Patterson? Where does he like to go for vacation?" Kyle questioned.

Tony frowned. "He had a family funeral."

The family funeral had turned out to be a distant cousin, and none of the family recalled seeing Patterson after the services. The doctor had simply slipped out of town. All his instincts warned the clinic's chief physician was involved in Anna's disappearance. Dugin might have taken Anna, but Patterson wasn't clean, either.

Kyle took out the mug shot of Jesse Dugin and showed it to Tony. "What about him? Ever seen him around?"

Squinting, the security guard studied the photo. "Maybe. Can't really tell."

The mug shot was old, when Dugin's hair was short and he was bearded. Next, Kyle showed Tony the updated computer-generated photo that showed Dugin with a baseball cap, longer hair and no beard.

The security guard's eyes widened. "Yeah. Him I've seen. Once, ah, maybe twice."

"How and where?"

"Two, three weeks ago maybe. He came in to treat a cut on his hand. I remember him because he insisted on seeing Dr. Patterson right away and not waiting. And the cut, it wasn't bad." Tony snorted. "I would have put a bandage on it."

Exchanging glances with Roarke, he pressed on. "What other time did you see him?"

But Tony could only recall that one time. It was enough.

Dugin had gone underground, with no visible way of finding him yet. Police were combing through the locations where Anna and her mother had lived, questioning residents. Yet they had no solid leads. Until now.

They had to find Patterson and bring him in for questioning.

Outside the interrogation room, Kyle made yet another attempt to contact the doctor. The call went directly to voice mail. He tried Clint North's cell phone. Same thing.

"No luck?" Roarke asked.

Palming his cell, he looked at the two-way glass. "Maybe. I know one person who could know how to contact Patterson."

Questioning her would take diplomacy and tact. Belle worked at the clinic that belonged to her family, and she had contact with all the parties involved in Anna's disappearance. She knew Patterson.

His gut warned that Belle was the key to all of this.

* * *

Working at the cardiology office on Monday proved a good distraction for Belle. Until her mother called and asked her to come over when she was finished her shift at three. There was a quaver in Shirley's voice she didn't like.

The normally quiet, tree-lined street where her parents lived was packed with news vans and media hovering outside the iron gates. Two security guards checked her driver's license and opened the gates for her.

Inside the house, her mother sat in the living room with Mindy Worthington. Shirley looked pale and far older than her sixty-eight years. Belle sat beside her, took her pulse.

"I'm fine. Medically. It's the stress. I asked Mindy to come over because I'm leaving town, Belle, and I have all my social obligations to meet." Mrs. North rubbed her temples. "Dealing with the media, the reporters camped outside the clinic and our house, has been dreadful."

Her genteel mother disliked the limelight. Belle empathized. "Hire more security guards to keep them away."

"Your father already did, but they pounce soon as we leave the property. I'm all but trapped here." Mrs. North sipped her wine. "Now they're saying our clinic and foundation are at the heart of the investigation. Our name will be ruined."

"After all that you've done for the community. All your projects, your charity efforts." Mindy tsk-tsked.

Guilt crept over her. She had been the doctor on duty who treated Anna. If she'd called the police with her suspicions that day, Anna might have been rescued. None of this would have happened.

"I promise you, I'll do everything I can to clear the clinic and our family name, Mom."

Her mother turned the wineglass in her hands. "I don't know what you can do, Belle. The matter has been taken out of our hands and it rests with the authorities."

"Don't discount the power of a smart woman."

The quip that she'd uttered in the past usually made her mother smile. At least her mother's lips lifted slightly. Then she set her wineglass down with a troubled look.

"I've had several threatening emails in the past day, saying the vilest things about our family taking advantage of people. Some suggested auditing the foundation, claiming it's used solely for tax evasion."

"That's preposterous. The attention will blow over, eventually. Maybe if the public put more effort into volunteering to find Anna instead of lambasting you, the FBI would have more leads. You're not to blame in this," Belle said hotly.

"They say I am." Mrs. North plucked at the sleeve of her silk blouse. "It's our family's foundation, and I am the chairman. Your father wants to take me out of town for a few days until all this blows over."

Belle clasped her hands. "That's a good idea, Mom. Take a little vacation. You and Dad deserve it."

Her mother's mouth wobbled. "It feels as if we are running away."

Throat closing tight, she fought to control her emotions. Shirley Vandermeer North had never hurt a living soul in her life. Her mother deeply cared about the causes she supported.

She had never seen her mother like this—frail and aged. Fear crept around the edges of Belle's confidence. Although she seldom was sick, what if the stress affected her mother's health?

Mrs. North rubbed her thin hands together. "I'm beginning to wish we had never opened that clinic."

"That's what happens when you try to help those kind of people. They take advantage of what you give them." Mindy poured herself more wine from the carafe.

Belle had a bad feeling about this. "Who exactly are 'those people'?"

"The kind the clinic aids. Why couldn't that woman have paid closer attention to her daughter?" Mrs. North burst out.

Mindy shook her head with a regretful sigh. "It's in the breeding, Shirley. There is none. So many transients, so many are prevalent here in Florida and they're ignorant. They simply do not know how to take care of their children. They let them run wild, fail to properly educate them. It's no wonder many end up in jail. Or in this case, get into trouble."

Mrs. North nodded. "If this Rosa had been more careful, and watched over her child, this never would have happened and our lives would have never been disrupted."

Belle blinked hard in dumbfounded shock, all sympathy for her family's plight vanishing. She understood her mother's desperate need to grasp at someone to blame for the chaos revolving in their lives, but to blame Rosa was unfair. And cruel.

"I can't believe you're both blaming the victim."

Mindy's lips pursed. "Belle, dear, who else is to blame but the mother? She should have been watching out for her child."

Stomach knotting, she fisted her hands. "How about putting the blame where it belongs? On the damn person who did this!"

"Belle," Mrs. North said, looking uneasy.

"Rosa Rodriguez lies in a coma in an intensive care unit. Someone tried to kill her. The same person who kidnapped Anna. And you're both placing the responsibility on Rosa."

She turned to Mindy. "Would you do the same if I were abducted? Blame my mother for my disappearance?"

"It's not the same..." Mindy began.

"It's exactly the same. You're both saying Rosa is at fault. You don't know her circumstances, anything about her life. How she lived, what she had to do to survive. Instead you sit here and point fingers at a mother who probably fought with her life to save her daughter."

Standing up, she swept them both with a look of contempt. "I never imagined you're so heartless."

Shirley took a deep breath. "That's a cruel thing to say about your father and me, Belle. We are far from heartless. I have to go pack." Her mother headed for the stairs, followed by an anxious Mindy.

There was nothing more to say.

Her hands shook violently as she jammed the key into the ignition of her Corvette. Belle accelerated and the car roared out of the circular driveway.

At the gate, she tapped her fingers on the steering wheel as the security guard pressed a button to release the gate. Television vans and reporters milled outside, some waving microphones in her face.

On impulse she stopped, rolled down her window to address the crush of media.

"I have a statement to make to the press," she told them in a strong, clear voice. "My family is innocent of anything having to do with this abduction. I promise you, I will help track down the person who took Anna and they will see justice. The power of my family's money is behind this. If we have to hire a squadron of detectives to aid the FBI, Anna will be found."

As they shouted more questions at her, she sped away.

On A1A, the serene vista of the turquoise ocean waters with their lacy whitecaps did little to soothe her raging nerves. She passed several expensive homes like her family's, all tastefully tucked away behind ornate steel gates.

Her world was far different from Rosa Rodriguez's. She'd never had to worry about a roof over her head, food to eat or money to buy basic necessities.

Belle Bluetoothed her phone and dialed Kyle's number.

"Anderson," he said in a clipped tone.

She took a deep breath. "I've had a nasty fight with my mother. But that's not why I'm calling. I made a statement to the press and I thought you should know."

"Saw it on the news."

The media wasted no time.

"I thought we agreed you'd avoid talking to reporters." No recrimination in his voice, which was refreshing.

"I felt I had to say something because the public is censuring my family and it's deeply upsetting my mom. Dad is taking her out of town until the feeding frenzy dies down. I wanted the media to know our family stands with the FBI in doing all we can to find Anna."

Silence for a few seconds, then he spoke in a gentle voice. "What happened? You sound rattled, and it isn't about the press coverage."

Tears burned in the back of her throat. Belle gripped the steering wheel so hard her palms hurt. Driving like this could get her into an accident.

After pulling into a shopping-center parking lot, she guided the Corvette into an empty space and sat, engine running. Belle wiped her eyes.

"Mom and her friend blame Rosa for Anna's disappearance. Rosa, who lost her daughter and is still in a coma, damn it! My mother is a generous, kind person. Oh, she has her faults, but she's never been cruel or callous. Why would she say such things?"

"I've run into it more than you know," he said in his deep, soothing voice. "People want to place blame with someone because it makes them feel safe. It's an odd psychology. If the fault lies with the victim, then the person blaming them isn't vulnerable."

"When, in truth, we all are vulnerable. Because anything bad can happen to any of us. That's life." Belle thought of the cases she'd seen in medical school that seemed tragically unfair—from car crashes to cancer.

"To think the alternative—that the world isn't safe, no matter what precautions you take—is terrifying."

Fingers hurting as she wrapped them around her phone, she wanted to keep him talking. The disquieting incident at home had turned her happy illusion that her family was nonjudgmental into a spiderweb of cracked ideals.

When had they changed?

When had *she* changed?

"Where are you headed now?" he asked.

"The hospital." She took a deep breath. "I need to see Rosa. Then maybe a walk in the park. I'll call you if I get any news."

She hung up. Belle liked the agent, liked making him smile and laugh. And yet what he investigated was no laughing matter.

At the hospital, Anna's mother still lay in ICU in a coma. The charge nurse told Belle all her vitals were good. It was only a matter of her finally waking up.

Belle left the ICU deeply troubled. What if Rosa remained in a coma indefinitely? Or suffered brain damage?

She went home, changed into jeans, a comfortable long-sleeved shirt and sneakers, and clipped on Boo's leash.

"Come on, sweetie," she told her happy dog. "Walkies!"

Belle drove to the park. Yellow crime-scene tape still cordoned off the area where Rosa had been found. Belle parked across the lake, tucked a dog water canteen for Boo into her backpack and they began to walk.

Sun warmed her face as a cooling breeze blew across the lake.

The visit to ICU to see Rosa had deeply rattled her. She needed fresh air, a chance to purge the vision of Anna's pale-faced mother lying in the big bed, hooked up to machines keeping her alive.

Belle could only hope Rosa would make it.

She sat on the lake's bank, staring at the crime scene

across the water. Sunlight shimmered on the clear lake, and in the distance, she heard a child giggle. Families were picnicking, riding bicycles; men and women zipped along the mountain bike trail.

So normal.

So surreal.

"So many terrible things happen in this world, Boo," she told her dog, hugging him. "How can I fight them?"

Boo squirmed. As she released him, he turned and licked a stray tear trickling down her cheek.

"The only thing necessary for the triumph of evil is for good men to do nothing," a deep voice said behind her.

Belle blinked hard. "I heard Edmund Burke had said that. A nice sentiment. If only it were true."

She turned as Agent Anderson squatted beside her. In his charcoal-gray business suit, blue shirt and tie, he looked incongruous in a park known for mountain biking and hiking. His frown eased as he studied her face. "Why were you crying?"

Belle shrugged.

Kyle reached up, wiped away a teardrop with the edge of his thumb. His touch sent a shiver of awareness down her spinc. He had great hands. "What's wrong?"

His deep voice carried a note of sympathy, but she couldn't bring herself to fully trust him. "I was thinking about Anna, who's a little girl and too young to defend herself. And all the evil in this world. It feels overwhelming at times."

Kyle scratched Boo, who wagged his tail.

"Are you stalking me?" she asked him.

"Do you mind?"

Belle indicated the space next to her. He sat, rubbing Boo's ears. No point in asking how he'd found her. He was a skilled agent, and expert at finding people.

Except he hadn't found Anna yet. And until she was

found, nothing else mattered. Not her personal or professional life, or her feelings.

She stared at the water. "Do you believe it's true? Can good men doing something prohibit evil?"

"Better than the alternative. Terrible things are always going to happen in the world, Doc. And there are good people who will do what they can to stop them."

She moistened her lips. "I'm glad you're one of them."

A brief smile touched his mouth. "I do what I can." He sighed. "Sometimes it's not enough."

For a few moments they sat in companionable silence.

"I stopped by ICU to see Rosa. She's still unconscious. I wanted to see about paying for her medical expenses, but they told me someone already is." She turned and looked at him. His profile was sharply outlined against the bright sunshine. A hank of dark hair hung over his forehead, the breeze playing with it. It made him look younger, almost boyish.

"Your mother is paying the bill. All of it."

Unease shot through her. "How did you find out?"

"I checked when I visited Rosa yesterday."

Not good. Her mother was altruistic to a fault, but this put her family even more under the microscope as suspects. "She probably feels guilty because our clinic was connected to what happened to Rosa."

"Maybe." He looked at her, really looked at her. Such deep blue eyes, unfathomable like the ocean. "I did a little checking, Dr. North. Maybe your mother has another reason to help Rosa."

This couldn't be good. Belle stiffened. "Which is?"

"She should tell you."

More mysteries. She hated secrets.

"If you're going to be coy about it, why bother saying anything?" she snapped.

Kyle scratched Boo's head again. "Did you know you have a record with the FBI?"

Shock filled her. "That's crazy. I don't. And my mother has something to do with this?"

"Yup. It's a sealed file."

"I will make a point of asking her. So, why do you need to talk to me?"

"We brought your security guard in for questioning. He told us he'd seen Dugin at the clinic before."

Belle frowned, searching for memory. "Dr. Patterson usually treated Anna, but I didn't find any records on Dugin visiting him."

"Seems his visits were private. He specifically insisted on seeing Dr. Patterson." Kyle gave her a pointed look. "Your director, who seems to be missing, as well. And is not answering any of his cell phone calls."

Acid churned in her stomach. First the FBI record, now this. "So this isn't a social call. Or you want to accompany me on a hike."

"We could walk." He gave a languid stretch. "Fresh air might do us both good."

Insight struck her. "You waited to talk to me while I was alone. And not in my house or the clinic."

A half smile touched his sensual mouth. "You're pretty damn bright, Doc. Yeah, because I don't want other ears around. Let's walk."

He pulled her to her feet, his grip strong but not crushing. Belle gripped Boo's leash as they headed for a less-traveled hiking path.

"What do you know about Dr. Michael Patterson?" he asked.

Belle told him. No secrets there. Family friend for years, her brother had gone deep-sea fishing with him a few times on Patterson's boat, and when they'd needed someone to run the clinic when it opened last year, he'd asked for the job.

Kyle listened intently, saying little.

"Where does he go when he's not in town? Vacation home, anyplace special?"

This wasn't sounding good. "He was at a family funeral," she insisted. "That's why he was out of town."

"Maybe. But he didn't stay long."

Belle turned, glaring at him. "If you have something to say, say it."

He gave her a pointed look. "I told you before, I don't trust doctors and now your medical director has given me a new reason why. He had direct contact with Dugin, our suspect in this case. And now Patterson is 'unavailable.'"

"I can contact him for you. I'm sure if you talked with him, it would clear all this up."

"I'd love that."

Sarcasm dripped from his voice. Belle's fingers curled into fists. "I still wouldn't take the word of Tony, our security guard. Tony's only there because his wife begged my family for a job."

"Is your family always in the habit of doing charity and handing out jobs to unqualified applicants? Doctors, as well? Or do you have something else to hide, such as taking little girls?"

The insult stung. Belle stopped and faced him. "How dare you insinuate my family has something to do with Anna's disappearance," she said in a low voice. "And here I thought I liked you. You're impudent and boorish."

He considered. "Funny, my partner usually calls me a pain in the ass. I haven't been called impudent since my fourth-grade teacher."

The slight teasing tone confused her. "I'm sure your teacher was correct."

"Mrs. Lerner didn't like the frog I placed in her desk drawer."

Belle struggled against a smile. He was purposely disarming her again. "Agent Anderson, my family and the clinic have nothing to hide."

"Maybe," he said softly, getting in her face. "But I can't believe that until we can find Dr. Patterson and find out what the hell he was doing with the man suspected of taking Anna."

He was only doing his job. And she had to do hers. Belle gripped Boo's leash tight. "Then listen to me, because I'm telling you the full truth. I will do whatever it takes to find her. Understand? Even if it means my own reputation is on the line. Or my family's. I'm sure once you're able to contact Mike, you will receive his full cooperation."

He looked at her for a long moment. Then he nodded. "Okay, Doc. Then I'll need any information you have on Patterson. Phone numbers, places he likes to frequent. Everything."

Stomach churning, she nodded. "You really think Mike could be connected to Anna vanishing?"

"I'd bet my badge on it. Where do you keep all that information on him?"

"It's at my house." She gave him a pointed look. "I could request you obtain a search warrant."

Kyle leaned close enough for her to count the slight bristles on his chiseled chin. "You could. But it would save a hell of a lot of time in finding Anna if you simply invited me over."

She ended up doing just that, leading the way as he followed in his SUV.

The thought of her mentor being involved in this abduction iced her blood. But better to find Mike, have him clear his own name, than make excuses.

On the way to her house, she phoned her brother. Voice mail. "Clint, call me ASAP. I need to find Mike."

Belle couldn't relax once they were inside the house.

Agent Anderson was larger than life, taking up all the space inside her small home. He filled the air with sheer male vitality, and there was no denying the chemistry sparking between them.

Chemistry that wouldn't go anywhere, because she sensed he didn't want this attraction any more than she did.

She led the way to the living room overlooking the lanai and the turquoise pool water. Kyle moved aside a multi-colored throw and sank down into the couch with a soft curse. Belle laughed.

"I should have warned you. It swallows you whole. You can get lost and they'll have to send out a search party."

Her smile faded as she remembered the reason why he was here. "I'll get you those files."

In a few minutes, he was sifting through the information she had on Mike Patterson. Mike had mentored her, taught her a few things about medicine long before she'd started college.

From the file he lifted out a photo of Mike and her brother on a tropical beach. On the back was penned "Bahamas."

"Mind if I take this?"

"Go ahead. I don't need it." She went into the kitchen and returned with two glasses of iced tea.

Kyle set down his glass. "Tell me about your dog."

"Boo isn't a purebred. Well, he might be. I found him wandering in a parking lot down south. He was hungry and dirty." She rubbed the dog's ears. "Saving dogs is a passion of mine. Too many are abandoned. I have a pet project I support that rescues them."

"Pampered Strays," he said, not missing a beat. "You sit on the board of directors."

Belle blinked. "How did you know... Oh. You investigated me."

Of course. She was probably still considered a suspect. And there was the matter of that mysterious sealed file with the FBI. She made a mental note to ask her mother later. "Did you find out all my dark secrets? Discover all my dirty laundry? What's next, wiretapping my phone?"

She said it in a light tone, but it disconcerted her to think Kyle had dug into her past.

He stretched out his long legs and rolled a shoulder. "Naw. Wiretapping's a pain, so unless there's a good reason for it, I avoid it. Background checks are easier. Less cumbersome. You have quite a shocking past, Dr. North."

"Good thing you never found out about how many times I played truant from finishing school."

Kyle took a long swig of tea, his throat muscles working. She watched with fascination. He set down the glass and gave her a solemn look. "I know. There's no statute of limitations on that, Doc."

As her jaw dropped, he laughed. His laugh, so hearty and carefree, lifted her spirits. Belle suspected this FBI agent seldom laughed while investigating cases. "I had an excuse. I sneaked out with my girlfriends to hang at the beach."

"And here I thought you were a perfect lady." Kyle scratched Boo's ears as the dog jumped onto the sofa.

"I'm not always a lady, and far from perfect." She glanced ruefully at her mussed clothing. "My mother would be appalled at my appearance right now."

His warm gaze swept over her. "You look pretty good to me."

Heat crawled up her throat to her face. Compliments from admiring men, she could handle those. But this one was different. It wasn't empty flattery to coax her into bed or get something else from her. Sincerity toned his voice.

Belle sensed he didn't give compliments often, but when he did, they were like rare gems.

Much to her chagrin, she liked this agent. Bad news. *Don't fall for the man investigating you and your family.*

She glanced at her cell phone. As much as this man intrigued and aroused her, they were too different. And she knew he still regarded her as a suspect.

"I have to visit my parents before they leave."

Kyle nodded. "I'll need all their contact information and where they'll be staying."

Police cars blocked the road to her parents' house, allowing access only to residents. They allowed Belle through. Her mother was upstairs, packing, looking worn-out.

Belle sat on the lounge chair by the window, watching. "Do you need anything from me while you're gone?"

"No. Your brother has arranged everything and we've paid the staff and gave them time off."

Belle toyed with a pile of scarves on the bed. "Mom, how well do you know Mike Patterson?"

Mrs. North snapped the suitcase shut. "We've known his family for a long time. Why do you ask?"

"The police can't seem to locate him."

"He's probably in hiding after all this dreadful publicity surrounding the clinic."

"Do you trust him?"

Shirley turned and frowned. "I don't know him well enough, Belle. Your brother does. He's friends with him."

She watched as her mother went into the dressing room and emerged with a small Louis Vuitton cosmetics case.

"Mom, what happened to me that I have an FBI record?"

The case thumped to the floor. Shirley rubbed her hands together. "That's preposterous. Why would you have a record?"

"I don't know. But you do. Apparently I was too young to remember what happened to me." She jumped up, picked up the case. "What happened?"

Her mother rubbed her forehead. "Belle, must we talk about this now? I have less than two hours to pack before we have to leave for the airport."

Belle held on to the case as her mother reached out for it. "Yes, we do. What happened to me? Was I witness to a federal crime?"

She sighed. "We'll talk, Belle, I promise, but now is not the time."

Knowing her mother wouldn't discuss it further, she changed the subject. "Paying Rosa's medical bills is very generous of you. Why are you doing it?"

"I paid Rosa's medical bills because when that poor woman awakes, she'll be going through hell," Shirley said softly. "The guilt and self-blame, the terrible fear that something awful happened to her baby and there is nothing, absolutely nothing, she can do about it."

Such a far cry from her mother's accusations earlier, blaming Rosa for losing track of Anna. "From what you said before, you blamed her for Anna disappearing."

Her mother shrugged, her expression impartial once more. "Perhaps I misjudged her. Besides, I know your generous side. You'd be paying Rosa's medical bills yourself and you need all your cash for the move to Boston when the residency comes through."

Oh. That. Belle picked up a pile of cashmere scarves, carried them to the suitcase. "Do you need any help?"

"No. Go downstairs—see if Clint is here yet. He promised to drive us to the airport. I don't dare call a taxi or an Uber, having them find out we're besieged by the media."

Belle understood. Her mother needed time to regain her lost composure, repair the armor of cosmetics and grooming that shielded her from the world.

If only it were that easy for her. But the greater question remained—why wasn't Mike Patterson back yet and what did he have to do with Anna's disappearance?

Chapter 10

By Thursday, Belle reasoned the media frenzy would have died down outside the now-closed clinic. After leaving the cardiology practice, she decided to stop at the clinic to look for the missing files once more.

Maybe they could even reopen tomorrow.

Always an optimist. But the community needs us and needs our services.

As she drove, her thoughts drifted to the attractive agent. Such a paradox. Growly and distant one minute and then compassionate and gentle the next. She itched to dig beneath the prickly outer shell to find the man beneath.

See what he was really like. Sure, he was hot. Sexy in a subtle way, with his urbane charm and quiet dedication. He made the other men in her slim social circle seem inconsequential and shallow as a puddle.

Her cell phone beeped. Belle pressed the Bluetooth button on her dashboard.

"Dr Pepper, where you at?"

Kyle's deep, laconic drawl sent a tingle rushing down her spine. The pleasant sensation made her squirm with anticipation. The man had a voice that could seduce a celibate.

"In my trusty little red Corvette. Why?"

"Thought we could get together, go over the details of

all the other girls that you can recall. And then maybe grab a bite to eat."

A date. Sort of. Not really. "Sure. Good timing. I'm going to check on things at the clinic."

Instantly his voice became alert, his tone sharp. "Are you driving there alone?"

"Yes. I figured the media circus would have departed town by now."

"They have, but there's another circus taking their place. Turn around. Don't go."

"I'm almost there. It'll only take a minute."

"Wait for me. I'm getting in my car now."

He hung up. Odd. She turned right onto the back road of the clinic, saw a commotion down the street.

Maybe the media frenzy hadn't died down yet. There was always the back gate.

She pulled up to the back, unlocked the gate and pulled her car inside, before locking the gate behind her. A crowd gathered in front of the clinic outside the gate. The back door was bolted from the inside, so she'd have to go around the front.

Dismay and regret filled her as she walked around the building.

Dozens of people lined the metal security fence outside the clinic. They held signs and waved them. Some held candles. A few people held up photos of Anna printed in the local newspapers.

As she stared at them, the crowd spotted her and began to point and shout.

"That's her! I saw her on TV! She's the doctor who owns this place!"

"Dr. Death! What did you do with Anna!"

"Child snatcher!"

"How many more of our kids are going to disappear?" one woman screamed.

Angry voices, filled with grief and rage. Now was not the time for reassurance. They needed an outlet for their emotions, and she was it.

Why hadn't she listened to Kyle?

Too late now. She'd just run inside, comb through the files and then dash out.

Keys rattled in her hand as she unlocked the front door.

When she returned outside, the crowd had grown. Six local police tried to keep order. Perspiration trickled down her back and her palms went clammy. Bright sunshine showed the angry faces in harsh relief.

She wanted to run and hide, but forced herself to walk slowly outside. Heels clicking on the concrete, she locked the front door and closed the steel grate.

Smile and wave.

Belle waved but could not smile. Not when her stomach churned and she felt nauseated.

She didn't need these people to point fingers and make accusations. Not when she'd already wallowed in the pool of self blame.

Screeches and shouts increased in tempo and volume, blending into a chorus of rage.

"Hey, Dr. North!"

Automatically she turned. A rock whistled through the air. Sharp pain exploded on her temple as she gave a startled cry. Belle touched her head and her fingers came away stained red. The red blossomed, and warmth trickled down her cheek.

She was a doctor, accustomed to healing people and being thanked for her services by patients. The vicious burst of violence jolted her. Not since a playground fight with Roger Brown had anyone tried to deliberately hurt her.

Immobilized with disbelief, she could only stare at the roaring crowd.

She might have stood there for a while longer, but a black

SUV pulled to a screeching halt on the street outside, along with four police cars. Kyle pulled to a stop, jumped out.

"Clear this area," he ordered the police.

They moved the crowd back and Kyle opened the gate before driving through. He parked inside the complex, turned and faced the people.

"Get back, all of you, or I'll haul you in for trespassing," he said in a deep voice that carried clear across the parking lot.

Maybe the crowd recognized him from the press conference. Or maybe it was his natural air of authority. They eased away as he came toward them.

"This clinic is where they took Lucy," one man protested. "It's all that rich doctor's fault. They're stealing children!"

"She's the one treating your children, not hurting them. Dr. North and her foundation have been the cornerstone of low-cost medical care for your community. She's provided us with valuable information to help find the girls. And this is how you treat her?"

He was magnificent the way he stood up to the angry mob. Never had someone defended her with such bravado and confidence.

Kyle went to her, slid an arm around her shoulders. Inside, she felt queasy with anxiety. Belle struggled to maintain her composure. His touch was an anchor in a maelstrom of emotions.

Some looked shamefaced. A couple of mothers started to weep.

Belle wanted to weep with them. *I have to stop this. It's tearing this community apart. We have to find Anna or no one will be safe.*

"All of you, go home. I told you last night, the FBI is on this case and we will not stop until Anna is found. Standing here and shouting insults will not get them found. Is this the example you want to set for your own children?"

They began to drift away. Kyle gripped her shoulders, studied her face. "They hurt you."

He removed a clean white linen cloth from his inside pocket, dabbed at the cut.

"It's only a small laceration." Belle took his handkerchief, pressed it to the wound.

"Infection, remember, Doc? Never mind." He glanced at the people drifting away. "We'll treat it at my place. Best to get you out of here."

Hand on the small of her back, he guided her over to the SUV, opened the passenger door for her. "In."

"My car…"

"I'll have someone drive it to my place after the crowd fully disperses."

Too exhausted and numb to argue, she climbed inside, clutching her purse strap in one hand, holding the cloth to her temple with the other.

So much anger.

So much violence.

They don't hate you. It's not personal, Belle. They are terrified of losing their own children.

Dimly she became aware of Kyle quietly talking on the phone to his partner, asking him to take care of her car. Belle turned away, staring at the passing buildings as he sped past.

Hope had buoyed her these past few days that Anna would be found soon so her family's name would be cleared. She'd temporarily forgotten the horrific impact on other lives—those living in the community who worried about their own children.

Belle pulled the handkerchief away from her throbbing temple. The bleeding had slowed a little.

"Keep pressure on it," he advised, getting on the freeway.

"Now who's playing doctor?"

"I've suffered enough bullet wounds to know about first aid." Kyle reached over, clasped her hand. "Want me to stop at a fast-food restaurant and get you a soda? You're pale and trembling. Could use the sugar."

"No, I'm fine. Did you learn about sugar to treat shock and raise blood sugar from getting so many bullet wounds?"

He winked at her. "I learned it from an arrogant, pretty doctor after a gun battle at the international airport."

Belle sputtered. "Arrogant!"

"Well." He considered. "More pretty than arrogant."

"Says the agent who walked around with a bullet wound."

"It's just a flesh wound," he said in a high falsetto, and she laughed.

"I love Monty Python movies." Belle sighed. "It's been a long time since I've seen any movie."

"Stick with me, Doc. I'm better than Netflix." He grinned at her, and the grin faded as his sharpened gaze studied her temple.

Kyle's jaw tightened and a nerve jumped in his own temple. She could tell he was enraged, and controlling it.

"They didn't mean to get violent," she told him. "They're scared."

"Do you always make excuses for everyone who hurts you?"

Bitterness tinged his deep voice. Belle glanced at him, lowered the cloth from her temple. "Do you always castigate everyone who makes a mistake?"

"Some mistakes cost lives."

"Is that what you learned on the job? How long have you been with the FBI?"

"Eight years. I started at the academy when I was twenty-three. A little later than most."

"Decided to see the world first?"

"Got my degree in criminal justice, spent a year working for a buddy in Honduras doing security for a rich family." He glanced at her. "Bodyguard work, investigations into who was most likely to kidnap whom and why. My friend taught me how to look for signs of gang activity."

No wonder his Spanish was excellent. "Then why did you move here?"

A nerve jumped in his jaw again. "My wife. She was pregnant and it was too dicey in Honduras. Her family wanted her someplace safe."

He snorted. "Safe. She was safe from the gangs here, but not drunk drivers."

Silence draped between them for a moment. Kyle switched off the engine.

What a sad irony. His wife had moved to Florida to be safe and she died instead in a car crash.

"Was her family one of your clients in Honduras?"

Kyle nodded, not looking at her. "Caroline fell in love with me after I did a stint working security for her father. Family is all expats with a factory. Caro and I started dating, and she didn't believe in birth control and I was young and stupid…and she got pregnant."

Belle put a hand on his arm. "Everyone makes mistakes, Kyle. But not everyone owns up to them."

They had driven only ten minutes on the freeway when he turned off. Belle blinked in surprise. "I thought your office was in Biscayne Glades," she said, referring to the urban center where the FBI had a large field office.

"It is. I commute."

When Kyle headed for a quiet residential area where a few of her friends lived, Belle felt more surprise. He turned into a tree-lined street. Two-story homes flanked them as he drove past.

The houses here were definitely more expensive than her rental.

He pulled into a curved driveway before a turquoise two-story house with a metal roof. Keys jingled in his hand as he stared at the house before them. "She wanted to keep the baby and so did I. We liked each other, and I thought marriage wouldn't be a big deal. But I needed a more stable job with good benefits, so I joined the agency, trained at Quantico. By the time Kasey was born, I was a field agent specializing in abductions and child trafficking."

A sinking feeling began in her stomach. "Did Kasey die in the car crash?"

He refused to meet her gaze. "Ten days later, in the hospital. She never awoke from the coma."

Belle felt a sickening jolt. Losing a child had to the worst thing a parent ever suffered. "I'm so sorry."

His mouth compressed. "The doctors said the same thing. I didn't believe them. They weren't really sorry."

No wonder he disliked her on first sight. He probably blamed the medical profession for losing his daughter.

She had no words of real comfort, only that platitude of sympathy. Belle turned to him. "I can't imagine the pain you suffered, losing your daughter. And your wife. I won't even pretend to try. I used to try to make sense of tragedy and gave up. All I can do as a doctor is try my best to save those who can be saved. Sometimes, as hard as it is to accept, it's not enough."

Knuckles whitened as he clenched his keys. "The doctors who treated her could have done more to save her."

"Like you can with all the children you try to save?"

Kyle turned, scowling. "What the hell do you mean?"

"You're an FBI agent. You're a professional who does all he can to bring children home to their families. Not every case you solve has a good ending."

For a moment he sat there, his body tense. Then his broad shoulders relaxed a little. "You make a good point. C'mon. Let's take care of your injury."

She sensed there would be no further conversation about the matter, and was glad to drop it. Her head already pounded.

She got an impression of cool white marble tile, and an expansive living-and-dining area. The kitchen, immediately to the right, was modern and gleaming, with stainless steel appliances, an island with four bar stools and light granite counters.

Photos of sailboats decorated the walls. Belle swept an appreciative eye over the interior and the white sectional sofa overlooking the water and a pool in back. Yet for all the tasteful interior decorating, the house had the feeling of a designer showpiece.

Not a real home.

"Very nice."

He shrugged. "It's not mine. Belongs to a friend who uses it two weeks out of the year. I'm rarely here, anyway."

No wonder it lacked personality, especially his. Belle suspected Kyle was the kind of man who kept his professional life neat and clean, and kicked off his leather loafers while at home.

"Go into the guest bathroom. Second door on the right. Be there in a minute. Have to lock up my gun."

She found her way there, a long, elegant bathroom with a door leading to the pool. More white cabinets, gleaming counters and stainless steel. She pulled out a bamboo stool from the shower and sat.

Kyle came into the bathroom, rummaged through a bottom cabinet.

Gray trousers stretched tight over his butt. Terrific butt, too, all taut muscle and round. Admiring the scenery, she startled when he straightened and turned. A blush suffused her cheeks. He noticed, gave a crooked grin.

"Checking me out, Doc?"

Belle shrugged. "If the view is perfect, why not?"

Now it was Kyle's turn for his cheeks to turn ruddy. He set a bottle of peroxide and a first-aid kit down on the counter. "Can't believe you called my ass perfect."

"Don't get a big head over it, cowboy agent." Belle winced as he dabbed liquid on her wound.

"Sorry," he murmured. "I'm trying to go easy."

"S'okay." He had big hands, but he was gentle as he cleansed the laceration. Strength in those hands, but he knew how and when to wield it.

Bet he'd be great in bed with those hands.

Another flush ignited her cheeks.

Kyle applied antibiotic cream and a small bandage. "You okay, Doc? You're flushing."

"Fine," she said tersely.

He left and returned with a glass of water and handed it to her, along with two painkillers. Belle shook her head. "I don't take pills."

"Sorry, I'm fresh out of morphine."

At her raised brows, he flashed a brief smile. "Joke. It's just aspirin."

Fine. She did need something, even if pride prohibited her.

Kyle squatted before her, his blue gaze intense. "Feel up to going over details of what you remember from the other girls who went missing?"

"Of course. Anything to help."

They went into the living area in the back. Kyle loosened his tie, unbuttoned the top button of his shirt.

"I wondered when you would unwind. Do you ever take off the suit jacket?"

"Only when I get shot."

Belle rolled her eyes as he grinned. Then he shrugged out of his jacket, draped it neatly over a dining room chair. She sat on the sectional as he grabbed a pen and pad.

"Let's start with the medical file first. What do you re-member?" he asked.

Belle went over to him. "No, first I want to see your arm. The one with the bullet wound."

Stiffening, he snorted. "It's fine. Didn't even need stitches."

"I'm a doctor," she said serenely. "I want to see for my-self. Call it a free house call."

Grumbling, he tossed the pad and pen aside, removed his tie and took off his starched white shirt. Belle's heart skipped a beat. For a moment, she forgot she was a medical professional as her hormones kicked into stride.

It was challenging to be professional and objective when faced with all that tanned, smooth skin and muscles.

Kyle Anderson had a fine physique, trim and athletic. A sprinkling of dark hair covered his chest. His arms were muscled, but not bulging. He had the tone of a runner, not a weight lifter.

She inched closer to him on the sofa, breathing in the delicious spice of his cologne. Belle lifted the bandage and studied the wound, her pulse racing. Not from the injury, but his nearness.

"What does it feel like to get shot?"

"I didn't even know I'd been hit. Not this time. Too much adrenaline. The other two times it was like getting smacked with a hot iron. Hurts like a bitch, but when you're in the middle of gunfire, you kick into survival mode. The pain starts later, when everything calms down."

"It's the body's way of compensating, to keep you alive."

Her gaze swept over his body. Two other scars dented his skin. One round and small on his collarbone, the other lower, ragged and large.

She gently probed the scars. "More bullet wounds?"

Kyle glanced down at her hand. "Large one was a bullet. Other one was when some perp stabbed me with an ice pick."

Belle touched the larger injury, the puckered pink flesh on his shoulder. "And this?"

"Shootout on a drug case."

"Looks like it hurt. A lot."

"The psychological trauma is worse. I kept thinking that I couldn't leave my partner, had to stay there and give him cover. Roarke told me later that I never even said anything, even blinked. He hadn't seen it since he saw a buddy shot in Afghanistan."

"Roarke served? Army?"

"Navy SEAL."

She lifted the bandage on his arm. The ugly ridge marching through his tanned arm had turned pink, but looked healthy. No infection.

"Healing nicely. The ER doc did a good job."

Kyle's gaze locked to hers. "You have a nice touch, Doc."

Unable to resist, she slid her fingers up and down his biceps. "You're young and strong and have a good immune system. There should be no lasting effects."

"Maybe not from the bullet graze, but my heart is racing pretty damn hard right now," he said softly. "Has a habit of doing that when you're around. Gets worse when you touch me."

"I like touching you," she whispered.

Sparks sizzled between them, a natural chemistry her brain recognized as purely sexual. She tried to remember it was biology. Science.

Her body nudged her closer. *Go for it.*

Belle moistened her lips as he stared at her mouth. He wanted it as badly as she did. One kiss. What could happen? *Plenty.*

Then Kyle's gaze flicked away and he reached for his shirt.

"The girls," he said in a ragged voice. "Tell me what you know."

Work. Belle retreated a safe few feet away and closed her eyes. But as she recalled the details, disappointment filled her.

She hadn't been this attracted to a man in a long time. But Kyle Anderson, as rugged and charming as he was, wasn't here for socializing.

Neither was she.

Chapter 11

Ninety minutes later, feeling as if her brain had been wrung dry, Belle was ready for food. The bright blue sky turned leaden with sunset, and her stomach grumbled, reminding her she'd forgotten to eat lunch.

Kyle shut his notebook. "Thanks, Doc."

"Now what?" She sipped the water he'd fetched for her.

He scanned the notes. "I'll type up my report, send this in."

"Anything useful?"

Hope faded as he shook his head. "Afraid not. Looks like standard medical information, childhood colds, immunizations. Nothing unusual."

He tapped the pen against the pad. "We haven't been able to get ahold of Dr. Patterson."

Mike had not returned to the clinic since Anna's disappearance. But he texted Clint, her brother and his employer, to tell him he was taking vacation time. The clinic had been closed since Anna's disappearance.

"He took an extended vacation." Belle shrugged. "He's entitled to it."

"Fine. But we need to question him, and he seems to be out of reach."

Surprise filled her. "Did you try his cell?"

Even if Mike was out of the country, he always answered his cell phone. Like her, he had an international calling plan.

"Voice mail." Kyle looked thoughtful. "Either he's loath to talk to us, or he's out of reach if he's traveling. Any idea where he headed?"

"He usually likes warmth this time of year."

"Doesn't everyone?" he asked dryly. "We'll find a way to touch base with him."

"Why?"

"Routine." He leaned forward, his gaze intent. "We questioned everyone who works at the clinic, except him. And he's the chief physician, the one person who should know everything that happens at that place."

"I can try to reach him for you."

"Promise?"

Belle hesitated. "I will call him later."

Kyle smiled at her and a tingle rushed down her spine. When he lost the serious look, the man was downright devastating.

"What should I do next?"

"Feel like grabbing a bite?"

"Definitely. I'm starved. What do you have?"

Those lean cheeks grew ruddy again. "Not much, I'm afraid, except for old cans of Spam left over from last hurricane season. Pickings here are slim."

"Spam in a can or on a computer isn't my favorite," she said lightly. "Know a good place that has fajitas? I have a craving for sizzling food."

Kyle flashed his charming grin. "As long as you don't mind hockey games."

"Not at all."

The sports bar he selected was crowded. Wide-screen televisions blared basketball and hockey games. Kyle slid into a wood booth and she sat across from him.

She liked a well-dressed man, and Kyle Anderson definitely dressed well. But here in this casual atmosphere, Belle wondered what he'd look like in shorts and a T-shirt.

Or better yet, nothing at all. The upper half of him certainly looked yummy.

When the waiter came over, she ordered the chicken fajitas and white wine. Kyle ordered a draft domestic beer, an appetizer of fried pickles and the grilled chicken dinner. Belle raised her brows.

"Fried pickles? I can hear your arteries hardening already."

"I don't always eat like this, but man, their fried pickles are sinful. You have to try them. Or don't you like anything sinful?"

In his deep, sultry voice, Kyle made *sinful* sound absolutely...sinfully tempting. She leaned on the table. "Like your fried pickles, the occasional indulgence never hurt me."

"Interesting," he murmured. "I know a few things that are much more pleasurable than eating fried pickles."

It felt wonderfully freeing and enjoyable, flirting like this in a crowded restaurant. The gleam in his blue eyes, the way he caressed her with his gaze made her feel fully feminine and aware for the first time in months. Work and volunteering and worry about her future had consumed her.

Belle drew in a sharp breath. "It feels wrong, being here, when Anna is still missing."

Kyle reached out, rested his hand atop hers. "Stop blaming yourself for eating a meal. One thing I've learned on the job, Doc, is you have to take a break once in a while and indulge in self-care or you'll burn out."

The waiter brought their drinks. Kyle didn't even look up, or reach for his beer, only continued holding her hand. It felt wonderful and calming, and yet not calming. Her body hummed with happiness.

Anticipation.

Fascinating how holding hands with a man made her heart beat faster than some men did when they were engaged in much more physical contact.

Although intense and dedicated, Kyle wasn't demanding. Belle had met other men who were high-maintenance and pressured her before she was ready.

She liked his sense of humor, and the way his face lit up when he smiled.

And he smelled wonderful, like a day at the beach.

Although she considered herself independent and didn't need a man's protection, his chivalrous attitude proved endearing. But most of all, it felt good to have a guy treat her with respect, as an equal and still show the same interest in her she felt for him.

Belle squeezed his fingers. "You have a nice touch, Kyle."

With his other hand, he picked up a pickle slice, dipped it into sauce and held it to her mouth. "One slice. Once you try it, you'll never forget it."

Her mouth parted and his eyes darkened as he slid the pickle slice past her lips. Belle chewed, swallowed and licked her mouth.

"Anything else you suggest I try?"

It might have gone further, except a loud "Kyle, what are you doing here?" interrupted them. He slid his hand away, scowled at Roarke, who sauntered up to the booth.

"Unlike you, I'm not pretending I'm on vacation," he told him. "What the hell is that?"

Roarke looked down. "Clothing."

Belle suppressed a laugh. Kyle's partner wore a bright red-and-yellow Hawaiian-print shirt, black shorts and sandals.

"And here I thought you only ordered takeout." Roarke slid into the booth next to him. "Then again, even workaholics have to eat."

Kyle glowered at his partner. "You look like a beach bum."

"And you look like a fed. Once a fed, always one." Roarke helped himself to a fried pickle. "Hey, these are pretty good."

Belle slid the dish closer to him. "Help yourself."

"You have a habit of showing up in all the wrong places at all the wrong times," he said, eyeing his partner.

Roarke nodded at Kyle. "He's always this grumpy when he's hangry."

Belle smiled, but she also felt a stab of disappointment at his partner showing up. She'd been looking forward to dinner alone with Kyle. Dinner and something else?

If it went further, she definitely would not be disappointed.

Roarke was cute. Quite cute. With his dark hair and fascinating green eyes, he could even be considered devastating. But he didn't interest her.

Kyle did.

"I'm always grumpy when you're around," Kyle muttered.

"People who complain all the time are sexually frustrated. They should be making love instead of griping," Roarke said in Spanish, grinning at a scowling Kyle.

Belle bit back a laugh.

"Sex is your answer to everything," he muttered in the same language.

"Not everything. More people should make love. So much better than taking out your frustrations on your work partner."

"I take my frustration out in the gym when I kickbox. Want me to take it out on your face?" Kyle offered.

Roarke's grin widened. "You'd be better off, and much happier, my friend, in bed with a pretty woman. And if you're too sour to seize the opportunity, I'll be happy to oblige."

He glanced at Belle as he continued speaking in Spanish. Belle bit her lip.

"Stay away from her," Kyle growled.

Enough. "I can stand up for myself," she told Kyle in English.

As his brow wrinkled, she added sweetly in Spanish, "Speaking in another language to exclude an English speaker is considered rude."

His jaw dropped. "I didn't know…"

"That I'm fluent in Spanish?" She folded her hands primly on the table. "Did you think that because I went to finishing school, maybe I wouldn't want to learn the same language many of the clinic patients speak?"

Roarke laughed again. "I knew I liked you, Dr. Belle North."

But her attention riveted to Kyle. "You kickbox for fun? Or to work out?"

"Both. Ever tried it?"

Belle shook her head. "I work out, but nothing martial arts."

"You should try Krav Maga. A pretty woman like yourself needs to know self-defense." Roarke helped himself to another pickle.

The scowl on Kyle's face almost amused her. Almost. She didn't mind flirting, but she wanted to flirt with Kyle, not Roarke.

"I'm capable of defending myself. I don't need anything fancy."

"It's not fancy," Kyle told her. "It's a simple technique for self-defense used by the Israelis to be easy and learned by anyone. I'll teach you."

"He does have a black belt in Krav Maga," Roarke said, grinning. "Not bad for a fed. He does make a good sparring partner."

"And I suppose you have a black belt as well in one of those things," she told him.

Roarke's smile dropped. "I have a black belt in survival."

Their food arrived and she dug into her salad as they argued about the best self-defense techniques. Then Roarke ate another pickle, dusted off his hands and saluted her.

"Thanks for the food, Doc. Gotta run. Enjoy."

With a grin at his partner, the federal agent pushed off toward the crowded bar.

"He's not a bad sort, just has poor taste in dress. If only I could get him to stop frequenting surf shops," Kyle joked.

Belle laughed.

"Belle North, such a pretty picture you make. I can't believe you're slumming in a place like this."

The blond man saying this stood before their table. Sudden disquiet curled through her. Belle's laughter died. The excellent salad turned to cardboard in her stomach.

"Hello, Evan." She gestured to Kyle. "This is FBI special agent Kyle Anderson. Kyle, this is Evan Worthington."

The two men silently sized each other up.

Evan ignored her dining partner. "Mother told me your residency should come through any moment now. Maybe you'll get a match near me. I'm based in Boston. Mass General has an excellent cardiology department. Even a little lady like you has a good shot at one."

His words slurred, clearly indicating he was more than a little drunk. Tension radiated from Kyle, but he remained silent. She gave him credit. If she weren't a lady, she'd deck Evan right now.

"I may not get a cardiology match," she murmured. "Have a nice evening, Evan. Do say hello to your mother."

"Well, if you're planning to hang around town longer, we should see each other."

"I'm busy," she said tersely.

"Oh, come on. You can't work all the time. Mother says

the clinic is closed now, so you should have free time. Maybe we could play doctor again, like we did when we were younger." Evan winked at her. She wanted to slap him.

"The lady said she's busy." Kyle gave him a long, cool look. "If you don't mind, we need to finish our dinner."

Evan scowled. "Cool it, G-man. Was I talking with you?"

As Kyle started to slide out of the booth, she interjected. "Evan, you'd best leave. Now."

The man shrugged. "Lots of other women. Who wants a cold fish when you can have a warm one? Goodbye, Belle. Have a nice life."

When Evan sauntered off, she released a deep breath. "What an ass."

Kyle eyed her. "Old boyfriend?"

"Hardly. We grew up together, had one date in college. He's the son of my mother's good friend. He's not my friend."

Instead of answering, Kyle peered out the window as Evan staggered out of the bar. He watched. Belle turned her head. To her relief, she saw a car pull up front and Evan climb inside.

"You were waiting to see if he'd take an Uber," she said gently.

Kyle's gaze hardened. "I don't tolerate those who drink and drive."

Belle nodded. "Evan's an ass, but he's not stupid. His blood-alcohol level was probably up there in the ozone layer. I hope the driver doesn't faint from the fumes."

At last he smiled, lines forming at the edges of his eyes, the shadows vanishing from his eyes.

"So tell me, Doc, what made you want to work at the clinic?"

The question surprised her. "I like working with people."

He looked puzzled.

"I thought about cancer research. But getting stuck in a

lab all day with test tubes and microscopes isn't for me."
Belle stared at the hand covering hers, the dusting of dark
hair across the back, the tanned skin and strong fingers.
"But I like working with children too much to stay stuck
in a lab. My parents are pushing me into cardiology. Surgery. Any day my cardiology match should come through."

Kyle frowned. "A heart surgeon when you enjoy working with kids? Why not pediatrics?"

It was a question she'd pondered herself. The answer
shamed her.

"I don't want to disappoint them. They think I need a
specialty that is more elite and will earn more income.
Most pediatric doctors don't earn anything close to what
a cardiologist does."

"You always do whatever your parents want?"

The question stung, and yet in an odd way, she'd expect
nothing less from him. It was direct and blunt, reassuring.

Typical of this hardened agent with a gentle heart he
tried hard to hide from the world.

"When they're footing the bills, yes."

"So you'd rather be a frustrated cardiologist than a happy
pediatrician. Don't residencies pay?"

They did. And she had secretly gone over the figures if
she'd gotten the one she'd applied for in Washington, DC,
fretting over how she could afford a place of her own while
working insane hours that would mean some nights spent
at the hospital.

Still, the chance to work with children in need, to maybe
diagnose them early and give them a fighting chance…

Belle slipped her hand free of Kyle's grip. "I'm finished
and I need to get home now."

End of conversation. Always, it worked before in the
past with a date she'd wished would end. Problem was, she
didn't want the time with him to end.

Just this uncomfortable conversation where she'd had to examine her own motivations and future.

Kyle glanced at his phone. "I have to get back, as well." He signaled for the check, which the waiter immediately brought.

As she started to protest, he shook his head. "You're a witness and I need to feed you, Miss North."

"Thank you, Agent Anderson."

So they were back to that again—last names.

"I need you to call Dr. Patterson soon as possible and let me know where he is." His gaze searched hers.

"I will. I promise."

He dug a credit card out of his wallet, slid it into the vinyl folder holding the check. "You surprise me, Doc," he said quietly. "When I first met you, you seemed like the type of woman to go after whatever it is she wanted and not give a damn about the expectations of others. Do you really think pleasing your parents is more important than selecting a career that will fulfill you long after they're gone? Who are you living for then?"

Belle gritted her teeth. "Is it really any of your business what I do with my life? Is your life so sterling that you can criticize mine?"

"Not criticism, just an observation." His expression shuttered. "Maybe you're right—what your family wants is more important than what you want. Maybe if I had paid more attention to my home life instead of trying to advance my own career, my daughter wouldn't be in her grave right now."

Kyle shook his head. "Forget I said it. Your life is your life."

Her heart twisted at the pain he must have suffered. She suspected this man seldom let down his barriers…and perhaps regretted saying what he did.

As they left the restaurant, he held the door open for her and checked the parking lot, sticking to her side.

Even though they'd disagreed, he still looked out for her. Belle enjoyed being with a man who was both courteous and protective.

Yet she found herself wishing she had never met Agent Kyle Anderson.

Because he yanked open a door she'd tried to keep closed for a long time, and seeing the tantalizing glimpse of what lay beyond made her frustrated and wistful. It wasn't merely a future with a pediatric residency in a busy urban hospital.

It was a relationship with an intriguing man who truly knew her—maybe even better than she knew herself.

Chapter 12

Belle couldn't sleep that night. She rolled over, glanced at the clock on the nightstand.

Two in the morning.

Her conscience kept nagging her. She'd promised Kyle she'd contact Mike Patterson, and yet, she felt the need to keep her brother in touch with everything that happened.

When she'd called Clint after arriving home, he'd told her not to worry. Mike would be in touch.

It wasn't the same as direct contact. Her older brother had been brisk and eager to end the conversation. And for once, he didn't nag her about her personal life.

It made her wonder what was going on. Part of her didn't want to get involved.

Yet she'd promised Kyle she would find out.

I always keep my promises. I'm not breaking this one.

Rolling over, she fumbled for her cell phone and dialed Mike's number. Voice mail.

"Mike, this is Belle. Call me on my cell. It's urgent."

She hung up. That would motivate him to call. If he didn't, then she'd have to drive straight to Clint's house and demand to know what her brother knew, and she did not.

Sitting up, she reached for her bathrobe. At the bed's foot, Boo stirred. She patted him. "Back to sleep, sweetie. It's too early."

Her cell phone chimed. Mike.

"Mike, where are you? Why are you ignoring the FBI's phone calls?" Her fingers gripped the phone.

"In the Bahamas." He gave a breathy, humorless chuckle. "Staying at my vacation house for a while until all this blows over."

Her stomach knotted. "All this has to do with missing children, Mike. You need to return to the States. The agents need to question you. You might have information that can help us find Anna."

"Us?" His voice sharpened. "You're helping the feds?"

"Why wouldn't I?" Her heart raced. Belle switched on the bedside lamp, but the soft light did little to chase away her bout of sudden fear.

"Did they search the place?"

"Yes. And your house, as well."

"Find anything? Anything at all?"

"Nothing out of the ordinary. They could search again."

"Doubt they'd waste time. Time is money, Belle. I'll never forget that." The sharp tension eased from his tone.

Tired of his usual platitudes—how often did she have to listen to him drone about examining patients, make a diagnosis and then move on to the next—she sniffed. "Time is money, but a little girl's life is at stake. And the clinic remains closed, Mike. We need to open it again, show the community our support."

"Let it stay shut. Patients can find someplace else to go. I'm staying the hell out of it and as far away from that clinic as possible. And if you know what's good for you, Belle, you will, as well. Before you end up missing."

The phone clicked off.

Heart racing, she stared at the phone's screen. Mike Patterson had always been an efficient doctor and seemed to care about patients. The clinic's foundation had paid him a good salary, but not equal to what he could make in his own practice. They'd thought he'd asked for the position because he was semiretired and wanted to still practice medicine.

What if Mike was involved in something far more sinister? What if he was at the heart of these disappearances?

All this time she'd thought everyone at the clinic was beyond suspicion. But if Mike wasn't, then she needed to alert Kyle.

Fingers on her cell phone, she hesitated.

If the clinic was at the heart of the disappearances, and the police hadn't found anything, why would Mike seemed relieved?

Unless there's something he is hiding, and it's so well hidden, no one can find it except someone familiar with the building...

She stared at Kyle's number on her cell phone. The right thing to do would be to call him, let him know there was something else there.

It meant another, more thorough search. More publicity. More attention.

If she searched the building first, without Kyle, and did it quietly, she'd avoid all that.

And if she found something?

Of course I'll call him.

Belle picked up Boo, cuddled with the sleepy dog as she snuggled back into the covers. She finally fell into a restless sleep, filled with dreams of being chased by sexy agent Kyle Anderson.

In her dream, he drew her into his arms to kiss her. And then he frowned, telling her that he knew her.

"You did this," he said in his deep voice. "You're responsible for Anna. Tell me where she is."

"I don't know," she screamed.

"Tell me!"

But there was nothing to tell and deep inside, she knew he was right.

She was responsible for what happened to Anna Rodriguez.

As guilty as if she'd kidnapped the little girl herself.

In the morning, after coffee, giving Boo his walk and breakfast, she drove to the clinic. The Corvette's engine purred reassuringly, and her iPod blared Imagine Dragons. Music usually soothed her.

Today nothing would soothe her. Her mind kept envisioning the battered teddy bear in the backseat of the car they'd found in the abandoned nursery.

The bloodstains in the front seat of the car. The prim, neat area where Anna and her mother had lived in hiding.

Thankfully, the clinic parking lot was empty upon her arrival. But soon it would crawl with police and detectives investigating every square inch. Already the clinic was under suspicion. Now even more so.

Inside the clinic, she turned on the air conditioner. Stale air circulated as the system coughed into life.

Belle switched on the lights, wincing as the fluorescent bulbs buzzed like a swarm of bees. The clinic building was old and needed updating.

If they ever opened again.

She headed directly for the doctor's office she shared. Nothing looked out of place. Nothing odd. The police had searched it thoroughly after they'd found Tony's lunch tote and the hidden drawer in the desk.

The hidden drawer didn't have any mystery attached to it, either. The desk, she'd told the police, came as a donation from Clint. He once used the desk in his business and hid important files in the false bottom because "I had a nosy secretary."

The police had been most thorough.

Still, what if they missed something?

"I don't have time for this," she said aloud.

Belle glanced at the clock on the wall. She'd hated that clock ever since Mike ordered Tony to hang it.

"Time is money," Mike was fond of saying.

He'd said the same thing last night. Dread raced down her spine. Belle shot out of her chair, reached up and grabbed the clock.

The police had lifted it from the wall and looked at the back, but everything looked normal. She studied the clock's back.

The front facing. Then she shook it.

Nothing.

Belle turned the clock over. The second hand stopped.

Bringing the clock back to her desk, she set it down. Belle rummaged in the office's junk drawer for a Phillips screwdriver. She unfastened the screws and lifted the back off the clock.

At first she saw nothing. Belle turned the clock over. Held it to the light.

Something glinted on tape. She worked at the tape and then freed the object.

The key tumbled into her palm. Fingers trembling, she examined it. It had been painted black, to match the clock's interior. Why would Mike hide a key in a clock, unless it was something he really needed to keep hidden? And where?

Sweat dripped down her forehead. This office was old, the air-conditioning system never working efficiently here. Tony had blamed the ventilation system and the air ducts leading to the office.

He'd always seemed to be working on the filter…

Key clutched in hand, she went to the air-conditioning return grille opposite the desk. It was partly blocked by stacks of boxes containing files.

She pushed them aside, and unlatched the grille and

pulled off the filter. It was clean. Of course. Tony had only changed it three weeks ago.

Belle found a flashlight, shone it into the empty space beyond the grille. It looked normal, she guessed.

Running her fingers along the boxed confines, she found nothing.

Frustrated, she banged her fist against the wall.

Something rattled.

Belle pushed hard with her fingers and a panel came loose. She removed it and shone the light on a steel fireproof box lying beyond the false panel.

Stomach knotting, she took the box to her desk. The key fit perfectly. She unlocked it.

A manila envelope lay inside. Her fingers shook as she opened it. The contents spilled out onto the clean white desk blotter. Photos. Dozens of photos of young girls, some as young as six. All of them pretty, with green or blue eyes and dark-haired.

All of them taken at the clinic. She recognized the backdrop of the room where they conducted pediatric exams. Each girl was fully clothed but sitting on the table. Belle's heart dropped to her stomach as she sifted through them. A clear invasion of privacy, and yet the girls didn't look camera shy.

It was as if they didn't realize someone took their picture.

"Oh God," she whispered, dropping one of Anna.

Anna had been here before. There had been no record of her. It had been purged from the system.

This photo showed Anna without her teddy bear, wearing a green-and-white shirt and white shorts. She was cleaner, smiling and clearly not afraid.

Either she knew the person taking the photos or…

Hidden camera.

Recognizing the sky blue wallpaper with the clouds, she dropped the photo and raced into Exam Room 4, the room where they treated pediatric patients on overflow days. Cabinets faced the long exam table. She opened each one, pawing through the contents.

The cabinet below the sink was locked. She didn't have the key. Clint would and so would Mike, and perhaps George.

Maybe she should call her brother. Her mind whirled with the implications.

This was not good for the clinic. There would be more media attention, fingers pointed at her illustrious family and more stress and pressure for her parents.

All of that mattered little. Finding Anna and the other missing girl mattered most.

But Clint needed to know this. Discover the truth from her and not get sidelined by the media or interrogation from the FBI.

Her brother answered his cell phone on the first ring. When she told him what she'd found, he went silent for a moment.

"Clint…did you know about this?"

Everything rebelled against asking that difficult question. Clint was family, and in her family, they came first. The Norths had a sterling, impeccable reputation. But Belle had to know.

"Damn it, Belle. I can't believe you would ask that," he finally said.

"I have to know. You're the foundation director and you're responsible for what happens here."

"It wasn't me," he snapped. Then he sighed and swore softly.

"Then is it Mike?" she persisted. "Someone must know about this who was in charge. You can't have this kind of activity taking place under everyone's noses!"

"Why not? You had no clue."

"Not fair." She bit her lip. "It took place in Exam Room

Four, the room Mike wanted painted, the room he liked to use. Is that why?"

"I don't know." Clint exhaled a sharp breath. "I'll talk to him."

"No, Clint, you need to wait for the FBI…"

Click. The phone went dead.

Now she'd done it. Put family first and Clint would alert Mike, and if Mike had a clue of the whereabouts of the missing girls, he'd clam up.

Time to pay the piper…

Belle called Kyle. "It's me."

"What's wrong?" The deep timbre of his smoky voice reassured her, centered her in the crazy spinning reality of what she'd just found.

Belle took a deep breath to steady herself. "I found something hidden in my office at the clinic. There's something you need to know…"

Half an hour later, the team from the FBI, along with the local police, combed over the clinic grounds and interior.

This time, they searched every square inch of every single room.

Kyle helped in the search. He was methodical, but brisk and professional. His angular jaw tightened as he examined the photographs, his fingers covered with a fresh pair of latex gloves.

He had said little to her since arriving. As if she were to blame for this.

"I called you as soon as I found the photos. I didn't take them," she told him as the police tore apart her office.

In his gaze she saw the silent condemnation.

"What made you come here early in the morning?"

Oh, he was direct all right. Belle bit her lower lip, not wanting to get Mike in trouble. Still, if he had done this…

Hard to believe a doctor with such high social standing

could sink so low. Was Mike dealing in child pornography? Was that why Anna had been kidnapped?

"Dr. North, what made you come here this morning?" he repeated.

Back to last names again. Kyle had turned from the friendly man with the discerning attitude and the sexy smile to the cold, impersonal FBI agent.

Belle gave an inward shudder. She'd hate to be on his bad side. Well, now she was viewed as the bad person. The suspect. "I talked with Mike, Dr. Patterson, last night."

He listened as she revealed everything about the conversation, and how she'd found the key and eventually, the hidden compartment.

"You didn't call me after talking with him."

Condemnation in that deep voice. Belle drew in a breath. "I wanted to check things out for myself first and not waste your time."

A partial truth.

"No, you wanted to protect your family name first."

"I did call you."

"And you alerted your brother first?"

His keen blue gaze searched her face. Belle sighed. "Yes, I told Clint. The foundation oversees the operation of this clinic. He deserved to know."

Kyle's jaw tightened. "You should have called me before telling anyone else what you found. This doesn't put you in a good light, Dr. North. You might be considered an accessory after the fact, especially if we can't locate Dr. Patterson."

Belle reeled. Her gaze whipped from the papers stacked up on the filing cabinets as police tore through the files, to the desk, to the light bulbs detectives removed from the overhead fixture. "Excuse me—I did call you. I could have tried to hide this. I want to help you catch whoever took Anna."

Lifting a few photos, he let them drop onto the desk.

"Even if this implicates someone close to you, like Michael Patterson? Or your own brother?"

Clint. Surely he couldn't be involved. Belle lifted her gaze to him. "I want to help you find Anna."

It wasn't an answer, and they both knew it. His expression shuttered. "Do you recognize the room where these were taken?"

"Exam Room Four. It's not often used." She hesitated. "I did look inside and found a locked cabinet. I don't know... where the key is."

"Show me," he directed.

Police swarmed all over the clinic, removing photographs from the hallways, even tearing off the cheerful animal wallpaper in one exam room. Belle fisted her hands in her lab coat pockets. They were tearing the clinic apart, but how could she blame them?

After what she'd found, she would have done the same. Who knew if finding the hidden photos might have come too late?

Kyle swept his cool blue gaze over the counter. He seemed distant, cold and professional.

Everything looked in place. A jar filled with tongue depressors, disinfectant and a tray of instruments.

"When was the last time you used this room to examine children?"

Children, not patients. Belle searched her memory. "Maybe two months ago."

"You haven't been in here since, except to look around after you found those photos?"

A faint flush heated her cheeks. "I used it two weeks ago to change into workout clothes. The room was empty and had more space than my office and the bathroom."

Belle pointed to the locked cabinet. Squatting down, he removed a tool from his pocket and jimmied the lock. A click followed. He opened the doors.

Boxes crammed the shelves. He opened each one. Each one contained medical supplies, from syringes to medication.

No camera.

"Those photos were taken in this room," she insisted. "I recognize the clouds on the wallpaper. One of them had a heart drawn in the middle, courtesy of a bored nurse."

Kyle dug deeper into the cabinet and withdrew a round black wireless speaker. "Do you recognize this?"

Not that she'd used this room often. Belle preferred the front room, with its softer lighting and larger area to work in. This one was too cramped. "It's a speaker for Bluetoothing music. Some of the doctors and nurses use it with frightened children to soothe them. We can program it from our phones."

"Do you use it?"

She shrugged. "The nurses might have turned it on the few times I've used this room, but I have other means to calm children."

"That's not all this is used for." Squatting down, he gestured to a small dot in the speaker's middle. "See that?"

Belle's heart dropped to her stomach as he unscrewed the top, revealing the mechanism inside. The hidden camera.

"You can buy these at any electronic store online," he muttered, his expression stormy. "It was right here in front of you."

"I never use it. It's always been there, like the tongue depressors. I use Boo to calm the children because…"

Judging from his cool look, Agent Kyle Anderson had placed her under suspicion again. Belle lifted her chin. "Dr. Patterson bought it for the clinic."

Oh, this was so not looking good for Mike. Inwardly, she cursed him. How had they been so blind?

Because he's a family friend and a distinguished physician.

"How long has this been here?"

She tried to remember. Her volunteer time had usually been during the week. "I guess about a month."

"One month." His jaw tightened. He went into the hallway, called to the crime-scene techs, "I need this room swept for prints, everything."

Belle backed out of the way, her throat tight with emotion. Bad enough she felt partly responsible for Anna's disappearance. Now the clinic was obviously the base where Dugin had operated in collusion with someone working here. All those days she'd been here, examining patients, working alongside the staff and she had never suspected anything.

"Your team will need to dust the photos and my office, as well," she said quietly. "My medical journal I use to record notes about patients is also missing."

Towering over her, he stared down with the same analytic coolness displayed yesterday on his arrival. "You've known there was a Bluetooth speaker in this room and never questioned it? Never inventoried it or recorded anything about it? Never inspected it yourself? This is your family's charity? How much damn control does your family exert, anyway? Or don't you even care?"

Resentment filled her. Belle sidestepped a man wearing an FBI jacket in the hallway and flattened herself against the wall. "I'm not in the habit of checking every single thing my coworkers do or the items they bring to the clinic, Agent Anderson."

"Maybe you should have."

How could she argue with such logic, when it was clear someone on staff had fooled them all along? Belle gritted her teeth. "You have the keys and the computer in my office is on. You're welcome to sort through all the files. Do you need me for anything else?"

"No." He turned his back on her, heading for Exam Room 4.

Fishing her phone out, she called her brother. Clint didn't answer, so she left a voice mail, alerting him to what happened.

She peered out the front door and saw news vans outside in the parking lot. The media crush had begun outside, but that was the least of her worries.

Belle popped her head into the room and saw Anderson dismantling the speaker. "When you're all finished here, drop the keys off at my house."

"It will be a long time before we do." Blue gaze filled with contempt, he shook his head. "Don't leave town, Dr. North. And tell your staff and your family not to leave, either. This clinic is now officially a crime scene. It's closed until further notice."

Chapter 13

The day had progressed from bad to worse.

Stale cigarette smoke clung to the jacket of the crime lab cybertechnician. Walls of the darkened room of the computer lab seemed to close in around him. Kyle hated this crypt-like room, with its buzz of computers and machines, lacking sunshine and daylight. But this kid was a whiz at Quantico, so they'd flown to Virginia to have him analyze what they'd found.

The room was a perfect place for vampires to hang out. And arrogant computer whizzes who thought they were invincible.

Kyle wrinkled his nose. "Dude, you should give up the cancer sticks. Nasty habit."

The thin, wiry kid—hell, he had to be no more than twenty—didn't even look at Kyle, but kept studying his computer screen. "You should criticize. Ever think of getting a new aftershave and stop borrowing from your father?"

At least I'm not setting one foot in the grave before I'm thirty. "I don't wear aftershave, and hurry up with that film. If you spent less time smoking on your break and more time processing, maybe we could get our work done."

The camera he'd found in the exam room had a sweet little SD card. They'd taken it back to the office, but the card was encrypted, protected by some complex code.

Code that Genius Boy boasted he could crack in no time. So what the hell was the holdup?

"You done yet?" he snapped at the tech.

"This baby has a virus attached and the wrong password could wipe out the entire card. Unless you'd care to try," the kid muttered. "Maybe you gorilla types should go back in the field, beat your chest some more instead of bothering the hell out of me."

Roarke strode into the darkened room. "Ease up," he murmured. "It's a delicate process extrapolating the information to get the right password."

Kyle shrugged off his partner's hand. "I'll ease up when this case is solved. We should have immediately ordered the clinic searched from top to bottom."

"Dr. North didn't appear to have anything to hide."

Right. Except for her family's involvement. Finding the photos made him aware that the clinic had a sinister underbelly, a purpose that dovetailed straight into trafficking children. Need a photo of a cute kid so you can determine which one is best to abduct and send overseas? Why, step right into this room.

"She has plenty to hide," he countered.

"If she did, why would she call us?"

But Kyle wasn't in the mood for logical arguments. He'd let himself be distracted by a pretty face and a sparkling personality and pale, smooth skin as touchable as velvet. He'd wondered what it would be like to kiss her... her mouth so ripe and warm, tasting sweet, the softness yielding beneath the subtle pressure of his own.

He gave a disgusted snort. Served him right for thinking with the wrong brain.

Damn, he was upset with the world today, upset with himself and angry at Belle. He'd thought she was decent, started to have faint hope he could trust her.

Faint hope that she'd put the welfare of endangered children ahead of her own needs, including those of her family.

But instead, she'd lied to him. She'd deliberately caged the truth to give her brother time to get word to their chief physician so he could cover his ass.

They'd have a hard time finding the doctor now. Bastard was probably on his way to Indonesia by now, or another country prohibiting extradition.

Doctors always banded together to protect each other. Just as cops did and so did the military. Only he'd thought Belle was different from the physicians who'd screwed up with his daughter.

Should have known better.

His nerves frayed, he tapped his fingers on the desktop. "Any time now…"

The kid snorted. "You field agents have no respect for the delicacy of my work. One does not recreate a masterpiece in minutes."

Masterpiece? "This isn't art school. Get to it."

Roarke tugged him away from the desk. "Let him work. And you, cool down. You've been grouchy as a toddler at nap time. Give it a break."

Toddlers, naptime. Cute little girls, their dark curls tousled and held in place by bright pink butterfly barrettes. "No nap." Scowls. "No tired, Dada."

How many naptimes had he missed? How much time had he spent brushing his daughter's hair, or singing her bedtime lullabies to smooth away that scowl?

How many times had he just plain missed spending time with her, all because he was on the fast track to a brilliant career?

The job always came first.

But family mattered. No matter what, he had to reunite Anna with her mother.

Kyle paced the small room, his thoughts in a maelstrom.

"How could we have missed the camera? If we'd dug deeper, gone over every square inch in the search…"

"We had no reason to suspect the clinic. The security guard/maintenance guy had an alibi and Belle North was on the level."

"Not on the level. She'd lie to protect her precious family name and their rep." He rubbed a hand over the bristles on his chin.

"Maybe. Let's see what Junior comes up with on the film." Roarke perched on a stool, gnawed on a granola bar. He offered a piece to Kyle. "Lunch?"

He shook his head, half admiring, half impatient with his partner's ability to down food at the most stressful of times. Who could eat when they had a promising, hot lead right before them?

Then again, Roarke was a former SEAL. The man learned to refuel every chance he could.

The SD card could contain more photos of children who'd visited the clinic. Incriminating evidence. Maybe even documents or memos leading to the SOB who'd taken Anna.

If they were real lucky, they'd catch a break and have the good Dr. Patterson speaking into the microphone, saying how he orchestrated all of this.

Until Junior cracked the code, they didn't know what they had.

"Got it."

Whirling, he made it over to the desk before Roarke could finish cramming the last bite of granola into his mouth. Kyle leaned over the tech's leather chair as the video popped up on the wall-mounted widescreen.

Grainy footage at first. No, the room was dark. On the screen, a light snapped on. Kyle expected to see a nurse entering the room with a young patient.

Instead, Belle walked inside, carrying a gym bag. She dropped the bag on the floor, stretched.

His heart raced. *Oh damn, please don't tell me she's involved.* Did the bag contain money? Something else suspicious?

Throat dry, he watched, sweat trickling down his spine. The camera angle was wide, showing everything. Her hair was soft gold, spilling down past her shoulders as she released the clip holding it back. With a sigh, she stretched again, the move lifting her breasts. He felt like a voyeur, eyeing the screen, but this was the job.

Belle removed her doctor's lab coat, hung it on a peg on the back of the door. Beneath the coat she wore a simple green sleeveless dress. Nice arms, slightly muscled, well defined. The lady hadn't lied. She did work out, even if it was that CrossFit that was all the rage these days.

His sport of choice was kickboxing with an opponent who could kick his ass.

Silence filled the room as they watched the screen. Then an annoying crunch. Kyle's glance flicked sideways.

Kid was munching on chips. Annoyed, he returned his attention to the screen.

Belle sat on the doctor's swivel stool in the room and bent over, kicking off her sensible heels.

Okay, this was odd. Was she going to nap in the unused exam room?

He studied the contours of her legs, clad in stockings. Such nice legs, long and with just the right amount of curve and muscle. So feminine. He liked that she wore a dress and pearls. It fit her elegant, refined personality. Yet part of him longed to see her in casual clothing, maybe shorts and a sleeveless top. He could envision her on a sailboat, wind teasing color into her cheeks, her hair blowing back, a laugh on her lips…

Sailing with her would be fun. A challenge he'd enjoy…

"Holy crap," the kid said between munches.

Kyle stared.

Holy crap indeed. Belle had hiked up her green dress, and proceeded to wriggle out of her pantyhose like a snake shedding a skin. Fortunately, she was quick, showing only a glimpse of forest green panties…

"She's a little old to be a victim of child trafficking," Junior said, munching on a potato chip. "But wow, what a bod…so hot…"

She folded the hose and placed them in the gym bag. He had a bad feeling about this. Wanted to shut off the camera. Kyle drew in a deep breath.

Next she withdrew black yoga pants, a pink T-shirt and what looked like a black sports bra from the bag, set them on the stool. Heart in his stomach, he clenched his fists. *No, get a call, get turned away, don't do this, don't do this…*

But she did. Unzipped her dress and drew it over her head.

"Wow," the kid said. "Nice!"

Jaw dropping, he could make no sound. Instead, he clapped a hand over the kid's eyes. Roarke leaned over, depressed a key to pause the video.

"Hey! What gives?" the kid yelled.

"Shut up," Kyle said softly.

"I need to see this. I need to tell where the footage is from…"

"Do you like DC?"

He could feel eyelashes blink against his palm as if the kid was confused. "Yeah. I love it here. Great nightlife."

"Then shut up and keep your eyes closed or I'll have you shipped to a field office in Nebraska and you'll freeze your balls and your social life."

The kid shut up. When he removed his hand, the kid's eyes remained shut. Scared. Good. He wasn't in any mood to tolerate sass or commentary.

Just in case the kid got ideas…

He pivoted the kid's chair around so he faced the door.

He nodded at the grim-faced Roarke, who let the video run again.

Belle stood before them in a lacy forest green bra. The undergarment exposed the top halves of her breasts, rounded and soft-looking. She had a perfect hourglass figure, her hips rounded but not too big, covered in matching lace panties. She looked like a Victoria's Secret underwear model.

She went to the mirror on the wall, stood before it, frowning. Why the frown? He didn't get it. She was gorgeous. Perfect. A teenage wet dream.

"Yeah, I need the workout. Too many late-night snacks, my girl," she said in a clear voice to the mirror.

With an index finger, she poked at her hips. "Wide as a house! Extra cardio today. You can do this," she told the mirror.

Wide as a house? He adored her hips. They were perfect as is…

Belle left the mirror and faced the camera again. His glance frantically shot to the clothing pile on the stool.

Clearly she was headed for a workout. Using the room as a changing room before she went to the gym. *Dear Lord, please don't let that be a sports bra, don't let that be one… get dressed…hurry up…hurry up…*

But the good Lord wasn't listening to him today because she reached behind her, unclipped the bra and pulled it off.

All while facing the camera on the counter.

Mouth dry, he fought to control a sudden surge of lust, and then felt an equal surge of disgust. He felt like a damn Peeping Tom, staring at her half-dressed.

She should be in his bedroom doing this as he watched. He'd gently tease her, encourage her, bringing a shy blush to her cheeks, a sparkle to her eyes…

Out of respect, he forced his gaze to examine other areas on the screen. The table behind her, and the edges of her toes. Hot-pink toenails. She liked her pedicures, he guessed. Her nails were trimmed and clean, but not painted, as if she worked a lot with them.

He reached over to end the video. Stomach clenching, he wanted to rip the SD card from the computer and pound it into oblivion.

Roarke stopped him.

"We have to watch it all, Kyle," Roarke said tightly. "Evidence."

He swore under his breath. Nodded.

Unfortunately, as he straightened, his eyes shot right to where he'd been trying to avoid. Her breasts. Kyle sucked down a deep breath, forced his gaze upward to her lovely face.

Pearls around her neck. Small, round and perfect. Glinting in the harsh fluorescent light.

I'd ask her to keep the pearls on when we made love. She would look so sexy, her hair spread out on my pillow...

Fisting his hands, he swallowed hard against the lust spreading through him. Kyle looked down, looked up.

Now onscreen Belle stood at the sink. The camera angle wasn't as clear, thankfully. He heard water running, and then a paper towel dispenser clicking.

Back to the camera, she went to the stool, dressed in the sports bra, yoga pants and pink T-shirt, then donned socks and shoes. She picked up the gym bag, left the room, clicked off the light.

The room went dark and silent once more.

The video kept rolling, and then went dark.

Kyle's mind clicked back to pro mode. He rolled Junior back to the screen. "What else is on this card?"

Junior typed in a few commands, scanned his monitor.

"Nothing. Just the video. Want to watch it again to make sure…"

Kyle reached over, snapped off the monitor.

"Hey," the kid protested.

Ignoring him, he removed the card from the desktop. "I need the password to the SD card."

"You have no right…"

"Password."

"Tell him, son," Roarke said quietly. "You don't want to mess with him now."

"Antibiotic," the kid muttered. "I ran the program using medical terms, figured that…"

"Thanks," he said curtly and, clutching the card, left the room.

In the hallway, he and Roarke were stopped by a solemn crime-scene tech.

"Got something for you, Kyle. I traced the serial numbers from the camera." The crime-scene tech consulted his tablet. "Purchased by one Michael Patterson with his credit card."

Kyle handed him the SD card. "Thanks, Dale. I need you to tell me everything you can about this card. It's a vid of Dr. North getting undressed."

Thankfully, Dale wasn't immature like the kid. "Sure."

They followed Dale into his lab, where he inserted the card into a computer. Kyle gave him the password and Dale ran a series of programs.

"Huh. Interesting." Dale pointed to a series of numbers on his computer screen. "I pulled the metadata from the SD card and the vid was recorded two weeks ago. It was taped over something."

"Can you go deep and find out what was erased?" Roarke asked.

"I can try. I'll get back to you."

They left Dale to do his work. Kyle headed for the

kitchen. He needed caffeine and a chance to clear his head, and sort through his jumbled thoughts.

"So Dr. Patterson used the camera to photograph children in the clinic, and caught Belle on camera as she undressed." Roarke handed Kyle a paper cup filled with black coffee and then got a cup for himself.

"The big question is why did Patterson do it?" he mused, stirring the barely warm liquid.

"Maybe Patterson has a thing for her. She is a beautiful woman," his partner pointed out.

What he wouldn't give to have Patterson here. He'd question him, maybe with his fists. On second hand, good thing the doctor wasn't here.

What kind of sick jerk was Patterson? Did he use the hidden camera to record photographs of children to kidnap them? If so, why keep the vid of Belle? To watch it later?

Maybe the bastard had a hidden obsession with Belle. His mind raced over the possibilities. To his shock, jealousy flashed through him. Patterson and Belle, laughing as they worked together…

Get a grip, Anderson.

This is what you get for getting involved, for letting your feelings interfere with a case. She's a beautiful woman. You're a guy. Control yourself.

Yet there was no denying the sparks flying between them when they were together. He was attracted to her on a deeper level, and not for her body. Her intellect and strong personality and dedication intrigued him. Until he realized her desire to protect her family overrode her desire to find the missing girls.

He wondered if he'd been wrong, and she was a victim, as well. Had he been so eager to find fault with her, blaming her profession, because he didn't want her to be innocent?

Cast blame on her because his attraction to her made

him uncomfortable? Made him think of things that seemed impossibly out of reach?

Things like a real relationship with a woman, not simply a one-night stand.

Things like home and family instead of career and hard work.

A life.

Kyle scoffed. He was getting too damn introspective and his life wasn't on the line. An innocent little girl was missing and if not dead yet, perhaps shipped out of the country even as he stood here like a dumb ass.

"Earth to Kyle?" Roarke waved a hand in front of his face. "Dude, you here?"

"What?"

"The fact that the card was still in the camera indicates whoever did this, most likely Patterson, didn't see the video yet. It wasn't in the hidden compartment with the photos of the children."

True. He felt for the coin in his trouser pocket, brought it out and flipped it. There were plenty of sick people in this world who would never hesitate to hurt someone else. Was Belle an innocent victim?

There was something innocent in the way she undressed, the critical self-exam in the mirror and her lack of guile that told him she was unaware of being recorded.

"Patterson is our link," he muttered.

Roarke took out his phone, made a call. Sure enough, just as Kyle suspected.

"The doctor might have told Belle he was in the Bahamas, but the phone company pinged his iPhone and he's still here in Florida. His location keeps jumping from Miami to the Keys."

He blinked fast. "Find him. Put out an APB. I want that bastard caught before he even flashes his passport. He's our link."

"Dr. North's footage has to be accidental. Maybe he planned to return later for the SD card."

Roarke's suggestion made sense. Yet his gut said otherwise. "I think he was totally aware of Belle undressing in that room, and kept the card."

"Why?"

"That's something only Belle can answer. Did he tell her to use the room, knowing the camera recorded? What's the extent of their relationship and what does it have to do with the missing children?"

"She's not a suspect anymore."

"Not for the moment. But we need to question her because Dr. North is in the thick of all of this. And she may have answers, answers she doesn't even realize she knows."

Chapter 14

It had been a long, tiring day at the cardiology practice and Belle was ready to kick off her heels and relax.

For some reason, her mind constantly drifted to Kyle. It hurt to know he considered her as a suspect, someone who would be so low as to conspire to photograph innocent children. Maybe even help kidnap them.

She liked him. Really liked him, more than as a person. The chemistry between them sizzled and made her feel alive and aware in a way no other man had made her feel in a long time.

Stirring a pot of spaghetti sauce on the stove, she tried to lift her spirits. Music blared on the speaker Bluetoothed to her iPod, a lighthearted jazz tune. At her feet, Boo wagged his tail in hopes of a treat.

"Not yet, sweetie."

Belle sighed. She hated leaving him alone all day while she was gone, and though Boo was fed and walked by a pet sitter, he was still lonely.

Maybe she'd take her dog over to her cousin Myra's house for a visit. Boo adored playing with the two other rescue shih tzu dogs Myra and her husband owned.

The treats were kept in a ceramic jar on the counter painted with paws. Belle tossed a dog biscuit to Boo, who caught it in midair. As he munched, Belle tested the sauce.

Almost ready. All these carbs were going to be hell on her hips, but she needed a treat after the strain of the past week.

A soft chime sounded at the front door. She turned down the heat under the sauce, wiped her hands and consulted her phone to see the video camera on the doorbell.

Her heart skipped a beat. The black SUV in the driveway, and the two men standing on her porch would make any woman's heart beat faster, but the FBI agents were not here to socialize.

Now what? I didn't do it.

Steeling herself, she opened the door.

"Gentlemen. How may I help you?"

Inside, she winced at her cold, stiff voice, what Clint called her social-chastising tone.

Kyle inclined his head. "We found something. May we come inside?"

Equally formal, but gone was the coldness of yesterday, the accusing glare. Confused, she stepped aside. Boo raced into the hallway, barking, tail wagging as a greeting.

Roarke stooped down and petted him, but Kyle did not.

Then he focused on her. She became too aware of the intensity of his gaze, and flushed. Belle swept a hand over her jeans. Bare feet, too. And yeah, there was a red stain on her gray shirt.

"You caught me in the middle of making dinner. I don't usually look like this."

More formality. Awkward. *If you plan on hauling me to the police station for questioning, maybe you'll let me change.*

"You look wonderful," he said softly.

That deep voice, so sexy and gruff, made her melt. *Don't think of that. You're a suspect. The enemy.*

Refusing to look at him, she instead studied the laptop in his hands.

Hope sprang inside her. Maybe they found a lead? "Is it Anna? Did you find her?"

"No." Kyle's mouth flattened. "We have something to show you. It's not good, I'm afraid. But it has nothing to do with Anna."

Belle led them into the kitchen. "May I get you a cold drink? Water? Tea?"

"No, thanks," Roarke said.

"I'll take a bottled water."

Surprised Kyle wanted a drink, she got him one as he set the laptop on the kitchen table, typed in some commands and then pulled out a chair.

"Please sit," he ordered.

No refusing the command in his firm, yet gentle voice. Belle handed him the water and sat. Kyle and Roarke took seats across from each other. Kyle opened the water and took a long swig.

"Whatever you're here for, you need to know I had nothing to do with the hidden camera or the photographs. I may have called my brother to alert him about it, but I swear I would never condone such activity, or hide it from the authorities. I'm not in league with whoever set up that camera."

"I believe you."

Belle watched Kyle's expression turn sympathetic. Oh, this was not good. What was going on? Even Roarke stared at the floor as if finding it suddenly fascinating.

"You do? Yesterday you were ready to throw me into a jail cell." Belle folded her arms across her chest.

His gaze riveted to the pearls around her throat. "Yesterday we didn't know about this."

Kyle popped the SD card into his laptop, typed a command.

"We found an encrypted SD card still in the hidden

camera in Exam Room Four," he told her. "Our staff found the password to unlock it."

"Footage of Anna? Do you need me to ID her?"

"No." He took a deep breath. "Footage of you."

Belle fingered her pearls, a gift from her late grandmother. Seldom taken off, they were a comforting reminder of decorum blended with love. Her grandmother had loved her dearly, and if Belle played in the mud or was a little naughty, her grandmother never scolded or chastised, warning her to be a lady.

Her grandmother let her be herself.

Kyle's mouth thinned as he depressed a button and the video began playing on the laptop screen. Roarke looked away, his expression tight. Kyle focused on her.

She watched.

Oh dear Lord in heaven. Her heart dropped to her stomach, and she struggled to breathe.

Exam Room Four two weeks ago, when she'd spent a weary day seeing patients and had to force herself to go to CrossFit classes. She'd changed in the room as motivation, because it was empty...

Although slightly distorted, the video showed her undressing, kicking off her wide high heels, removing her lab coat and then...

She forced herself to watch the rest of it. Humiliation crawled through her. Mercifully, the video soon ended.

Nausea boiled in her stomach. Through sheer determination, she kept her gorge down, swallowed hard. The room felt hot, too warm, and the entire house smelled like the spaghetti sauce simmering on the stove.

Dimly she thought from now on she would forever associate the smell of spaghetti sauce with seeing herself half-naked on tape.

Someone had violated her privacy, her trust, and filmed her when she was most vulnerable. She didn't know whether to be more embarrassed by the monologue before the mirror or the fact she'd bared her breasts.

It made her angrier when she realized how vulnerable the children had been in that room, children who trusted them as physicians and nurses and physician assistants to heal them.

Not hurt or humiliate.

She lifted her eyes to Kyle. The anger in his own eyes surprised her. She expected to find sympathy or the cold FBI agent once more. Not this glittering fury, as if he wanted to throttle whoever did this.

The thought comforted a little. Only a little. She clutched her pearls, feeling each one by touch, thinking of her dignified grandmother and what Poppy would do in such a situation.

Help them find whoever did this.

Her hands dropped to her lap as she realized the pearl-clutching damsel in distress look was too clichéd. They probably thought she would wring her hands next. Poor, violated Belle.

She wanted to vomit again.

Instead, she cleared her throat. "I imagine you have questions for me."

Roarke blinked, but a small, satisfied smile touched Kyle's full mouth. "Yes."

But instead of grilling her, he coaxed Boo over, picked up the dog and scratched behind his ears. Boo's tail beat the air. Agent Anderson certainly had a way with dogs.

When he settled Boo into her lap, she wasn't surprised. If he was a dog person, he knew petting her dog would lower her blood pressure.

Fingers shaking, she stroked Boo's short hair. Her mother never understood why Belle kept a shih tzu in a puppy cut, but then again Boo was a rescue and...

"You ready for this?" Kyle asked softly.

She gave a jerky nod.

"When you went into the room to change, did you tell anyone?"

His keen blue gaze remained steady. Like a lighthouse beacon on a turbulent, dark sea tossing whitecaps back and forth, she focused on his calmness.

"Um." Belle rested her hand on Boo's back. "Yes. No. I mean, I had finished my shift and Mike, Dr. Patterson, was there working on files. He told me to use Exam Room Four—no one was in it and it had more privacy and space than the bathrooms."

Anger shot through her, vibrating like a tuning fork. "He told me I should go work out as planned. He knew how tiring it was after a long shift, but exercise was important to relieving stress."

"Bastard," Kyle grated out, but his voice remained soft. "Did you see him after you left? How did he act? Pleased? Secretive?"

"He acted…relieved." She frowned. "If he did this, why would he be relieved? I'd think he wanted a tape of me undressing, he'd be happy, smirking or trying hard to hide his emotions. I thought it terribly peculiar at the time, but I was in a hurry to get to class."

"Maybe it wasn't a video for him to watch." Faint color touched Kyle's high cheekbones. Such aristocratic cheeks. She wondered what his heritage was.

"He could have wanted you to undress in that room and kept the video as blackmail." Roarke exchanged glances with Kyle and stopped scribbling in a notebook. She hadn't even noticed he took notes.

Did the agent take notes while watching the video of her? The thought proved unsettling.

"Blackmail?" Belle was proud her voice didn't quaver.

"In case you found something out he didn't want discovered." Roarke started to speak, and Kyle's cell phone rang. He excused himself and walked over to the sliding glass doors, talking quietly.

Roarke tapped his pencil on the pad. "These days, it's all too easy to upload something this incriminating to social media and just the threat might be enough..."

"Incriminating?" She set down Boo, and he loped over to his pillow and lay down, watching them. "I was undressing. Am I the suspect here?"

Red suffused Roarke's face. "Uh, no, Dr. North, I meant it's a video Patterson could have used against you to keep you silent."

"Silent about what?"

"About anything. Most likely the photos of the children we found."

She was glad when Kyle returned to the table. "Lab called. They ran the prints on the photos of the children and Patterson's are all over them." He regarded her with a steady look.

"Our crime lab discovered footage of another video on this same card. The one of you copied over it. We weren't able to discern much.

"We ran Patterson's information through IAFIS and found his prints." Kyle tucked away his cell. "It's our national fingerprint-ID system. He pleaded guilty to dispensing medical marijuana without a license in New York two years ago."

Stunned, she sat back.

"Did your family do a background check on him?" Roarke asked.

This was getting worse by the minute. "I assumed Clint did, since he's in charge of the foundation and the foundation does all the hiring." Fingernails dug into her palms. "Mike is an old family friend, though, so probably not. My parents are friends of his parents and they socialized in Upstate New York."

She almost feared to ask him. "Do you think Mike took Anna?"

"At the very least, he had something to do with her kidnapping. We'll find him. He's still here in the States."

Kyle's words unsettled her further. "He told me he was in the Bahamas, headed to Europe."

"Pings on his cell show he's in Miami and headed for the Keys. We'll catch him." Kyle reached over, slid his palm over hers. "You okay?"

Part of her liked the comforting feel of his hand over hers, his quiet voice soft with concern. The other half recalled how he had labeled her a suspect simply for calling her brother before the FBI.

Belle yanked her hand away. "Am I still a suspect?"

His expression shuttered. "You've dropped way down on the list."

"Because of this." Disgust filled her as she pointed to the video. "You were ready to accuse me, until you saw this?"

"Yes."

At least he was honest. But that wasn't earning him any points. Incredulous, she struggled with her rising temper. "Just because now you see me naked on a video, I'm innocent? Your logic is inane, Special Agent Anderson."

"I'll use any logic I damn well please to catch whoever is behind these kidnappings, and find Anna."

Roarke held up his hands. "Think I'll take a stroll outside, look at the perimeter."

He went out the sliding glass door as Kyle drained his bottle of water. Slamming it down on the table, he glared at her.

"Look, I didn't want to believe you had anything to do with the kidnappings. But I have to do my job. My first priority is finding those girls."

"Mine, as well. And if you'd stopped jumping to conclusions about me, and my family, simply because we have money…"

"Money has nothing to do with it. I don't give a damn if you're rich as Midas. It's…" He took a deep breath, seemed to struggle with his own temper.

"It's what? Because I'm blonde? Because I have faults like other people? What is it?"

"I don't trust doctors."

Kyle rubbed a hand over the bristles on his chin. "And your Dr. Patterson gave me another reason for that mistrust."

Belle stared. "Must be hard when you need medical care."

"I make damn sure I don't."

Kyle flexed his fingers. "I like you, Belle, I really do. I don't think you had anything to do with this. We're going to need your help to reel in Patterson. He's the only solid lead we have so far and each day that goes by it gets less likely that we'll find Anna alive and well."

That made no sense because Patterson hadn't abducted Anna. "What about Jesse Dugin?"

Muscles jumped in his tight jaw. "Vanished. We've searched last known location, offered a reward. Combed the community where he lived. Nothing."

But he wasn't telling everything and she had to know. "You don't think he was behind all this. There's something greater."

"I can't discuss that."

"You can level with me if you want me to help catch Mike."

Kyle's gaze flicked to the sliding door, where Roarke paced outside. "All right. Dugin was the middleman, hired for the abduction and to kill Rosa. Patterson is the one who arranged everything. On the day Anna vanished, eighty thousand dollars was wired to Dugin's account from a bank in the Bahamas."

Somehow she wasn't surprised. "And with Mike having a vacation home there, that puts even more suspicion on him."

"Correct."

"And my brother, for hiring Mike, and not checking his background?"

"Somewhat. We have a team now questioning Clint."

Her brother wouldn't cooperate fully. Clint and Mike were fishing buddies. Probably Clint knew about the conviction and decided to hire Mike to give him a chance.

The action tarnished her brother's sterling reputation. She was glad her parents had gone away for a few weeks. Mom would be even more upset with what'd developed.

Because the clinic and now the entire foundation were entrenched in this situation, and their family reputation?

Didn't matter.

Not while there was a missing girl and a slim thread of time for her to be found safe and alive.

She forgot her anger and her earlier embarrassment. "What do you want me to do?"

Kyle studied her, his expression softening. "You're not like any doctor I've ever met, Belle North. Most of them are too busy and dismissive to take time to help."

"Then I'd say you haven't met many in my field, Agent Anderson." She wasn't ready to forgive him yet for his earlier suspicion. "Widen your horizons and it'll do you a world of good."

"Maybe. But I'll still stop at an office supply place to staple my own wounds."

He winked at her as she rolled her eyes, but his teasing tone brought a smile to her face.

Kyle stuck out a palm. "Truce?"

She held out her hand. "Truce."

For a minute, he held her hand, and then lightly squeezed it. A shiver of pure awareness shot through her.

"What do you need me to do?"

"Come to the station and look at mug books. See if you recognize any of the associates of Dr. Patterson's who may have come to the clinic." He pointed to the stove. "Sorry for making you miss dinner."

She went to turn off the spaghetti sauce. It was ruined, anyway.

Who could have an appetite after watching something like that?

Kyle kept his mouth shut and watched Belle as she turned the pages of the mug books. After nearly a half an hour of looking, she'd not identified a single one. Not that it surprised him. Patterson was clever, and not the type to openly associate with criminals at his workplace.

She closed the last book. "Now what?"

For a moment he hesitated. The next step involved risk to her, and he hated exposing her to it. Yet they had the advantage now.

"Call Patterson. Tell him you need to meet him in a location halfway for you both. Tell him the police have named you as a suspect and you don't know where to turn."

She looked doubtful. "You really think he'll care?"

"Make him care. Keep him on the line, however you can. We'll trace the call and get his exact location. His cell keeps bouncing."

Belle still looked doubtful, the cute little frown line indenting between her silky dark gold brows. She dug her cell phone out of her Gucci bag, and then glanced around at the busy police station.

"Not here. And not your cell phone." Kyle led her to a quiet conference room filled with equipment where men monitored the phone calls.

She picked up the conference-room phone, dialed Mike's number as the men waited. But the call went to voice mail.

"He's not picking up."

Belle dialed again. Nothing.

She tried her cell phone. Same thing. This time she left a message, asking him to call her on the station phone number.

Kyle's expression tightened. "Either he's not picking up the phone for anyone or..."

"Or what? He's already left the country?"

"Doubtful. We have alerts at all the airports to search for him. Unless he left by boat."

"Mike doesn't have a boat. He used to, but sold it about two months ago..."

Her expression fell. "Oh, that sounds terrible. Suspicious. He told me his boat needed too much work and he didn't have the time or the energy for it. Do you think he sold it for money?"

Kyle nodded grimly. And wondered if Patterson was in deeper financial trouble than they'd realized. Which made him a perfect accessory for someone wanting to kidnap a little girl from the clinic...

He drove her home in the sleek black SUV. Belle kept checking her cell phone. Finally when they were almost at her house, it rang.

"Patterson?" Kyle asked, not taking his eyes off the road.

Belle nodded. She'd given them permission to wiretap her phone. At this point, anything to catch whoever did this.

If it was Mike, she'd have her own special way of dealing with it. One that involved lawyers.

Taking a deep breath, she answered. "Mike, where are you? I'm in real trouble."

"Belle. I'm sorry. I really am. I can't help you."

"Can't or won't? Mike, what the hell did you do?"

Perhaps the fact that she swore, a rarity for her, stunned him into silence. Or perhaps he was simply scared. Heavy breathing came through the line.

"Mike, I'm not taking the fall for this. I can't. I have my future ahead of me. Remember what you told me about becoming a doctor? I wanted to be like you."

Out of the corner of her eye, she saw Kyle nod and mouth, "Good." He made a stretching motion.

Cue for keep Mike talking so they could trace the call.

"I'm afraid you'll have to, Belle. You and Clint. I may... not survive this."

For the first time, real fear shot through her. Mike didn't sound pompous or dramatic. He was scared. Terrified.

"Where are you?" Fingers tightened around her phone. "I'll tell Clint to pick you up."

"No. I don't want him involved." Worry riddled his tone, as if the man were sitting next to her. "Cops with you now?"

She hesitated.

"Level with me, Belle. I need to talk to them. I have information they need. I want to make a trade. Put me on speaker."

Taking a leap of faith, she did.

"Who's with you, Belle? The feds?"

"This is special agent Kyle Anderson of the FBI, Dr. Patterson. What information do you have to offer?"

"Not here, over the phone. In person. I'll give you everything. Names, dates, where Anna is."

Belle bit her lip. He knew, the bastard. He knew everything.

"She's alive? Where is she? Is she okay?" she blurted out.

Kyle put a hand on her arm. "Easy," he mouthed.

"She's fine." Mike sounded impatient. "But they're going to move her out of the country in a few days and you'll lose her forever."

She could only think of one reason to get Anna out of the

United States—a child-trafficking ring. Her mentor was involved in with criminals who stole children and sold them.

"Mike, how could you do this?" Belle's throat closed tight. She trusted him so much in the past. To find out he participated in stealing Anna was like finding out her own brother was a criminal.

A heavy sigh. "Nothing is as black-and-white as you make it out to be, little Bluebell," he said, using her childhood nickname. "Especially with family."

The remark made no sense. "You mean your family?"

"No." The word was curt. "Stay out of this, Bluebell, before you get hurt. The people behind this have money and power and they'll stop at nothing to get what they think is theirs."

"What do you want, Dr. Patterson?"

How could Kyle remain so calm, his voice so even? Her heart raced a mile a minute and she wanted to scream at the phone.

"I want to cut a deal. My testimony and the information I'll give you in exchange for I don't do any time. For anything."

"I can see what can be arranged."

"Do it."

"Where do you want to meet?" Kyle asked.

"The Old Pine Tree Motel in Dade Town on US 27 in one hour. Room Six. Only you. And Belle. No other cops or feds."

"No." For the first time Kyle's voice sharpened. "I'll meet you but not with Belle. I'll need more than an hour. It will take that long from where I'm at. Two hours. Eight p.m. sharp."

"Fine. Two hours. But bring her or there's no deal and I won't say a damn word."

The phone clicked off. Belle stared at the screen.

Consulting her GPS, she sucked in a breath. "It's a good

forty-five minutes from here. Looks like the motel is a truck stop. Why would he stay there?"

"Truck stops specialize in anonymity. Like no-tell motels."

"Oh." Of course. Glad he couldn't see the heat suffusing her cheeks, she studied the map. "If you take the interstate down to…"

"You're not going."

She halfway expected that. "Mike said to bring me or no deal. Will you risk Anna's life? He won't talk unless I'm there."

"I won't risk yours." Kyle shook his head. "He's desperate and could be armed and dangerous."

"I'm going."

"You'll stay at your house."

Belle set her cell phone on the dashboard. "You don't have time to drop me off and meet him there."

"Yes, I will. I'm not going in alone. I'll have backup."

"Backup as in other police? No, you'll risk Anna's life!"

Kyle's voice remained level and calm. "Trust me, Belle. I know what I'm doing."

"And I know Mike. He won't talk to you alone. He'll want me there as a negotiator."

The glow of dashboard lights showed his expression tightening. "Negotiator?"

"He knows me, knows my family and, most of all—" she sighed "—he knows our family attorney. And he knows Clint will hire our attorney in order to protect the clinic's name."

Kyle cursed softly, got into the right lane to head for the interstate. "All right. But you do exactly as I say. Has Patterson ever been to that motel before?"

Emotion tightened her throat. "I'm not sure. But I know that area. Clint and Mike used to go bass fishing there in the Everglades. They took me a few times."

She only prayed Mike would talk and they'd get to Anna in time to save her.

Kyle didn't like this.

He'd stopped at the FBI command center first to organize backup, outfitted himself and Belle in Kevlar vests. No way in hell was he walking into a potentially deadly situation without backup. Going alone was risky enough. Taking Belle with him ground on every last nerve.

But she had a point. Patterson wouldn't talk without her.

Belle wore the bulky vest beneath an oversize sweater a police officer loaned her. His was over his shirt in plain sight. Kyle poked at the vest, wishing he'd taken the time after the last case to get it properly fitted. But in this case, it would suffice.

She insisted Mike wouldn't hurt her.

He lacked such faith. Patterson was now a fugitive and desperate men did desperate acts, such as shooting old family friends.

They pulled into the parking lot of the Old Pine Tree Motel at exactly eight o'clock. The motel was a seedy one-story building that clearly had seen better days, maybe back in the 1970s. Sodium parking-lot lights cast a dull orange glow over the two trucks and a beaten-looking sedan.

And standing out like a debutante at a senior citizens' dance, a late-model black Jaguar coupe.

"That's Mike's car." Belle started to open her door.

Kyle put a hand on her arm. "Wait."

At least she didn't argue with him. Belle looked at him. "What do you want me to do?"

"I'll go in first. If he's there, he and I will have a chat. And then I'll bring him out here so he can talk with you."

The Dade Town Police and federal officers stood by in the abandoned warehouse building next to the motel. They'd move as soon as he gave the word.

"It won't work. He's probably already seen your vehicle and knows you're here. He'll want to at least see me, Kyle."

Much as he hated this, Belle was right. They couldn't risk Patterson clamming up and refusing to reveal what he knew. Yet he wasn't about to let her stroll out into the parking lot as an open target. Everything inside him bristled at the idea of her being at risk.

With a start, he realized it was more than his protective nature. He'd started to care for Belle in a more meaningful way. Time enough to ponder that later.

He looked at Room Six across the parking lot. No light shone through the closed curtains, but that meant nothing. Patterson could be inside, hiding, waiting for them to show up.

Kyle checked his sidearm. "He can see you when I say he can see you. For now, you stay here. Lock the doors. If you hear anything, shots fired, anything, you get down. Got it?"

She nodded.

On second thought…he reached into the glove box and withdrew a Glock. "Have you ever fired a gun?"

Her pert nose wrinkled. "Once or twice on a hunting trip. Not…that."

"Here." He showed her the safety. "It's loaded, ready to go. Semiautomatic. Point and shoot. At the bad guys, not me, okay?"

Belle managed a faint smile. "Got it."

Unable to prevent himself, he touched her cheek. "You're something else, Doc."

Then he opened the door and slammed it, striding across the parking lot to Room Six.

And possible danger…or the information they needed to finally retrieve Anna, safe and alive.

Chapter 15

Her cheek felt warm where Kyle had touched it. Only two weeks ago she'd thought him arrogant and cold when they'd first met at the airport. Now she knew that the icy exterior hid a warm man inside, who deeply cared about his job and the children he tried to help.

Face it, girlfriend, you're starting to fall for him. Hard and fast.

Belle gripped her hands in her lap, watching Kyle walk across the blacktop. Worry needled her. If Mike was armed, he could panic and shoot Kyle if provoked. He wouldn't hurt her because it would be like shooting his own sister.

Once she thought she had known Mike as a calm, collected professional, a doctor she respected for his thirty years of working as a healer.

Now? Her safe, secure world spun on its axis. She didn't know who to trust anymore. Could she even trust her own brother, who had arranged for Mike to be chief physician?

Belle focused on Kyle. She trusted him. The agent risked his life to protect others and took an enormous gamble now.

Her gaze scanned the nearly empty parking lot. That Jaguar... Mike had always boasted about it, how sweet it handled, how he liked to crank up the speed on the highway. He'd even arranged for a vanity plate.

Alarm raced through her as she stared at the Jaguar's

tail end. She couldn't see entirely from here, but those first three letters weren't *DOC*.

Kyle ordered her to remain in the vehicle. But if that wasn't Mike's car, he could be walking into a trap.

Leaving the door open, and clutching the pistol, she slipped out of the SUV and walked backward to the right to get a better view of the Jag's license plate.

Her heart dropped to her stomach. Not *DOC PAT*. This license plate was ordinary. There were many other black Jaguar coupes in the area.

Why hadn't she noticed before and warned Kyle? Damn it, she'd been trained to use all her good sense and the first thing she'd failed to do was see the car wasn't the right one.

Was Mike even here?

Belle glanced at Room Six. Weapon held outward, Kyle knocked on the door.

Nothing. No barrage of bullets, thankfully. But no answer. No lights on in the room, either. Something was dreadfully wrong.

Kyle ducked into the room.

Cupping her hands, she peered into the Jaguar. Hard to see in this light. Belle used the flashlight app on her cell phone.

The car's interior was pristine, with shiny leather seats. But dangling from the rearview mirror was a pair of earphones. Mike always put them there for phone calls because he once lamented that he lost earphones more times than most people lost their television remotes.

It had to be his car, but that license plate… Why would he change it?

Kyle needed to know. Torn, she lingered. Finally Belle scurried across the parking lot after him. He emerged a minute later as she reached the door.

Scowling at her, he lowered his weapon. "I told you to wait in the vehicle."

Belle told him about the license plate. "The car looks just like Mike's, but it's the wrong plate."

Speaking into the hidden microphone on his tie, Kyle's brow furrowed. "Roarke, Patterson isn't here. I need you to run a plate for me."

They hurried over to the Jaguar and Kyle rattled off the numbers. A minute later he rubbed his forehead. "The plate belongs to a 2016 Nissan stolen a month ago. You sure this is his car?"

"Pretty sure. His headphones are on the mirror. I wouldn't be able to tell until you opened the glove box and pulled out the registration. Why would he put another plate on the Jag? Because you were searching for his car?"

"Most likely."

She put a hand on Kyle's arm. "Mike was here."

"He might still be around." Kyle gestured to the SUV. "Go. Get back in the vehicle."

"No. I'm telling you, if he's here and scared, seeing me is the only thing that will get him to talk."

He could have gone out, but she doubted it. Not when he knew they were headed to him.

Belle went to the SUV and waited as Kyle checked around the front of the motel. It was quiet but for the hum of insects in the nearby swamp and the traffic from the distant roadway.

Kyle returned to the SUV and climbed inside, radioing his partner. "Roarke, check the back. Go silent. This guy could still be on premises and if he has Anna, we don't want to spook him."

He waited for a few minutes and then touched his earpiece. "All clear. Stay in position. I'll contact you."

Turning to Belle, he pointed to the car. "Is there anyone else Patterson knows who could have accompanied him here? Anyone he could have been working with, whom he trusts?"

"My brother." She dialed Clint's number. It went to voice mail.

"Clint, call me ASAP." Belle hung up and stared at the motel. So frustrating. Her skin itched with impatience. Anna seemed within distance of rescue, yet the man who knew everything was missing.

Or hiding.

"Was Mike even in Room Six? What about his clothing?"

"There's a suitcase in the closet." Kyle tensed. "And a set of girls' clothing in the dresser."

Her heart sank. Mike looked guilty. Still, Anna mattered most. "I can't see him killing her. He's not like that. He heals children."

Kyle snorted. "Not all doctors heal, Belle. Don't be so naive. Some kill."

Ow. That stung, deep. "You surprise me. You didn't strike me as the type of man to let your personal prejudices interfere with the job."

He turned to her so quickly, quietly, it was like watching a cobra strike. Yet in the dim light she saw anguish, not anger, on his face.

"I don't. But damn it, your friend is key to finding Anna and if we don't find him, our chances of finding her shrink, especially if she's moved. It's too damn easy to smuggle children out of this state. Florida's surrounded by water. She could be in the islands and on a freighter while we're sitting here, doing nothing."

He was equally frustrated as her. The only solution was finding Mike. Belle searched her memory. Mike liked to fish in the Everglades, and he kept his promises. "He's not stupid, so if he said he had information to share, and wanted to cut a deal, he was ready to talk. Something must have interrupted him."

Kyle went still. "Or someone."

"Or he was working with a partner." He radioed his own partner. "Roarke, meet me at the motel office."

As he started out of the vehicle, she joined him. Kyle glared at her. "You, back in the vehicle."

"No. You need me."

She scurried after him as Kyle started across the lot for the motel office.

"Do you think we were too late?" she asked him. "He wanted to see us in an hour and you delayed it."

"No. We needed that hour. Something else is going on."

In his bulletproof vest and suit, Roarke stood in the motel lobby, his gun holstered. He shoved an impatient hand through his dark hair. "I've rung that damn desk bell for two minutes. Guy's ignoring me."

A noise in the back alerted them to the clerk's arrival. Middle-aged, with gray shot through thinning hair, the man looked as if he'd been sleeping.

Kyle flashed his badge. "Special agent Anderson with the FBI. I need to know who checked into Room Six."

The sleepy clerk blinked, shuffled to the computer with sloth-like speed. He squinted at the screen. "Room Six. Michael Dawes, paid cash. Checked in earlier today, paid in full for the night."

"Dawes is his mother's maiden name," she told Kyle.

"What time did he check in?" Kyle asked.

Yawning again, the clerk studied the screen. "Three thirty. Scheduled to check out tomorrow."

"I need the names of those currently occupying the rooms on either side of Room Six." Kyle demanded.

The clerk frowned as he scanned the computer. "Room Seven is empty, but it says that someone checked into Room Five two hours ago."

"Do you record license plates when someone checks in?" she asked.

A small laugh. "Lady, this ain't the Hilton. People come

and go and like their privacy. Long as they pay the bill, that's all we care about."

"I need the skeleton key to Room Five."

"I don't know…"

"Now."

The deadly stare Kyle gave the clerk made Belle glad she was on his side.

Paling, the clerk fished out a metal key from a desk drawer and handed it over. "Okay, okay."

The door banged behind them as they rushed out of the office. Belle tailed behind, watching Kyle move with purpose. She'd hate to make an enemy of him. The very traits that others perceived as a threat enabled Kyle to focus with single-minded determination on finding a child.

It was because of him, and his partner, that Anna's chances of being found increased a notch. She could forgive his earlier remarks about doctors. She could forgive a blizzard of doctor insults as long as they found Anna, alive and well.

"Stay back," Kyle warned. He drew his weapon. "FBI."

"Screw the key," Roarke muttered and broke down the door.

Kyle, Roarke and the police rushed into the room. A few minutes later she heard "Clear" and ventured to the doorway.

"No one's here," Kyle announced. "Belle, stay here. If Patterson booked this room as well, I'll need you to ID his clothing and any personal items."

The motel was standard, nothing expensive. Cheap green carpeting instead of floor tiles matched the green drapes at the windows. A mirror hung over the main bureau, and a television was tucked into an armoire. Thin blue bedspreads covered two queen-size beds. A round table sat beneath the window. Twin lamps with dusty shades decorated nightstands on either side of the beds.

Mike would never sleep here, unless he was desperate and hiding out. A self-professed travel snob, he bragged about his elite status with a few upscale hotel chains.

"One-story motels are too lowbrow for Mike," she murmured. "Even for a one-night stand."

"Or a one-hour stand?" Kyle suggested.

Warmth suffused her cheeks. "Plenty of privacy at his house."

"He wasn't here because of an affair. He was here hiding out. These places are notorious for cash payments and discretion."

The few items in the bathroom were ordinary and she couldn't tell if they belonged to Mike. But the shaving cream was an off brand and she knew he enjoyed the luxury of expensive things.

Belle looked at the clothing in the closet and wrinkled her nose. The suitcase was filled with wrinkled shirts and shorts of various colors.

"Do you recognize anything belonging to Patterson?" Kyle asked.

She shook her head. "It's all too small. He's more than six feet tall and bulky. And he's picky about what he wears. Mike would no more wear a gaudy Hawaiian shirt than he'd be caught dead in cheap sandals. Mike is tidy, no matter where he stays."

They returned to Room Six. Police combed through the closet, examined the warped desk drawers. Her heart sank when they carefully lifted out girls' clothing from the dresser drawers.

"That looks like Anna's size," she told Kyle.

Hovering, Belle wished she could help. The room was plain and smelled slightly moldy, despite the window air conditioner running full blast. Had Mike taken Anna and kept her here in this damp, stale room?

But the clerk insisted he hadn't seen any children today.

The motel was not exactly family friendly. A child would have stood out.

Why the clothing? Did Mike buy it to take to Anna before she left the country?

She backed up against the bed closest to the bathroom. Her shoes made contact with something wet and squishy. She glanced down.

Maybe the bathroom leaked. Belle squatted down and touched the wet carpet.

Red stained her fingers. Breath hitching, she stared at the carpet.

Please don't let it be Anna. Please let her be alive. Throat tight, she could barely breathe or talk.

"Kyle," she whispered, pointing to the carpet. "Blood. It's coming from the second bed."

Gaze sharp, he crouched down. "Roarke, help me lift the mattress."

They lifted the mattress and set it against the wall. Beneath was a splintered wood board instead of a box spring. Belle's heart raced as the men lifted the board.

Eyes open wide with terror, Dr. Michael Patterson was curled into a fetal position, staring sightlessly at nothing. Someone had stuffed a white hand towel into his mouth. His wrists and feet were bound with gray duct tape.

A star-shaped bullet wound marked his high forehead, where the hairline had severely receded. There was little blood, except for that pooling beneath him. He wore a navy polo shirt and dark trousers and leather loafers. Her gaze whipped down to his feet. Socks with little gold anchors on them.

She'd once joked with him about those socks. He was absurdly proud of those socks and liked to wear them in the clinic.

They weigh you down because a boat is just a hole in the water where you pour money, Belle had once teased him.

"I guess we were too late after all," she said softly.

Roarke cursed. "I'll call for the corner and CSU."

He walked away, talking into his microphone.

Kyle remained with her as she stared at her brother's friend. Trembling, she checked his pulse, even though she knew he was dead. Kneeling beside the bed, she looked at the man who had helped inspire her to become a doctor.

Forget the fact he had aided in Anna's abduction.

Forget the fact he once sat at her family's dinner table.

Forget the fact Mike was like an older brother.

They had shared meals, laughs, helped diagnose patients and they'd been deep-sea fishing together.

Mike had been her mentor.

Belle cleared her throat. "The body is dead less than two hours. Without a thorough clinical examination, my estimate is he was killed an hour ago."

Kyle squatted down next to her. "Looks like a .45."

"Rigor in the fingers and jaw, but the body is still warm to the touch." She studied Mike's forehead and the gunshot wound, using her training to think of this as a case, a dead body. Total objectivity. *You can't help anyone if you fall apart.*

Mike's own advice to her echoed in her mind. Belle shoved aside the memory and focused on the wound. "The body is pale from blood loss, and there is periorbital ecchymoses to the eyes. Bruising around the eyes from the gunshot wound. The orbital plates looked fractured."

"Execution-style gunshot wound. Whoever did this pressed the muzzle against his forehead."

She pressed on, glad for Kyle's steady, calm tone. He was thorough and professional and his composure loaned her strength to keep talking. "Cause of death most likely is a large-caliber gunshot wound to the forehead at close range. The skin is bruised, and there is a muzzle imprint and gunpowder residue. A pattern of small abrasions on the skin at the entrance wound confirms close-contact range of the weapon. The exit wound is present…"

Belle glanced at the blood pooling beneath the body. "Of course, an autopsy will prove cause and time of death."

She looked at Kyle. "Do you want me to check for lividity or should you wait for the ME?"

Kyle tugged at her arm. "C'mon, Belle. The ME will take care of it."

Outside, she took a grateful gulp of fresh air. Belle leaned against the exterior wall, hugging herself. Mike was dead. Anna still missing, and they were running out of time.

Thoughts raced through her head. Clint had to be told. Yet she hesitated to call her brother in front of Kyle.

She glanced at her shoes, the bloody footprints she left behind and shuddered.

Kyle's jaw tightened. "Come on, let's get you cleaned up."

Belle kicked off her shoes and carried them, following him to the motel manager's office. The man was far more cooperative now, letting them into a bathroom in his office.

After she washed her hands and splashed water on her face, Kyle handed her paper towels. Belle tried to calm the rapid pounding of her heart. This wasn't her first dead body. She'd autopsied them in med school.

But it was the first dead body belonging to someone she knew.

When they returned outside, Belle pulled out her cell phone. "Can you hunt me down a bottle of water?" she asked Kyle. "I have to make a call."

As the agent walked off, she dialed her brother. He answered on the first ring.

"Mike is dead. We found him in the motel room, Clint. He was murdered."

She expected shock, grief, even silence. Not the string

of curses that followed. Her suspicions grew. Did Clint know anything?

"Why would anyone kill him, Clint?" She walked off and lowered her voice for privacy. "What was he involved in that you're not telling me?"

Silence for a minute. Then Clint's voice cracked. "Damn, Belle, I can't be certain, but I know he had financial trouble. Big trouble. As in owing a lot for gambling debts."

Belle went still. "Did you loan him money?"

"I've been loaning him money. Finally had to cut him off. He didn't linger at that family funeral, Belle. That's not why he took time off from the clinic. He flew to the Bahamas to sell his vacation home. Came back two nights ago." Clint's voice dropped. "Mike told me he'd gotten involved in something shady, but said it would all work out."

"Why didn't you tell me?"

"I promised him I'd keep my mouth shut."

Slowly it dawned on her. "You knew I was in the thick of this, getting flak for being the last person to see Anna alive and you chose to protect Mike? And not tell me?"

"I didn't think he'd had a hand in kidnapping that little girl, Belle. That's not like him."

Yelling at him would accomplish nothing. Remembering Kyle's calmness and professionalism, she kept her voice steady. "When did you last hear from Mike?"

Clint sighed. "I called him tonight."

That was news. "When?"

"Three hours ago. Left a voice mail and then he texted me around seven and said you were closer to Anna than you think. I thought it meant you were on the verge of finding her." A heavy sigh from her brother. "I'm sorry, Belle. Where are you? I'll come pick you up. You shouldn't be alone."

"I'm with the FBI." She didn't want to go home to her

dark house and the memories dancing on the edge of her thoughts. Grief and anger were for later.

Helping the FBI with the investigation kept her focused. Kept her from thinking how her brother with his sterling reputation for honesty had been less than honest so he could protect a family friend.

Kyle returned, a bottle of water in hand. She took it, nodded her thanks.

"You can go over to my house and take care of Boo. Can you keep him overnight at your place?"

"Sure. Anything else?" He hesitated. "Should I call Mike's parents? They're down here for the season."

"No. The police will inform the Pattersons, but I'm sure his parents will need emotional support after they find out. I'll call you tomorrow, Clint. And don't go anywhere. I'm certain the police will want to question you. This is a murder investigation now."

She hung up.

"Stupid, stupid, stupid," she whispered, clutching her cell phone. "Clint, why didn't you tell me what happened?"

A warm, steady hand on her arm. Kyle. His touch centered her, allowed her to gather her lost composure and scattered thoughts.

"You okay?" His gaze remained calm and steady. A lifeboat in a turbulent sea. For a minute it seemed like the bustle around them, the flashing lights, the stream of police into and out of the room and the voices faded into gray. There was only Kyle, and his oh-so-blue eyes and his concerned expression.

Belle fought the impulse to sag into his arms, let him lead her away from the nightmare inside Room Six.

"Yes. I was talking with my brother to let him know what happened."

"What did Clint tell you?"

Family loyalty always came first in the past. But she'd

realized that while her loyalty might remain with family, her own family had different ideas.

Belle told Kyle everything her brother said. When she finished, Kyle's expression tightened, though his tone remained calm. "We'll need to question him. Tonight. We'll handle it. First, though, I'm driving you home. I'll drop you off before Roarke and I go to your brother's house."

A few minutes later, she sat next to Kyle in his SUV. Belle uncapped the water and took a long drink.

The darkness of the Everglades flanked them like a cloak as Kyle drove north. She blinked back tears, remembering past times here at night with Mike and Clint, staring at the stars.

Belle wiped her eyes. "You can question Clint and I'll call my parents. They'll come home on the next flight, I'm sure. Mom…she's close to Mike's mother and she'll want to help…plan the funeral."

The time was past for any members of her family to hide away from the police and the press. They had to face up to their responsibility. Dr. Michael Patterson was their employee. Anna had visited their clinic before she vanished.

Mike was dead.

And Belle had the bad feeling if they couldn't find Anna soon, there could be another death on their consciences.

Chapter 16

The funeral three days later was an ordeal. Belle managed to get through the service without any display of emotion.

But the reception afterward required all her strength to greet guests and play the part of the soothing cohostess as her parents circulated among the crowd.

Her mother had faults, but she had a generous heart. The North mansion had been opened to everyone who attended Mike's funeral. Of course, the funeral was closed, with only family and friends attending, the elite Mike frequently socialized with.

As always, her mother's amazing ability to entertain, no matter what the occasion, impressed Belle. In the time since she'd flown back, her mother had organized the caterer, valets for parking and flowers, and had the house scrubbed by cleaning staff until it shone.

In the cool elegance of her parents' living room she lingered over a cheese puff, staring at it, willing the tears away. Crying was confined to bathroom and in the privacy of one's bedroom. Even at funerals. This room with its blue wallpaper and tastefully expensive white-and-blue furniture reflected the ocean vista gleaming through the floor-to-ceiling windows. With the white-gloved waitstaff, they could be at one of her mother's social galas.

No one knew Mike had been murdered. There were

whispers, but the media had been kept out of it. Most people believed that Mike had died from a heart attack after bass fishing all day.

"Hi, Belle."

Startled, she glanced up at Evan Worthington. Not drunk this time, not obnoxious as he'd been in the restaurant when she'd dined there with Kyle. Instead he was somber in his charcoal-gray suit and dark blue tie, hands clasped in front of him as if he didn't know what to do with them. His black hair was slicked back from his forehead. The hairstyle made him look younger.

"Evan."

He took her hand and attempted to shake it, but his clasp was more than a polite squeeze. Evan seemed to hang on for dear life.

A waiter stopped by with a silver tray of hors d'oeuvres. "I'll take one," she told him, and Evan finally released his grip.

She selected a cheese pastry and bit into it. Delicious. Of course. Her mother would never allow mediocre food to touch anyone's palate within the confines of the North mansion. Even if she'd had only two days to plan the menu.

"Terrible about Mike's death. But a nice way to remember him. It was good of your parents to host this." Evan snagged a glass of wine from another passing waiter in full dinner dress.

Black-tie funeral. Mike always lived in style. Now he was sent off in style. Belle tried to push aside the last image of Mike, hands and feet bound, facial features frozen in horror, eyes glazing over.

"It was nice of your mom to help mine," she told him, spotting Mindy Worthington in the crowd, talking with several friends.

Mindy looked like an elegant grandmother, with a strand

of polished pearls around her neck that matched the ones in her earlobes. Gray hair swept back in a bun, Mindy looked equally at home at a funeral reception as she did chairing a charity gala. Her black dress was Chanel, and her pumps Manolo Blahnik.

Evan's mother was as polished and ironed as most of the other women present. But her son wasn't as neat. His black suit was rumpled, his tie askew as if he'd tugged on it too much.

"I hate funerals," he muttered. "I'm glad you're here." Evan downed his wine.

He handed the glass to a passing waiter and helped himself to another one.

She gave him a pointed look. "Don't imbibe too much more, Evan. Drinking too much isn't a good accessory for you."

He had the grace to look abashed. "Yeah, sorry about that at the bar. I was on a tear with the guys, first time I've really had a chance to let loose since I went into remission."

Fishing around for common ground, she gestured to his mother. "Your mother was wonderful to help with this reception."

He nodded. "Mom has always liked to organize everything. She didn't mind, especially since Dr. Patterson's parents are in shock."

And throwing this reception took not only organization, but money. It was a drop in the bucket to people like her mother, and Mindy. Like her mother, Mindy enjoyed the privileges accommodating a wealthy lifestyle. But Mindy had always put her son first. Evan was an only child, doted upon by his mother. The pampering had grown worse after Evan's father died five years ago.

As a teenager circulating in the same tennis-and-polo set, Belle once envied Evan for his mother's devotion. He could do no wrong, unlike Belle, who never managed to do anything right. Mindy would do anything for Evan, whereas Belle's mother was more concerned with maintaining her own lifestyle and social obligations, and making sure her daughter had an equally shining social presence. As she grew older, Belle realized the kind of helicopter parenting Mindy had perfected before the term grew popular could be equally damaging as absentee parenting.

Her own parents weren't terrible. She'd wished her father had spent more time with her, though. But at least her parents listened to her at times. Sometimes she suspected Mindy only lectured Evan to do as she wished. Evan had broken free for a while when he moved away to pursue a successful investing career. And then the cancer attacked him.

She felt sorry for him, but not enough to socialize. When Evan got drunk he turned ugly. He wouldn't dare drink too much here and make a spectacle of himself.

Evan cast a nervous eye at the clusters of people quietly talking. "I always imagined Mike to be invincible. One of those older doctors who eats whole foods and lives in the gym, with a heart that would never give out. He never did seem to have fun."

Belle shrugged. Last thing she wanted was to philosophize with a man whose idea of fun was chugging a six-pack. Her own feelings right now were so complicated regarding Mike.

He'd been her mentor, a physician and family friend to hold in high regard. And now she realized he hid plenty of secrets.

Mike had died without revealing one critical secret—Anna's location.

"Say, Belle, I really am sorry about how I acted in the bar. I was obnoxious and you were with that FBI guy."

She relaxed a little. Maybe Evan wasn't all that bad. Cancer changed people, and the grueling chemo treatments might have refined his cruder edges.

"Apology accepted. The FBI guy is Agent Anderson, who's working on finding Anna."

"Right. You have a thing for him?"

Startled, she nearly spilled her champagne. "A thing?"

"The way you two were staring at each other, it seemed like he was more into you than as just a fed."

Yes, her heart agreed.

No, her mind protested.

Not that I'd tell you anything that personal or private. I guess you really haven't changed. "I'm doing all I can to help the federal authorities find Anna, since I was one of the last people to see her."

A diplomatic answer. Her mother would approve. But though it seemed the right answer, it gave Evan the wrong idea. He grinned, and his green eyes sparkled.

"Good. Then you're not seeing anyone and neither am I. Maybe we can start over again. Go out on a real date. I know a great French restaurant that's quiet, intimate and has a wonderful wine selection."

Belle stared. They were at a funeral reception, and he was hitting on her. "I don't think so, Evan."

"Just one date. Give me a chance. You're so beautiful and smart, and I might learn something from you." He grinned, showing perfect teeth. Perhaps that smile might charm other women.

It did nothing except irritate her.

Thankfully Mindy, Evan's mother, drifted over, a cloud of French perfume following in her wake. "Evan, darling, there you are. Are you all right, dear?"

She clucked and cooed over her baby chick, secretly amusing Belle as Evan looked uncomfortable. "I'm fine, Mother. Chatting with Belle."

Mindy's gaze grew bright. "I always thought you two would make a darling couple, Belle. Have you ever considered staying here instead of going away to do that medical thing?"

That medical thing. As if practicing medicine was a hobby like knitting. Laughing would be inappropriate. "I don't think so, Mrs. Worthington. Evan and I aren't quite compatible." She smiled to diffuse the sharp rejection.

If he felt rejected, Evan didn't show it. Instead, he nibbled on the edge of his thumbnail. Mindy's smile grew tight. "Dear, stop that nasty habit. Well, that's too bad, Belle. You're giving up the chance of a lifetime."

Fingers tipped with glossy red nails curled possessively around Evan's upper arm. "Come along, dear. I have someone for you to meet."

Belle released a relieved breath as they wound through the living room. Tense already from smiling and trying to mask her feelings, she didn't need Mindy pressuring her.

Another waiter passed with a silver tray of canapés, but she had little appetite. Mike's dead face kept floating before her. Belle wished for a friendly face, a person who could relate and not someone she'd felt forced her into polite conversation. Her skin felt stretched too tight, her smile ready to crack her face.

Out of the corner of her eye, she spotted a light in the dark tunnel entering the bright living room. Kyle Anderson.

In his black suit with a solid navy blue tie, absent of the whimsical patterns he usually sported, he blended well with this crowd. The dark suit complemented his inky black hair, and the gray lock of hair made him look distinguished.

She was definitely caring too much. Maybe even falling in love with him.

The thought startled her into almost letting her wineglass tilt. Love wasn't on the agenda. Career came first, and her own family and their expectations.

Kyle was the last person she'd anticipated claiming her heart. On the surface, they had nothing in common. Yet she realized their differences provided a balance that could layer a firm foundation to a serious relationship. He was gruff and brisk, she was soft and understanding. Kyle helped her to see beyond her family's expectations to steal a peek at her future, a future where she could not only be fulfilled, but happy.

He encouraged her to be independent and face her deep fears about rejection from her family. Kyle was right. If her family truly loved her, and she knew they did, they wouldn't shun her for disappointing them.

Kyle had taught her much in the short time she'd known him. In turn she wanted to help him through the aching pain and grief he'd refused to surrender to after his daughter died. Let him know it was healthy to finally let it go.

Even though the chemistry between them sparked, it could never work out. The job came first with him, and she'd take a backseat to his career. She wasn't the type of woman to sit around pining for her man while he saved the world. Not when she herself could do some saving.

Seeing her, Kyle shot her a smile that lit her up inside, warmed her where she had been ice-cold.

Belle threaded through the crowd. Tempted to hug him tight, she nodded instead. "Agent Anderson," she said in her best hostess voice, "so good of you to come. Is your partner accommodating you?"

"Thanks. Roarke is in the garden."

He and Roarke had been present at the service. Kyle had texted her yesterday that they would attend the funeral to survey the attendees for any suspicious behavior, but still, Kyle's presence filled her with a small, secret joy. When she saw him, her heart beat faster in a way that had nothing to do with the recent tragedy.

Silly of her. He had a job to do, and little time for a social life. He wore his badge clipped to his suit jacket usually. Today it hung on his belt, tucked away discreetly.

She'd been deprived of male company for so long and decent, engaging conversation with the opposite sex that it wasn't surprising her hormones leaped every time Kyle was around. Yet it wasn't his hot body or his good looks.

He cared. He might have a barbed-wire exterior, but inside beat the heart of a man who would risk all to save an endangered child.

"Is there anything you need? I can make introductions if you wish," she asked. She lowered her voice. "I do understand if you and your partner wish to remain in the background because you're here in a professional manner."

Kyle took her hand. Such a simple gesture, yet it seemed much more. His touch was light as his grip. If she wanted to pull away, it was easy enough to do so, unlike Evan's viselike pressure. "We do. But I also came to see how you are, Belle."

His eyes were so very blue, and they caressed her in a long, lingering stroke. Evan's scrutiny made her uncomfortable. This man's masculine interest made her blood run hot.

Belle bit her lip. "Thank you. I'm fine."

He said nothing, only studied her. She sighed. "I'm not, but I'm holding it together. I don't have a choice."

Warmth filled her as he stroked a thumb over the back of her hand, his expression filled with concern. "You're an extraordinary woman, Belle North. Strong and capable. But even the strong need a rest once in a while."

Unlike Evan's hollow compliments, this praise sounded sincere. Coming from a man who prized professionalism, it meant a great deal.

"I'll be all right. Later, I have a hot date with a bottle of chilled white wine and maybe a pizza."

His mouth twitched upward. "I still owe you a dinner for burning your spaghetti sauce."

"Deal," she said lightly, alarmed at how the promise in those words made her heart skip a happy beat.

They walked to a quiet corner near one of her mother's prized Chinese vases. "Do you have any suspects? Or any additional information about Anna?"

"No." He glanced around the room. "Are most of these people your family's friends or friends of Patterson?"

"Both. His parents are here as well, but you've already met them." She wondered what they could divine from this reception. "Do you truly believe the killer could be here?"

"Perhaps," Kyle murmured. "Often criminals put themselves into the investigation, acting as if they wish to help. Sometimes it's to throw law enforcement off the track, sometimes it's the thrill. This reception is a good place to circulate and observe any odd behaviors. Has anyone asked you any direct questions about Patterson's death?"

"My brother." Realizing how suspicious that sounded, she hastened to add, "Clint knows Mike was murdered and he hasn't said anything. He's as eager to catch whoever did this as he is to find Anna."

Both Kyle and Roarke had extensively questioned her brother shortly after Mike's body was found. Clint had been too shaken to be of much use.

He'd admitted that Mike had acted suspicious and when pressed, Mike only said he had some money troubles.

"Did you ever find out how much money Mike owed?" she asked.

Kyle's gaze sharpened. "Clint finally told us Mike said he owed more than two hundred thousand."

More shocks. Belle's stomach roiled. The foundation had paid Mike a handsome salary to run the clinic, but gambling debts could mount quickly. "Owed to whom?"

He searched her expression. "Everyone, it seemed. He

maxed out his credit cards and there's a matter of an infusion of cash into his bank account we can't quite trace. It came from an overseas account."

"A loan shark?"

"Maybe. Your brother said Mike came to him asking for a year's advance on his salary, and he couldn't do it under the foundation rules. He offered to give Mike a fifty-thousand-dollar loan. Mike took twenty-five thousand and said he'd be in touch about the other half. A few days later, he called Clint and said he'd found another way to settle things. He was coming into some money."

Her skin began to itch, a sure sign that her instincts warned Mike had stumbled onto something shady. "When was this phone call?"

"December 16."

"It wasn't a Christmas gift." Belle bit her lip and set down her champagne before she spilled it. "December 17 was the first time stamp on the photos."

"Yes. It's obvious someone paid Dr. Patterson to secretly record girls in the clinic." Kyle frowned and rubbed his jaw, as if thinking hard. "What we can't figure out is if whoever is behind Anna's kidnapping wanted to abduct girls for sex trafficking or to send overseas, why only take one girl?"

"It could have been the start of something," she pointed out. "If Anna hadn't warned me she was in danger, who would have missed her? She was living on the fringes of society with her mother. They had no real friends or neighbors. The tent was paid for so when they left the campground, the park rangers wouldn't have thought anything was wrong until they came to clean up the grounds and saw all the clothing. And by then, the kidnapper would have removed all the evidence."

"Would have, except for your intervention. By your alerting me, you helped to spotlight what was going on. I don't think I ever thanked you."

His deep voice sent a shiver rushing down her spine. "I did what any responsible citizen would do."

"Sadly, no. Some wouldn't want to get involved." He took her hand again and leaned close.

"I'm glad I did," she told him softly.

"So am I." He stared at her mouth as if he longed to kiss her. She wanted the same thing.

And then she saw her mother approach, and she realized where they were. Mortified, she backed away.

Shirley held out her hand. Kyle shook it.

"Thank you for attending, Agent Anderson. If there is anything my husband and I can do for the FBI, please let us know. Anything."

With a nod at her, Shirley Vandermeer North walked away.

Her mother's attitude surprised Belle. "You made a good impression. My mother is usually not so friendly with, ah, people she considers public servants." She gave a little laugh. "I used to envision her breathing fire at civil servants if they failed to do what she wished. I used to feel sorry for whoever had to deal with her at the driver's license bureau."

Kyle studied the room. "Your mother isn't the ogre you think she is, Belle. She does care."

Odd remark. Clearly he knew something she did not. But this wasn't the place for such discourse. "Mom does want Anna found. But probably more to clear our family name."

"Maybe. There's something that bothers me about this case," he mused. "Why Anna? She's pretty, but there are other girls who are prettier, and younger. They would fetch a great deal on the black market. If that was the kidnapper's intent."

Kyle's cell phone rang. He answered in a terse voice, "Anderson."

Belle's heart dropped to her stomach at his tight expression.

"No, stay where you are. I'll head over there now." He hung up, drew in a breath.

"What happened?"

"Rosa's awake. And she's talking."

Chapter 17

He hated hospitals. Part of the job, interviewing witnesses and medical professionals, but he had never liked it, even before Kasey died.

Elevator doors opened with a whoosh, and he walked onto the ICU floor, Belle at his side. Funny how having her with him lowered his blood pressure. She'd insisted on accompanying him.

Kyle glanced at her. She was sexy as hell and smart, but yeah, her calm demeanor settled his raw nerves. Belle wasn't afraid of hospitals. This was her turf, her world, and she navigated it well.

Downstairs, he'd flashed his badge to the bored receptionist, but it was Belle who asked the questions, ordering the receptionist to get the charge nurse to meet them outside Rosa's room. She did it with cool efficiency and professionalism. He admired her take-charge attitude. No sweat on her forehead.

Him? Perspiration ran down his back as if he'd done an hour session at the gym, gluing his shirt to his skin.

An officer greeted him in the hallway. "We have a twenty-four-hour guard on her. I called your partner soon as I heard the news."

He thanked the deputy. "Good job."

Outside Rosa's ICU room, a petite redhead in blue scrubs

greeted them. "I'm Candy, the charge nurse. You have ten minutes with her. She's been drifting in and out of consciousness and we won't risk upsetting her and increasing her blood pressure."

"Thank you, Candy. I'm Dr. North, one of the cardiologists on this case working with the FBI. May I see her chart?"

Candy went to get the chart. Kyle raised his brows. "Now you're a cardiologist?"

She shrugged. "If it gets us in there quicker and lowers her worry about Rosa's heart. I do work for a well-known cardiology practice. The night shift is working now, so we shouldn't have to worry about her physician interfering."

"Good." He ran a hand through his hair, realized what he was doing and shoved his hands into the pockets of his trousers.

In his right pocket, he touched the silver coin he always carried. Touching it grounded him in reality, reminded him he had a job to do.

Candy rolled over a computer stand with a laptop attached to it. Belle thanked her and scanned the screen, asking Candy questions. He peered through the glass door at Rosa. Damn, he knew she wouldn't be sitting up and animated, but when the deputy phoned that she was awake, he'd hoped for better than this.

She opened the door to the room and she and Kyle approached Rosa's bedside.

Beeping machines were hooked up to the woman and tubes snaked out of her. His gorge rose and he forced it down, concentrating on Rosa's pale face.

"She's not intubated anymore, so she can talk, but it won't be easy," Belle warned. "Her throat will be sore and she'll be scared. Her vitals are strong, which is good."

He leaned close, the antiseptic smells strong in his nose, the memories equally strong. Kasey had a pink blanket in

Pediatrics when she'd been in the ICU. The nurses thought it would make his daughter's appearance less harsh.

Pink. Blue. Didn't matter, because in the end, blankets and machines hadn't done a damn thing.

"Rosa, can you talk?" he urged. "Do you know what happened with your daughter?"

Rosa moaned. "Anna, Anna."

Monitoring the beeping machines, Belle shook her head at him. "You need to go slower. Let me try."

Placing a hand on the woman's forehead, Belle spoke in a low, soothing voice. "Rosa, it's me, Dr. North, the doctor who treated your daughter. I'm working with the FBI to try to find Anna. It's all right, Rosa. We'll get Anna. Can you tell us about the man who was with you when you were attacked?"

The woman's eyes opened, but they looked unfocused, as if Rosa struggled between consciousness and staying asleep. "*Mi corazón*, where is she? My Anna?"

"We're trying to find her, Rosa. We need to know about the man who attacked you. We think he took her." Belle never raised her voice.

Inside, he screamed with frustration. The woman on the bed knew the answers, and he felt desperate to coax them out.

"Was it Jesse Dugin? The man who was hiding you?" Belle asked in Spanish.

Rosa nodded, licked her lips.

"He…promised to keep Anna safe. Promised…take us away and hide us. Has a boat…would take us away from Florida. Not more running."

Kyle's alarm grew. "Hide you from what? Who was threatening you?"

The woman's eyes closed.

"Rosa, honey, Anna was scared in the clinic. Why were you running? From the law?" Belle pressed.

"Yes," Rosa mumbled. "No, no. Police on his side. Powerful. So scared he take Anna."

"Who wanted to take Anna?" Kyle demanded in English. "We need to find your daughter. Who wanted her?"

"Stop it," Belle hissed. "You're upsetting her."

"Get the padre," Rosa gasped, sitting up and reaching for Kyle. "Not safe. Anna. Save my baby, please!"

Alarms sounded on the machine as Rosa collapsed back to the bed. Candy rushed in. "That's enough. Out, now!"

Belle tugged him away as the nurse bent over her patient. Outside the room, he paced. "We were so damn close."

"Not close enough. You shouldn't have done that, Kyle. You scared her," Belle said softly.

The gentle criticism proved too much. Memories assaulted him—the medical team badgering him about Kasey and letting her go because there was no hope. None. *Her life could save others.* Urging him to end the vigil at her bedside, shaking their heads, saying Kasey would never wake up. No brain activity, kept alive by machines.

Pressing a finger to his temple, he glared at her. "I scared her? I'm the one trying to find her daughter. She's our only witness, damn it!"

Wisely, she left him alone, and headed to the horseshoe-shaped desk. "She called for a priest," Belle told a nurse. "Can you send the chaplain up to see her?"

The nurse nodded.

Send a chaplain. More memories. Kyle wanted to rage and scream. All his emotions zigged all over the place. The chaplain wouldn't solve anything. They needed to find Anna, save her.

Save my baby. Please.

I can't save her.

Squeezing his eyes shut, he tried to force the memories back. But the sounds of clicking and beeping machines, the smells of disinfectant and the drone of nurses in the background taunted him with the past.

I can't save her.

When Belle returned from the nurse's desk, he managed to speak in a cracked voice. "I have to get the hell out of here."

Her dark brown gaze sharpened. "All right. Go. I'll take an Uber home."

Kyle fled the hospital as if the hounds of hell snapped at his heels.

Just as he had that long-ago day when he'd ordered the machines turned off, the silence in Kasey's room deafening after he'd kissed her goodbye one last time.

He kept running, did not stop until he reached his SUV and slammed the door shut. Shaking, he stared at the black steering wheel. He did not start the vehicle. Nowhere to go. What was the point? Go home to an empty house?

I can't save her.

The passenger door opened quietly. He was barely aware of Belle sliding into the SUV, closing the door shut.

God, please, don't say anything because I'll shatter. But she said nothing, only sat quietly.

He licked cracked, dry lips.

"Kasey was two years old. Her mother and I were on the verge of a divorce. But we wanted it to be amicable, because of Kasey. She meant everything to us. My wife told me I was married to my job, not her. She was right. Career meant everything to me. That night…I was working at the office. Damn paperwork. Better than being home, fighting with Caroline. I should have known better."

Belle waited.

Kyle squeezed his hands tight around the wheel. "I got the call around midnight. She'd packed up, took Kasey and left. Headed to her mother's. On the way, she swerved to avoid a drunk driver and a truck hit them, spinning her out of control into the southbound lane. A tractor trailer T-boned them. Caroline was killed instantly. Kasey, our baby, my baby, was in the backseat and still alive."

A sharp intake of breath from Belle, but still she said nothing.

How long had it been since he'd talked about this? Never, he realized with a start. He wanted to make the words vanish, but they spilled out of him like water. He could not stop. Didn't matter that he was losing it. Losing it in front of a woman he truly respected.

A doctor, like the ones who'd turned into enemies that day. Doctors who failed to save Kasey. Couldn't do anything.

But he kept talking, spilling it out, feeling as if he was gonna puke if he held it in any longer.

"Four weeks in the ICU, hooked up to those damn machines. Every day, every single day she was alive, I was there at her bed. Reading to her. Holding her hand. Talking to her. Praying, crying, begging. She never woke up. That smell...it got into my clothing, my hair. I'll never forget it. Disinfectant. Bleach. Sickness."

Belle finally spoke in the darkness. "She never woke up."

Kyle squeezed his eyes shut, seeing Kasey's pale, still face, her tiny head wrapped in bandages. "Irreversible brain damage. Trauma, they said, caused by the crash. She'd never live off the machines. They were doing everything for her."

"But you couldn't let go."

Eyes flying open, he jerked his head in a violent nod. "Kept hoping and hoping. Until that day I knew there was no hope."

Belle sucked in a deep breath but said nothing.

"She was just a baby," he whispered. "They told me it was best to turn the machines off. I didn't want to do it. I couldn't. But there was another kid who was a perfect match. They wanted her heart. My baby's heart. She was only two years old. I told them yes. There was nothing I could do to save her. I was her father. I should have saved her."

Belle said nothing, only held out her arms.

She held him close as he finally surrendered to the grief raging through him. Kyle cried. He didn't care that he was sobbing like a child in the parking lot of a hospital and he had a job to do, a child to find, a case to complete. His breath came out in great, hitching sobs as she stroked his back and let him cry.

After a few minutes, he finally pulled away. Reached for the handkerchief he'd always carried, and the coin in his pocket flew out. It made a tinkling sound as it hit the dashboard and then fell to the floor.

Belle picked it up and handed it to him after he wiped his eyes and blew his nose.

"This was hers."

He pocketed the coin, stuffed the soggy linen back into his trouser pocket. "Yeah. I used to do magic tricks with it. We kept it on her dresser where it was too high for her to reach. Every night she insisted on a magic trick with her *purty shiny.*"

His mouth twitched in a ghostlike smile. "Kasey used to clap and squeal every time. Same stupid trick, but she loved it."

"Because her daddy did it, it was magic," Belle whispered. "She loved you, Kyle. And you loved her dearly. It was an accident. There was nothing you could have done."

He'd spilled his guts to her. In that moment, Kyle had never felt more vulnerable, and yet no longer alone.

In that moment, he only wanted to purge the memories and lose himself.

Kyle pulled her into his arms and kissed her with all the ferocity of emotions penned up far too long. He kissed her as if she were a lifeline and he a dying man adrift on the sea. His mouth moved over hers as she sighed. So sweet, warm, pliant. He kept kissing her, feeling desire and need vibrate with every bone in his body.

When he finally released her, kissing the corner of her sweet mouth, his heart pounded and his body thrummed.

More. Damn, he needed more.

"I'm here for you if you need me. If you don't want to be alone tonight," she whispered.

Sex with her would be incredible. He knew it with every cell in his body. Combustible.

It wouldn't be fair because he couldn't offer her everything she needed right now. Belle North deserved more than a one-night stand. She was the kind of woman you stuck with for a long time.

Belle touched his arm. Kyle turned away, switched on the ignition.

"I'll drive you home. I have to get back to the office."

It was too intense. Too much. He needed to retreat into the safe, familiar world of his work.

But as they pulled out of the hospital parking lot, he felt his guts ache once more. Not only for what he'd lost years ago.

But for what he wasn't willing to take what she offered with open arms.

Chapter 18

The kiss the other night had been everything she'd anticipated, and everything she longed for.

And yet Kyle had backed off. In a way she understood. He needed space.

So she gave it to him and, over the past two days, didn't even contact him except to text to see if there were any more updates on the case. Or if Rosa finally talked.

His brief answers told her the basics, but little else. No emotion.

That night after a long day at the cardiology office, Belle looked forward to a swim in the pool.

As she unlocked the front door and dropped her bag onto a nearby chair, Boo ran into the foyer to greet her. Tail wagging, the little dog circled around her.

"Hey, sweetie." Belle picked up her pet, buried her face into the soft fur. "I've missed you."

The past two days had been pure hell. Everyone kept side-eyeing her, as if she were personally responsible for Anna's disappearance and Mike's death. Her own doubts about Kyle and her intensified feelings for him.

It felt as if she'd been riding on a roller coaster.

"Let's find you some dinner and find me some tasty adult beverages," she told her dog.

Boo's tail beat the air harder in agreement.

A while later, clad in a black one-piece bathing suit, she did her laps as Boo chowed down on kibble on the lanai. A bottle of chardonnay chilled in the outdoor kitchen, along with her favorite wineglass. Belle pushed herself to do another ten laps. Tired as she was, she needed the exercise to de-stress.

Gliding through the warm water, she kicked harder, thinking of Anna.

When she left the pool and dried off, a cool breeze blew from the east. Belle donned a cute cotton crochet tunic. She fished the wine out of the refrigerator, uncorked it and did a long pour. She took a tentative sip, and then another.

Delicious.

A loud barking distracted her as she headed for the sofa and chairs arranged around an outdoor wicker table. Neighbor walking the dog next door, which she'd privately nicknamed Space Doggie for its hairless look. Boo dashed past her and headed for the side yard.

Alarm shot through her as she set down her wineglass and followed. The gate stood open.

"Boo!"

Belle rushed after the dog, scooped him up. Holding the squirming pup, she frowned.

Odd. She never left that gate open.

A prickling began on her nape.

Judy—her pet sitter, who fed and walked Boo during the day—had her own key. Judy knew the gate was finicky and could swing open on a windy day. She also knew of the shared animosity between Boo and the Chinese crested next door and how Boo would bolt and challenge the other dog as it passed by on the sidewalk.

Belle pushed at the gate. It didn't close, so she marched with Boo in her arms back to the lanai to put him in the house. As she reached the outdoor sofa, a bout of dizziness made her stumble.

Barely dropping Boo safely on the sofa, she fought the lassitude in her arms and legs, the incredible drunken feeling.

It made no sense. Although she'd not eaten lunch and drank on an empty stomach, she'd barely touched the wine.

If I were out partying with friends, I'd swear someone slipped something into my wine.

The prickling in her nape intensified. Belle staggered to the counter, picked up the wine cork, sniffed it.

Nothing.

But she knew something was terribly wrong. Belle stumbled to her phone and dialed Kyle's number.

"Help me," she whispered. "I'm home."

Out of the corner of her eye she saw a shadow move, and then pain exploded in her head. Belle screamed.

Grayness clouded the edges of her vision, and then the darkness rushed up to claim her.

He would get the son of a bitch who did this.

Someone attacked Belle in broad daylight. Someone was either desperate or confident. Or both.

Good thing she had neighbors who kept watch.

Kyle swore under his breath as he tried to keep Belle from sitting up.

"Easy," he soothed. "You're safe now."

Lying on the outdoor sofa where she'd collapsed, she tried to sit up again, but he put his hands on her shoulders.

"You've got a goose egg, but you should be fine." Kyle bit back his raging temper that wanted to find the bastard who did this to her and haul him away in handcuffs.

"Your neighbor was walking her dog and heard you scream. She rushed in here with her pepper spray and scared the perp away. Said he climbed over the fence and ran into the woods. Good thing the gate was open."

Groaning, she put a hand to her face. "Gate was supposed to be locked. Always locked. Someone broke inside."

"Can you remember anything else?" he asked.

"The wine…it was spiked with something." Belle frowned. "Odorless. Tasteless. Ketamine, I think. Or Rohypnol. Made me dizzy. I only had a couple of sips."

The lab would process the glass and the wine. Already, the team had dusted for prints, but Kyle doubted they'd find anything relevant. "Whoever did this was a pro."

Belle rubbed the back of her head. "Whoever did this certainly doesn't want me around anymore. Or asking any more questions."

"Could have been a hired gun." Kyle uncapped the water, held it up for her. "Drink."

She sipped the warm water.

"Where does one hire a gun these days?" she asked. "And how does such a person advertise their services? Take out a newspaper ad? Fly a banner over the beach in an airplane?"

Humor helped her in the past, but this wasn't a laughing matter. Damn, ever since the other night's kiss, he'd done nothing but think of her.

Twice he'd been tempted to call her. He needed to see her. But not like this…

"Maybe I can hire my own hit man to take out their hit man."

He liked her sense of humor. So calming. Kyle gripped her hands as the medics finished up.

"She's fine, Should go to the hospital for a CT scan, just in case of concussion," one advised.

Belle shook her head. "I'm fine. It doesn't even hurt much. I passed out from the drug more than anything. I need food, not a hospital."

"There's a chance whoever did this will return. You're not staying here alone," Roarke decided. "Is there a family member in town you can stay with for a few days?"

"My brother, but I don't want to stay with him. And I don't want to leave Boo alone here." She shivered. "Let me call my cousin. She can take care of Boo."

Belle thanked the medics and looked at Kyle. "I can stay with Clint, but I'd rather not. He'll never stop pestering and worrying. I can find a motel."

The hell with that. No way would he allow her to be that vulnerable.

"No. You're coming home with me." Kyle decided for her. "Soon as you feel better, pack a bag and we're leaving."

Chapter 19

On the drive to his house, Kyle updated her on the case's progress. They had interviewed Rosa's friends who lived in the same trailer park and had a tomato-and-cucumber stand at the local farmer's market. The three women had worked with Rosa cleaning houses but offered little information.

His cell rang as he drove. Kyle listened, thanked the person and hung up. "Good news. We have a fresh lead on Jesse Dugin. He's the bastard who did this to you." Kyle pulled into the driveway. "His prints were on your mini fridge. Don't worry. We'll catch him."

Belle exhaled with relief as she walked into Kyle's house. Though it was a showpiece, the house made her feel safe. Most likely it was the man closing and locking the door behind her and gesturing to the living room.

"Make yourself at home. I'll put your suitcase in the guest room."

When he emerged from the hallway, Kyle tugged at his tie, removed his jacket, hung it over a kitchen chair and then kicked off his leather loafers. Belle laughed.

"I knew it."

His brows arched. "Knew what?"

"That you were the type to kick off your shoes soon as you came home."

The grin he flashed made him look younger, more boyish. "Stick with me, Doc. I'm all about kicking back and relaxing once I go through those doors."

She doubted it, though. Kyle worked hard and, like her, he let cases push beneath his external barriers. For most people, work ended at quitting time.

For Kyle and her, the work followed them home.

"Do you ever truly relax when you're on a case?" Belle removed her own shoes, placed them neatly by the door and went to the sofa, curling her legs beneath her. "Can you ever let go of it?"

After removing his tie and draping it over his suit jacket, he joined her on the sofa. "Not really. Not when I'm working a case. I'll try to take breaks, but it sticks with me. Sometimes I'll work on something else while I'm home and an idea will come to mind, a lead I never considered. So it's back to work."

Intrigued, she leaned back, studying him. "And what else do you work on while you're here? Another case?"

"Sometimes. Or I'll do chores, or indulge in playing."

He pointed to the baby grand piano in the living room's corner. More surprises. "Yours?"

"Came with the house, but the twelve years of lessons are all mine."

"Please play for me. I adore music, but my piano lessons always resulted in bribing the teacher to let me go to my room and study." She made a face. "You'd be surprised how far fifteen dollars and a pack of gum can go."

Kyle laughed. "Such a serious student, even then." He inched closer, touched her temple. "How are you feeling?"

"I'm fine. It was just a little bruise. Nothing big."

His big hand curled around her neck, massaging it. "That better?"

Unable to speak, she nodded, closing her eyes. He had amazing hands, kneading all the tension from her neck and sore shoulder. When she opened them, he had an intense look. Hungry.

Sexual.

Abruptly, he pulled away and went to the piano. "Classical okay with you?"

"Fine." *But I'd rather you remain here on the sofa with me. Maybe you could massage something other than my neck?*

Disappointment and need arrowed through her. Maybe it wasn't right, feeling something like this for a man utterly focused on saving a little girl's life. But time after time she'd shuttled aside her own needs to cater to the demands of others. Even her college boyfriend, who'd wanted her for sex and to show off at parties, hadn't truly considered what she wanted.

Time to please yourself, she urged herself.

Fingers rippling over the keys, Kyle played Chopin's "Raindrop Prelude." Head bent over the piano, he seemed to surrender to the music. Absorbed by the beauty he created, she closed her eyes, time and space vanishing. She was back in childhood, listening to her mother play the piano as Belle curled up on the sofa, home sick from school. It had been storming outside, droplets splashing against the windows and the intensity of the piece echoed the splatter of rain and the howl of the wind.

And yet she'd never felt more secure, more loved, because her mother had taken an entire precious day to stay home and care for her.

When the piece ended, she applauded. Kyle made a little bow.

"You're quite good."

He shrugged. "Maybe I'll never play at Carnegie Hall, but at one point, I had considered a career in music."

More surprises from this man, who had so many deep

layers to him. "That's a one-eighty from the FBI academy. What happened?"

Another shrug. "Music isn't my life. I enjoy it, but it's not my true passion."

"Saving lives is."

How well she understood this. Medicine was hers, a passion that some might claim bordered on obsession. Yet she never considered doing anything else with her life.

Kyle rubbed the back of his neck. "I do what I can."

Belle joined him at the piano. "Is that why you have this?" She touched the lock of gray.

He nodded. "Got it five years ago after a grueling case. We spent weeks on it…and after, it aged me."

"What compelled you to have this kind of life?"

He nodded slowly. "Yeah, you understand. It's not merely a job. It is a life. It becomes consuming at times, so much that you lose all sense of time and place until that case is resolved…"

"Or that patient is healed."

He gave her a long, thoughtful look. "I joined the academy because I have a simple sense of justice and right and wrong. Not black-and-white. Nothing is truly black-and-white. The world's a crazy place, Belle. You and I both know it. But if I can make a small difference, either bring a child safely home to a parent crazed with fear, or give them the information they need to begin the process of grieving and letting go, then it's worth all of it."

He depressed a key, making a tiny plinking sound. "I used to think of myself as a hero in a red cape, saving the day, until I realized one day that my zeal made me neglect, and eventually lose, what was most important."

Belle sat on the piano bench and touched his hand. "The accident wasn't your fault, Kyle."

Then, because it needed to be said, she added, "Kasey's death wasn't the doctors' fault, either. Bad things just happen, no matter how hard you try to prevent them. Or how much you work to save a life."

He looked down at her hand covering his. "Yeah. You're right. It's taken me a long time to realize that."

Her chest felt hollow at the sadness on his face.

"What about you? Why did you choose medicine?"

"I've never wanted to be anything but a doctor, Kyle. We're not perfect. We do everything we can. At times during medical school, my biggest fear wasn't that I'd make a mistake and get a bad score on a test. It was that I'd make a mistake and cost a life. I never told anyone this, but it's one of reasons I needed a gap year, to seriously think about what direction I wanted to head into. When you make a mistake in investing, you can cost someone money. But not their life."

She rushed on. "Seeing you, how intense and driven to save Anna you are, made me realize I've been selfish, thinking about my fears and me, me, me. If I have a gift, as you clearly have, then I need to use it. And trust in myself and the professionals around me to make the best decision I can at the time, based on the information I have. It's a reason why I haven't dated in a long time. I've been focused on medicine and learning as much as I can so I don't make those mistakes in the future."

Kyle said nothing.

Fine. She felt a little foolish, spilling her heart like this. You're like an open book, her brother often teased. Men can read everything about you because you wear your emotions on the outside.

Suddenly he reached out. Smoothing back her hair, he stared into her eyes.

"My life isn't terrific, Belle. I haven't been able to hold down a relationship with a woman since the accident. I have other dark secrets other than admitting to killing a few men, bad guys who deserved it. It's that I haven't wanted anything from women, other than casual sex."

Heart pounding, she gazed into his blue eyes. "What are you saying, Kyle?"

"That if you're willing to take a chance, so am I."

"Yes," she whispered. "I'm tired of not taking chances."

He lowered his head and his warm lips met hers. Her eyes closed as she slid her arms around his neck. As kisses went, it was sweet and lingering, flickering with a hint of leashed passion. Maybe he didn't want to put everything into the kiss. Maybe he wanted to be with her as much as she wanted to be with him, but he hesitated showing it.

So she showed him. Belle deepened the kiss, putting all her feeling behind it. Everything. Nerve endings tingled, drowning in sensation as he met her challenge, groaning and opening his mouth. She felt it with every ounce of her soul as he responded, holding her closer, stroking her tongue with his own. Maybe this wouldn't end. *Don't let it end, because for the first time in my life, everything feels complete.*

They broke apart slowly, the sounds of their ragged breathing filling the air.

"Wow," he muttered.

She agreed. "That was…incredible."

He searched her face. "You okay?"

"Never better." Belle felt her stomach grumble. "But I must confess, I am hungry."

Then he stood up and headed into the kitchen. "You must think I'm a lousy host, bringing you here and not even feeding you. I owe you a dinner. I make a killer spaghetti sauce."

Kyle found folding tray tables and they ate on the deck of the boat docked behind his house. Sunset had streaked the skies pink and lavender, and there was a slight chill in the air. A perfect winter night in South Florida. Water lapped at the boat's edges as Kyle's neighbors took their own crafts out, headed for the Intracoastal.

Belle speared a meatball piece and ate it, listening to Kyle talk about growing up in Upstate New York. They traded stories about their childhoods and a shared love of action movies. His parents lived in Upstate New York. Two younger brothers were in New York City, both working in finance.

"I'm the lone wolf when it came to a career in law enforcement. My family thought I was crazy, but they supported my decision." He regarded her over his glass of red wine. "Tell me something, Belle. You seem so conflicted about pleasing your family and choosing what you want to do. If today were your last day on earth, what decisions would you make about your career?"

Belle swirled the wine and frowned. "I honestly don't know."

She drained the vintage. "But I do know I'd order this. You have a good palate."

A soft smile rewarded her compliment. "Only the best for you."

After, she helped him bring the plates inside and load the dishwasher. Kyle leaned against the counter with a sigh. "Damn, Doc, that was a great sauce, even if I did make it myself."

Belle laughed. "So modest."

An impish twinkle shone in his blue eyes. "Always."

Then his expression shifted to something deeper, more serious. "How are you feeling? You okay here?"

Belle nodded.

"Ready for some lessons in self-defense?"

"Tonight?"

"No time like now. I'll feel better, letting you return home if I know you have a few ways to disarm someone."

He gestured to a door adjacent to the living room. "Wear light, flexible clothing. I'll meet you in the exercise room."

She changed into gray yoga pants and a sleeveless T-shirt. The exercise room turned out to be a garage converted into a makeshift gym, complete with air-conditioning, floor mats and workout equipment. Dressed in sleek black bike shorts and a tight black T-shirt, he handed her a black knife. Belle turned it over in her hands. It was plastic.

"It's fake. Come at me with it."

Okay, I can do this. She went toward him, knife pointed outward.

In a minute, he not only disarmed her, but had her on the floor. She blinked as he hovered over her. "I didn't even see you coming. How did you do that?"

"I'll show you."

Kyle taught her a couple of moves. "The important thing is to remember to get free and get away. Your goal isn't to engage your attacker, but throw him off, distract, hurt as much as possible to give yourself time to escape."

He came at her with a fake gun, showing her how to get away from a potential attacker. She memorized the move, twisting her body as he instructed. And then when they tried again, this time she not only freed the pistol from his grip, but used her legs in a quick move that caught him off-balance.

He tumbled to the mats with a hard grunt.

They worked at it for more than an hour before he called for an end.

"Shower, and then the entertainment? Unless you're tired. I have a great collection of classic action-adventure movies. I'll make the popcorn," he told her.

Belle brightened. "Sounds fantastic."

A while later, freshly showered and dressed in jeans and a lightweight cranberry sweater, she curled up on the sofa in the great room, a bowl of popcorn in hand as Kyle went around the house, drawing the blinds and securing the locks. Barefoot, clad in jeans and a baseball shirt, he looked totally at-home. Typical guy instead of serious FBI agent.

"How are you feeling? Any aftereffects? I didn't want to take it easy on you, but also didn't want to push you too hard."

"I feel wonderful. Thank you for letting me stay here."

His hand curled around her nape once more, lightly massaging. "No thanks necessary. You needed a safe place to stay, Belle."

"Because I'm involved in this case and you need me." A statement, but a question within it.

"No." Kyle's gaze was so blue as he studied her. "Because I've started to care for you, and I don't want to see you hurt."

A hitch of breath. Belle licked her lips, knowing he tracked every move. "The feeling's mutual, Agent Cowboy."

He glanced away. "I can't promise anything, Belle. My past is complicated and I'm not ready to move on. But damn, you have me tied up in knots and right now I feel like if I don't have you, I'm gonna die. So what are we going to do about this?"

The murmured question accompanied the sensual stroke of his fingers against her skin.

She lifted her face to his, studying his mouth. "My head is fine, but I'd feel much better if you kissed me."

"New medical treatment?" His voice was teasing, but his gaze turned sharp, hungry.

His mouth met hers in the softest of kisses. Nothing demanding. A slow exploration, sweet and almost hesitant.

When she slid her hands around his nape, he deepened the kiss. So good. She wanted to sink into it forever as the sensations spread throughout her body. In his arms she could forget all the day's trauma and her personal woes. This was living for the moment.

She had waited a long time to live in the moment.

When they broke apart, she felt a pang of emptiness, until he stood and held out his hand.

"Come to bed with me?" he asked in a soft, deep voice.

Belle took his hand. In his bedroom he switched on a lamp and took her into his arms again.

"I haven't done this in a long time." Belle felt bashful admitting this.

His blue gaze was steady. "Neither have I."

She felt her anxiety melt away beneath his tender gaze. Live for the moment. She'd been consumed by work, career and fulfilling the roles her parents, mainly her mother, molded for her. Now it was time to seek out her own needs.

"I don't want to be alone tonight." He kissed the tip of her nose. "But if you aren't ready for this, all you have to do is say good-night and march through that door to the guest room. I didn't bring you here to seduce you. I want you to feel safe and comfortable."

Belle pulled away, saw the sharp disappointment on his face quickly masked by the usual expressionless mask. She went to the door and closed it.

Then she returned to him, sliding her arms up his hard chest. "I'm ready now."

Kyle kissed her again, his mouth moving subtly over hers. She leaned into the kiss. She never knew how deep and rich a kiss could feel, how indulging and free-falling, and yet filled with tenderness.

His mouth moved across her chin, down to her collarbone as he dropped small, lazy kisses across her skin. Belle's body felt stretched too tight, her nerves humming with pleasure. She wanted him, but wanted to make this night last.

Because no one knew what tomorrow brought.

She pulled away and sat on the bed. "You promised entertainment, Agent Cowboy. Undress for me."

He raised his dark brows. "Giving me commands, Doc?"

Feeling bashful, she curled her fingers against the quilt. "I'm a doctor and when patients undress, it's purely professional. I can't indulge. And you have a terrific body."

She ducked her head. "I guess that confession sounds foolish."

Expecting a grin or an offhand remark, she was surprised to see him join her, cup her face into his strong hands.

"I have a confession to make as well, Doc," he said softly. "I've been attracted to you from the moment we met, but fought it. It was just sexual, until I got to know you better and realized you're a woman who understands what it's like to be steel on the outside and velvet on the inside. The kind of woman who understands what it feels like to wake up in the dark with the reality in your head chasing your nightmares."

Her heart ached at the somberness in his voice. She wrapped her hands around his wrists. "Yes. And on those nights, you long to have someone to hold you and tell you it's going to be okay, no matter what."

The moment hung between them, intense and still. Then Kyle slid off the bed and stood before her. "Want me to get the popcorn?" He winked.

She laughed. "No. I want you to take your time, though."

Belle watched, her body thrumming with sweet anticipation. Tugging the T-shirt off, he pitched it onto the floor. Kyle slid the belt from his jeans, unzipped them and slid them down past lean hips and trim, muscled legs dusted with dark hair. He kicked them away, standing before her clad only in snug black boxers.

Then he pulled off his boxers, freeing his erection. She licked her lips. Wow. Kyle Anderson had the sleekness of a runner's body, punctured by scars and testimonies of his courage. After jumping off the bed, she explored with her fingers, testing each old bullet wound, the whitish-pink scar from the graze at the airport. He closed his eyes, making a humming sound as she caressed his torso and the muscles rippling beneath tanned skin, and then playfully dipped lower to cup him.

Kyle's eyes flew open. "Your turn, sweetheart."

She'd undressed for a lover before, but always with urgency brought on by eagerness and a rush for time. Tonight they had hours and she planned to enjoy each exquisite moment.

Each move was accompanied by a little shimmy of her hips, a smile playing on her face. The hunger and anticipation on his own face made her feel more than beautiful.

She felt cherished.

As she joined him on the bed, she sighed. "I'm on the pill, but what about you?"

He grinned. "My friend who owns this house was in the military. His motto is Always Prepared."

With another wink, he opened the nightstand drawer to reveal it was filled with condoms. Belle shook her head in frank amusement. "As long as they're not expired."

Kyle held up a foil wrapper. "He restocks every few months just in case. Part of the hospitality of lending out his home." His grin faded and that serious look returned. "But I've never taken up on that hospitality. Never had a reason to want to do so, until I met you. You're beautiful, Belle North, inside and out. That's a rare find in a weary world these days."

He crooked his finger at her. "Get your sweet little butt over here right now and help me put this on."

Belle helped him roll on the condom. He kissed her then. His mouth felt wonderful against her, warm, subtle pressure. This wasn't sex, but something more, deeper and richer.

He crushed her against him, his mouth devouring hers as he cupped the back of her head. The sharp, painful ache between her legs intensified. Never had she wanted a man as much as she wanted Kyle. Needed him against her, skin to skin, their bodies sweat slicked and rubbing against each other.

They rolled together on the bed, tangling together in need.

He touched her, palms skimming up the small of her back. "You're so sexy," he murmured against her skin as he kissed her neck. "Scared the hell out of me when I saw you on the ground. I wanted to kill whoever dared hurt you."

"Hey." She rubbed her face against him. "I'm okay now. Let's not go back there. I need to forget, Kyle. Help me to forget."

Then he fisted a hand in her hair, bent her head back and kissed her with such passion, she could barely breathe. Belle could think of nothing but Kyle, his taste in her mouth as he kissed her hard and deep, his skin slick and firm against hers, the silky hairs on his naked thighs rubbing against hers.

She opened her thighs. Kyle slipped a hand between her legs and caressed her, drawing a finger through her swollen folds. Little gasps came from her mouth as she clutched him, her mouth tasting the salty slickness of the hard curve of his shoulder. Belle nipped him lightly, earning a hiss of breath. With a thumb, he teased her, then sank a finger deep inside. Every delicious stroke cranked the sweet tension higher and higher until she was panting, she was so close, close...

Kyle's mouth encased one hard nipple. He bit lightly.

She shattered, nails digging into the hard muscles of his back as she screamed.

Pride and masculine possession shone in his gaze as he sat back, watching her. His limbs were long and sturdy, roped with muscle. Wide shoulders gave way to the classic V of narrow waist and hips.

Then he was nudging her thighs open, before settling between them. Desire ignited his eyes, made his mouth sexy and swollen. Kyle laced his fingers between hers, his muscled weight pinning her down.

The position was sweetly intimate. Kyle's body on top of hers, his hard chest pressed against her soft breasts, his sleekly muscled flanks entwined with her slender legs, his heated gaze fused to hers.

Kyle lowered his mouth and dropped a singularly sweet kiss on her mouth.

His hardness slid against her soaked folds. The slow, teasing move made her grit her teeth. An impish grin, so typically Kyle, warned he knew exactly how the motion drove her crazy. Belle rolled her hips upward.

He thrust hard into her, pushing past the resistance of her tiny internal muscles, sealing them hip and hip. Belle flinched a little. It had been a long time since she'd had sex.

A long time since she'd opened herself up to a man, let him into the most private part of her body...her heart.

"You feel so damn good," he muttered. Concern flared in his gaze. "You okay?"

She drew a long, trembling sigh. "I won't be if you don't get moving, Kyle."

Pleasure rippled through her as he began to move. Slowly out, then back inside her, building the heat between them. All the while his gaze was warm and soft on her, the look on his face telling her this was more than sex.

More than making love.

It was reigniting a flame both didn't want, but both needed.

It consumed them, sending them spiraling together into erotic bliss as his hips drove harder and faster into her, her hips rising to meet his frantic moves. Belle tightened her hands around his as the crisp hair on his chest rubbed against her sensitive nipples. She squeezed hard around him, feeling the incredible pressure build higher and higher, the pleasure as sweet and hot until she cried out and climaxed again, gasping for air, feeling as if she were flying.

And would never descend.

Kyle closed his eyes and threw his head back, the corded muscles on his neck straining as he gave one last thrust. He twitched inside her as Kyle shouted her name; he came hard, breath rasping in ragged pants.

For a long time after they lay in each other's arms, drowsing. She didn't know what tomorrow would bring. Or if they would find Anna. But for now Belle was content to live in the moment.

Chapter 20

In the morning Kyle received a phone call that Jesse Dugin was in custody.

Kyle kissed her a swift goodbye, his blue gaze serious. "Even though we have him, be careful, Belle. Stay here if you can, and if you must leave, check in with me at all times."

She kissed him back. "No worries. I plan to call in sick and lounge around your house. Maybe catch up with some light reading."

"Medical textbooks?" he asked, his tone light and teasing.

When he kissed her again and left, Belle couldn't stop thinking about the loss of Mike Patterson and his connection to the case.

Something else Mike had said before he died nagged at her. Mike indicated that Anna was perfectly safe, but whoever had taken her planned to ship her out of the country.

Mike might have been a lot of things, but she knew he'd never hurt a child. Or participate in any criminal act involving a child. People did change, but Belle believed with all her heart that no matter how desperate for cash, Mike would never aid a kidnapping if the child would end up sexually abused.

No information had come out of questioning the women at the farmers market, Kyle had told her. The three workers had been tight-lipped. But maybe they would talk to her, as opposed to a federal agent…

Minutes later, showered and dressed in jeans, a long-sleeved baseball shirt and with her blond hair pulled back into a ponytail, she was out the door.

Belle took an Uber to the market. When she arrived, it was barely eight o'clock and only a few people frequented the stands. She walked to the tomato-and-cucumber kiosk.

The three Latina women smiled at her as she approached. Belle purchased a bag of tomatoes, admiring the rich red fruit. Belle breathed in the smell of fresh fruit and vegetables and fresh air.

"Are you Carmen, Rosa's friend?" she asked the youngest woman.

The two others, red bandannas over their graying hair, paused and stared as Carmen nodded. A volley of rapid-fire Spanish followed.

"I am not with the authorities," Belle told her in the same language. "I'm only trying to help Rosa find Anna, safe and alive."

Belle pulled a business card from her wallet and handed it to Carmen. "I'm a doctor. My name is Belle North. I work at the clinic."

Carmen relaxed, though the two others still tensed.

"You told the FBI agent who came to the trailer park that Rosa used to work with you cleaning houses. Surely she revealed a little of her personal life to you. You were friends."

Silence. Carmen fiddled with arranging the fruit.

"I know Rosa left her home because she couldn't pay the rent," Belle asserted. "But she paid for the tent at the park in cash and the clothing they found at the tent was expensive. Anna looked well-fed."

"Yes," Carmen finally admitted.

"Carmen, don't say another word," one woman admonished.

"Auntie, hush," Carmen replied. "We have to help Rosa. This lady can help her."

"I can. I only want to find Anna. What can you tell me about Rosa? Anything you can share will help us in the search for Anna."

"Rosa, she didn't leave the trailer because she couldn't pay the rent. She ran away because she was scared," Carmen admitted. "She told us she was running away from legal people and had to keep moving and keep hiding or they would find her."

"Running from the law? From police?"

The woman shook her head, making her black curls bounce. "No, no. Rosa had no problems with the law. Not afraid of police. She was afraid of Anna's father."

The mysterious father. Belle suspected the man was behind all of this.

"Did he threaten Rosa?"

"Yes. He's powerful man, has the law on his side," Carmen insisted.

Understanding flashed through her. "The court system. Rosa was afraid a judge would take Anna from her and give full custody to her father."

All three women nodded. "Rosa said that family wanted Anna. She had to quit her good job with the wealthy family and run away with Anna to hide her. Anna's father wanted her."

"Who is Anna's father?" Belle pressed.

Carmen frowned. "Rosa was afraid to say his name. She wouldn't tell us."

She started to ask more, but customers began flocking at the stand, and Carmen clammed up.

No further information would be forthcoming from the trio. Yet this was encouraging news. More than Kyle had managed to coax out from these women.

Anna's kidnapping might not have been to hurt her.

What if it was a custody battle and Anna's real father snatched her away?

Could Anna's father be Mike Patterson?

It made sense. Mike talked about wanting to have a family. He wasn't judicious in his affairs with women, and perhaps he'd had a fling with Rosa, resulting in Anna. And when Anna showed up at the clinic, bam!

Clutching the plastic bag of tomatoes, she took an Uber back to her house to get her car. Belle kept musing over what Carmen said.

Rich, powerful man.

Rosa feared him.

Anna liked gourmet food. Beef tenderloin with chipotle sauce. Where else would Anna taste such exotic food?

If Rosa worked for Mike, and he served dinners like that...

Beef tenderloin with chipotle sauce. They had the same menu at this year's fund-raising gala in Estancia Pointe for the clinic!

Mike had been there, of course. Maybe Rosa was a server. She didn't remember her, but she remembered the menu.

She had to talk with Rosa.

Sometime later, the nurse admitted her to Rosa's room. In her bed, Rosa sat up, watching television. Kyle had stopped by earlier to question her now that she was fully awake. Terrified of authorities, she'd refused to speak further with the police, the nurse told her. Only Belle had coaxed any information out of her.

They were moving her today from ICU into a regular room. Kyle had assigned a full-time police officer to guard her since security was less strict on that floor.

When she entered Rosa's room, the woman shut off the television and stared at her with wide eyes.

"Hi. Rosa. It's good to see you awake. I'm Dr. North, the doctor who treated Anna," she said in Spanish.

"I know," Rosa replied in the same language.

"Dr. Patterson is dead, Rosa. He can't hurt you anymore or take away Anna."

Rosa shook her head violently. "No. It's not safe. I can't tell you," she said.

"Who are you afraid of? I promise, we can protect you."

"No one can protect me. She has too much money. Did you find Jesse?"

"Yes, he's locked up and will never hurt you again. Why were you with him, Rosa?"

Rosa looked away. "He had money. I needed money to get away. Where's my Anna?"

"The FBI won't give up until Anna is found. But you have to tell us what you know."

Rosa compressed her lips. Her eyes darted back and forth as if expecting ghosts to emerge from all corners of the room.

"Did you work for Dr. Patterson? Is that how you found the clinic?"

The woman said nothing.

"Dr. Patterson was a friend of mine. He's dead, Rosa. If he is the one who threatened you, he can't hurt you anymore."

Tears filled the woman's eyes. "I wish I had never gone to your clinic in the first place. But I had no money and needed birth control pills."

Belle handed her a tissue to wipe her eyes. "You were serving at the fund-raiser for the clinic this year at Estancia Pointe, at the gold ballroom with the crystal chandeliers. You brought home a plate of leftover beef with chipotle sauce for your daughter. Anna loved it."

Wide-eyed, Rosa stared. She'd hit on a vein of truth. Belle continued. "You knew Dr. Patterson from somewhere, and you worked for a company that hired you to serve at the event. Who hired you, Rosa?"

Stomach churning, she leaned closer. "Is your real name Rosa or something else?"

The woman's body trembled. "Something else. Same as rich people's cars."

She racked her brain for Spanish names. "Mercedes?"

A startled blink. Bingo.

"Mercedes, who is scaring you so much? I'm sure that person is hiding Anna."

"Please," the woman whispered. "Find my Anna."

Belle leaned down, touched her hand. "We are trying everything. I promise you'll be protected. Who are you afraid of?"

Nothing. She tried again.

"Mercedes, I'm sure your family is worried about you. Do you want me to contact them for you?"

The woman's eyes filled with tears. "They don't care," she said in Spanish. "I left them when I was eighteen."

"Why?"

"They tried to force me into going to Chile to marry someone I didn't love."

"Your entire family is in Chile?"

Mercedes nodded. "I was born here when my parents lived in Florida. They're…wealthy. They moved back to their home country, but I grew up in Florida and didn't want to move back. Or get married."

"You do understand and speak English," Belle said slowly.

Mercedes nodded. "I'm sorry, Dr. Belle," she said in English. "I didn't mean to lie to you. But my Anna means everything to me. And I'm so scared of losing her."

"Then help me find her. Who is her father? Was it Dr. Mike?"

Mercedes's mouth wobbled. "You won't help me. Not

if you knew." The woman closed her eyes. "Go away. I'm tired."

"I will help you. I promise," Belle protested.

Nothing. Frustrated, Belle left the room and headed downstairs.

In all likelihood, Mike must have had an affair with Mercedes in the past, and the result was Anna. Maybe she worked for Mike as a maid. With the long hours at the clinic, and his gambling habit, Mike might have grown lonely for female company.

But it didn't add up. Anna was six years old. Why threaten to take Anna away now? Unless Mike hadn't known of her existence until recently.

And how did Jesse Dugin come into the picture? If Dugin murdered Mike, why attack me? Why am I a threat?

Everything was conjecture. The only clue she had was the fund-raising gala. Mercedes had been there.

Mindy Worthington had chaired the event. Her mother's friend would know exactly what caterer they used to serve the food.

Outside the hospital, she called Kyle. He answered on the first ring. "Hi, Doc."

Warmth pulsed through her at the sexy drawl of his deep voice. Forget about trying to remain impartial. She'd fallen head over high heels for this man.

Not that it would go anywhere. She had a career. And Kyle couldn't seem to move beyond his past.

"Hi, gorgeous," she said softly. "Any progress?"

"Dugin was trying to leave the country at the Miami airport, just as I thought. Homeland Security caught him, and Miami police are transporting him now up here. Should arrive in the next hour."

That meant Kyle was stuck at the police station. He would use all his powers of persuasion to coax information out of Jesse.

Belle relayed what she'd found out. "I think this is more a custody issue than any other kind of kidnapping. Rosa is afraid of Anna's father. Rosa's real name is Mercedes. I'm sure she changed it because she was running away. She has a wealthy family in Chile but ran from them when she was eighteen. She had to have worked for the caterer hired for the annual clinic gala. Soon as I find out who that was, I'm going to call them and talk to the owner."

A heavy intake of breath. "Be careful, Doc. Some of those companies pay under the table and don't like anyone snooping around."

"I'm not snooping. I'll ask about Mercedes because she was a hard worker and I'm interested in hiring her personally. I might even hire the catering company for a luncheon I'm hosting for my garden club."

He chuckled. "You'd make a good detective."

"I'd rather stick to medicine. Give me a good case of illness any day over this."

Silence for a moment. "I mean it, Belle. Be careful. The noose is tightening, and we don't want to risk losing Anna. Whoever has her must know that we're getting close."

"I will. Just think of me as your unofficial assistant."

"Report to me every place you go today. I want you to call. It doesn't matter if you go the beauty parlor or the grocery store, you let me know where you are every minute. Understand?"

Recognizing the sharp worry in his voice, she agreed.

"Gotta go, Doc. I'll see you later at the house." His voice softened to a sexy growl. "Maybe I'll give you that massage I promised last night."

She blew him a kiss and hung up.

Next she called Mindy Worthington, who answered on the first ring. "Belle, dear, how are you? I've been so worried since that terrible incident. I do wish you would have stayed with us."

Thinking of Evan and his attraction for her, she rolled her eyes. "I'm fine, Mrs. Worthington. But I need your help with something. When you hired the caterer for the Heart to Heart Gala this year, do you remember who you hired to cater the event?"

A slight pause. "Of course I do. Why?"

"Oh, just searching around for a good caterer for a luncheon I wish to plan. Who did you use?"

"Just a minute, dear. Let me find their contact information."

A minute later, Mindy got back on the phone. "The company I use is quite busy this time of year, dear. But there's another one I can recommend. Is there a reason you wish to use the same one?"

"I'm actually looking for a specific employee of theirs. Her name is Mercedes."

Silence a moment. "Oh, I see. Well, you can try them. All Star Fine Foods. I'll text the number soon as you hang up."

"Appreciate it."

"Hope this helps. I'm off to my spa day. Later, darling!"

Warm sunshine heated her face as she headed to her car. Florida in February was glorious, but she saw little of it because of work. She now had the opportunity to slow down, appreciate life. Appreciate not only the opportunities she'd been given, but contemplate the future with more confidence than she'd ever felt before.

A cardiology residency would set her on a path to a prestigious career with beaming approval from her family, and financial security for life.

A pediatric residency would set her on a path to a career she enjoyed, not as prestigious, and always, she'd have to deal with her family's disapproval. Their disappointment.

But it's my life. I have to live it, not them.

If today were your last day on earth, what decisions would you make?

Kyle's words from last night kept circulating in her mind. What decisions would she make?

Right now I'm deciding to find out if Rosa/Mercedes worked for All Star Fine Foods.

Inside her car, she dialed the number Mindy had texted her.

The phone rang a few times and went to voice mail. She left a message.

Now what? The company probably had a catering assignment and might not return her call until later.

But as she started up the car to leave, her cell rang. The number she'd just called.

"This is Ted Clare from All Star Fine Foods returning your call. You're looking for a catering company for an event?"

The man had a gruff voice, with a thick New York accent. Funny how certain professions evoked certain images. She'd envisioned a prissy, fussy man with a tall white hat, not a toughened type who sounded like a dockworker.

"Yes. Mindy Worthington told me you catered the gala for the clinic. There was a particular employee there, her name was Mercedes, you had hired. I'd like to know if you would recommend her because I'm looking for someone to cater an upcoming luncheon I'm hosting. Is she one of your employees?"

"Mercedes? Not sure. Got a last name?"

"It could be Rodriguez. I'm not exactly sure." Belle gave a description of Rosa/Mercedes. "Do you keep a list of people you employ?"

"We don't have permanent staff, but yeah, we have records."

Hope filled her. "Is there any way you can search for her for me? It would be extremely helpful."

"Yeah. I keep all the employee records at our corporate warehouse. Meet me there and I'll look through all of them and give you the ones you need."

He gave her the address and hung up.

Kyle didn't answer his phone, so she left a voice mail. "Hi, I'm meeting the owner of All Star Fine Foods at their warehouse in West Estancia Pointe. I'll let you know if I glean anything from the meeting."

Belle hung up and drove to the warehouse. It was across the railroad tracks, isolated, with a chain-link fence ringing the building. The building appeared out of commission. No sign, either. However, a sleek Mercedes was parked out front.

Unease crawled through her. For a thriving catering company, this business looked abandoned. Had the owner given her the wrong address?

On impulse, she used her cell phone to Google the catering company. They didn't have a website, but were listed as a catering company, and yes, this was their address. A few five-star reviews on Yelp, and about ten four-star reviews.

Well, at least they were legitimate.

A front door had been propped open, held in place by a rock. Belle walked inside. "Mr. Clare?"

The warehouse was cavernous, dimly lit, with lights glowing from a windowed office far to the left. Belle walked over to it and went inside.

"Mr. Clare?"

No answer.

Dust covered two desks. Stacks of files and papers tilted haphazardly to one side, threatening to spill over. If the owner expected to pull files from this mess…

If he kept everything on the computer, all she'd need was a printout.

Belle looked out at the warehouse. Crates were piled

high, floor to ceiling. Gray metal shelving held boxes and boxes. Curious, she walked outside and read one box.

Hill Country Chardonnay, the label read.

A tingling rushed down her spine. All Star Fine Foods wasn't a caterer. Mindy lied, or she didn't want to share the information. And why would they import wine if they were a food catering company?

She knew of one business in Estancia Pointe that did import wine.

Belle returned to the office and began combing through the shelves and desk drawers.

Midway through the second drawer, she found an invoice with Evan Worthington's name at the top.

Evan, the investment advisor. Evan, her childhood friend.

Stacks of wine magazines sagged on a shelf. Belle thumbed through them. One featured Evan on the cover, somberly staring at the camera as he held a bottle of wine.

She stared at the photo. Such a serious pose. Green eyes, that chin…

The magazine fell to the floor with a flutter of pages. "Oh dear God," Belle whispered.

The eyes. And then it slammed into her.

The way Anna nibbled on her thumbnail, just like…her father. Not Mike Patterson after all.

Belle ran out of the office, heading for the exit when a low chuckle came to her right. Frantic, she threaded through the crates.

She ran for the door leading outside, jiggled the knob. Locked from the outside. Trapped.

No way out. Whoever did this lured her here. So stupid of her to trust! A shadow moved in the dim light.

Screaming, she ran as the person approached. They planned this all along, to trap her here. Belle threaded through stacks of wood crates, desperately seeking another exit, fumbling for her cell phone to call Kyle. There, that reassuring red glow.

Energy flagging, she pushed on. Get away, her mind screamed.

This was the real enemy, who'd been standing before her all along. The one who would never let her speak the truth.

She darted around a stack of crates, zigged and zagged. Her lungs started burn as her heart rate accelerated. Can't do this much longer. A stitch began in her side, the muscle ache turning excruciating.

Maybe I should have worked out more in the gym. Belle almost laughed, but she hurt too much. Legs pumping, she ran. Up ahead, she saw the opened door of the warehouse. Someone would be outside, loading or unloading.

She opened her mouth to scream, using up the last bit of oxygen.

Gulping down a lungful of air, she flailed her hands. "Help me," she cried out, but the words came out as a whispered gasp.

And then she felt a prick in her arm and felt nothing more.

Chapter 21

Four hours of questioning and they'd gotten nowhere with Jesse Dugin. The man insisted on a lawyer and wouldn't say a word. Hands and ankles chained, he glared at them from the chair as Kyle sat across from him, the lawyer to Dugin's left.

Until Kyle laid his winning ace on the table—the DNA lifted from the motel room where Patterson had stayed.

"We have your DNA in Michael Patterson's room, Jesse." Kyle leaned close, maintaining eye contact. "You killed the doctor. There's enough evidence to send you away for life."

"Or to Old Sparky. Florida still has the death penalty," Roarke added.

Blood drained from the man's face. "I didn't want to do it. But the doc got scared, was going to blab everything. Had no choice."

"Jesse," his lawyer warned.

"No, I'm not taking the hit for this. You gotta work me out a deal."

"Oh, we'll deal. If you tell us what we need to know. Where the hell is Anna?" he demanded.

"No," the lawyer interrupted. "In return for Mr. Dugin's cooperation, we want a promise from the federal prosecutor of reduced charges."

"We'll work something out. But no deal until I know where the hell Anna is!" Kyle snapped.

Jesse banged his hand against the desk, making the handcuff rattle. "I told you I don't know!"

Kyle felt his impatience grow, forced it down. "Her name isn't Anna. What's her real name? We know what's going on. We know about the catering event, how Mercedes worked for rich people and then she had to bolt. And you were hired to find her."

The man's thin shoulders sagged. "Annalise. Kid's name is Annalise. The old lady wanted a family name. She insisted when Mercedes gave birth. It was part of the deal. The old lady controlled everything."

Alarm spread through Kyle. "Old lady. Related to Dr. Patterson?"

Jesse snorted. "You don't know squat. Patterson was same as me, hired to find Mercedes and the kid after they bolted. The clinic was a starting point because the old lady had sent Mercedes there to get birth control pills. Only the stupid photo the old lady gave me to ID the kid was so blurry that I had a hard time finding her, so I had to snatch other girls from the clinic until I finally got a photo of Mercedes from the ID badge she wore at the catering event."

"What was Patterson's part in this?" Roarke demanded.

"Patterson secretly photographed the kids at the clinic until we found the right one. Then he destroyed all the clinic medical records for Mercedes and Anna. I made my move on Mercedes, charmed her, gave her money and pretended to love her. She was desperate to get out of town and needed money. Patterson owed six figures and the old lady paid it all off."

"Who's the old lady?" Kyle asked.

Eyes darting to his lawyer, who nodded, Jesse sighed. "Mindy Worthington. She paid me to snatch Annalise and kill Mercedes."

Horror iced Kyle's spine.

"Don't you goons get it?" Jesse yelled. "Mercedes worked for the old lady and had an affair with her son. Worthington didn't give two squats how many bastards Evan fathered, until he couldn't have any more because of the cancer."

"The chemo made him sterile," he realized.

"Annalise is her only grandchild. She said her son got chemo and now he can never have kids and Annalise is her only hope of extending the lineage. When Mercedes wanted to take Annalise to Texas, the old lady threatened to sue for custody. Mercedes ran and Worthington hired me to find her."

"And kill Mercedes and steal Anna."

Jesse nodded. "The old lady's the real brains of that family, not her son."

Outside the interrogation room, he called Belle and got her voice mail. Then he checked messages, heard her sultry voice.

"Hi, I'm meeting the owner of All Star Fine Foods at their warehouse in West Estancia Pointe. I'll let you know if I glean anything from the meeting."

Minutes later, he did some checking through the Bureau's computer experts and found out not only the address of All Star Fine Foods, but that it was owned by...

Mindy Worthington.

Mindy was the one who had Anna. And Belle was walking straight into a trap.

Belle awoke feeling woozy and disoriented. Slowly, she forced her eyes open.

Think, think. Hard to recall anything, but every instinct screamed danger.

Belle went to move her hands and could not. Blinking to erase the head fog, she realized they were bound in front

of her with duct tape. Her legs, as well. She lay on a bed...
Craning her neck, she saw white walls. A white ceiling fan
spinning lazily overhead. Turning her head to the left, she
saw another room, without a door.

A single window displayed bright sunshine outside. The
air smelled slightly musty, as if this room had been unused
for a long time.

"Hello," she called out. Her lips were dry, cracked. She'd
have sold her soul for a drink of water right then.

Or an easy escape.

The door opened. Expecting an adult, or maybe even
that treacherous Mindy herself, the person slipping inside
shocked her.

"Anna," she called out in a hoarse whisper.

"Dr. North, why are you here?" The girl ran over to her.

"Help me. Get this tape off me," she urged.

She tried, but her thin fingers plucked uselessly at the
bindings around Belle's ankles.

"Try my hands."

After a few minutes, Anna succeeded in removing the
tape. Belle quickly undid her ankles.

She scrambled over to the window and her hopes sank.
A small patch of land outside, thick trees beyond. Beyond
the trees she saw a shimmer of sunlight on water.

Toto, I don't think we're in Estancia Pointe anymore.

"Water," she croaked.

Anna went into an adjoining room, returned with a bottle
of water. Belle drank it greedily, licked her lips.

"Where are we, honey?"

"I don't know. There's water all around us. It's like an
island."

The girl bit her lip. "It's scary at night. They told me to
never go out at night because of the mosquitoes."

Mosquitoes, water, probably someplace near the Everglades. Belle sat on the bed, rubbing her head. "How long have you been here? Are you all right?" she asked.

The girl looked fine. Her hair had been dyed blond, and she wore an expensive blue-and-white shorts-and-sweater outfit. Fear danced in her green eyes. But she was clean and looked well-fed.

"I'm fine," she said in rapid Spanish. "The lady, she told me to call her Grandmother, doesn't like me to speak Spanish. She said I have to forget that and my former life."

Not if I can get us both out of here. Belle opened the window, which slid upward only a few inches without noise. She pushed harder, but the window did not budge. No use trying to climb out.

Impact windows, with glass that would not easily shatter. She must still be in Florida. A chorus of insects hummed outside, accompanied by the distant croak of an alligator. The distinct roar of a generator filled the air, but no smell of diesel or gasoline, so the generator must not be by the building.

Wherever this place was, it was deep inside the Everglades. Or another swampy area, far from utilities.

"Anna, what did this grandmother tell you?"

The little girl chewed on her thumbnail. "She said my real daddy is her son and we were going to live far from Florida, in a place where no one would ever bother us."

Tears shimmered in Anna's eyes. "Grandmother said my mama is dead. Is it true, Dr. North? Will I ever see my real mama again?"

Belle hugged her. "It's not true. Your mama is fine. She's recovering in a hospital and they are taking good care of her. I'm going to do everything I can to make sure you see her again. Your mama misses you terribly."

"Why did this happen?" Anna whimpered. "Grandmother said I have to have private-school lessons and learn to be a lady, and in the place where we will live no one speaks Spanish. They changed my hair color, too."

"Anna, this is important. Do you remember anything about who took you here and how you got here?"

"No. All I remember is Jesse hurting Mama…" Tears swam in Anna's eyes again. "Then I felt this needle and when I woke up, I was here."

Dugin had drugged Anna and transported her here.

"Can you tell me anything at all about this place? Who's here during the day and night?"

"There's Mr. and Mrs. Clare are here all the time, except when my daddy visits. And my grandmother, but she never stays long. That's it, I think." Anna frowned. "Is he really my daddy?"

"Yes, I think so." The pounding ache in her head made it difficult to think. "Right now we have to figure out a way to contact the FBI agents who are looking for you. Who's here guarding you now?"

"Mr. Clare and Mrs. Clare. My grandmother has only been here once or twice during the day."

Anna's voice dropped. "There's a lot of alligators. I've heard them. Mrs. Clare says I can't play close to the water or they'll eat me."

Using a child's terror against her made Belle want to shake the unseen Mrs. Clare.

"Anna, do you know when they plan to take you to this place where you have to speak only English?"

Anna shook her head. "They wanted to go there last week, but my daddy said he had to set everything up yet. He argued with my grandmother that all the money wasn't in the right place yet and it would look too suspicious if she left all the sudden."

Before he died of a heart attack, Evan's father had purchased a palatial home in Switzerland. Evan must be transferring all the family money into a Swiss account for a permanent move to that country. If Mindy left in the middle of the social season, she'd need a good excuse.

Belle and Anna might have a little time to escape, but not much.

But how could they escape this house if there was no way in or out except by boat? Belle went into the adjacent bathroom. No door, only a curtain. She washed her face, dried it with a towel hanging on the rack to erase the grogginess. The bathroom, with its simple fixtures, was functional. Not upscale. But the mirror hanging over the sink was gilded and seemed incongruous.

Belle touched the mirror. *I've been here before.*

Motioning to Anna to remain quiet, she crept to the bedroom door, opened it and listened. Voices in the back, arguing.

Belle opened the door and slipped into the hallway. Oak flooring led to a living area. The voices were past the kitchen, and she could see two figures sitting on the screened-in porch. Two sofas in the living room and a square coffee table between them. Brown area rug, photos of fish and boats…

Evan's fishing camp house. She'd stayed here ten years ago with her brother, Evan and Mike Patterson. She'd been fifteen, tagging after her big brother and bragging she could outlast them on a fishing trip.

"It's a primitive house," Clint had warned. "Primitive for you, Belle. Generator, water pumped from a tank. No television. You might break a nail and then what would happen?"

It had only been for one night, but the memory stamped into her brain. The alligators surrounding the property were big and loud, but it was the snakes that scared her most. No road in. Without a boat, you were stuck.

Belle pushed past the pain in her head and inched her way to the kitchen to eavesdrop.

But she still felt dizzy and grabbed the counter, knocking over a pot. The people on the porch stopped talking. A door slammed and a bulky man in jeans, a grimy gray T-shirt strode in. A gun hung on a holster on his belt.

"You must be Mr. Clare," she guessed. "What do you think you're doing?"

"Keeping watch over you."

Belle backed away. "You truly think you can keep me prisoner here?"

"Not me. My employer. He's got plans for you." Clare licked his greasy lips and the glint in his eyes made her suddenly afraid. "You're going to be the good little wifey and please him in every way possible. Too bad, because you're really pretty. You and me could have a fun time together."

Wife? What madness was this?

Chin in the air, she glared at him. "Fun? With you? Doubtful."

"Maybe we still can, blondie."

Jerking back as his thumb traced her cheek, she shuddered. Kyle had touched her the same way, and the memory of his tender caress and the passion they'd shared fueled her resolve.

There must be a way to break free. I will see Kyle again. I will get Anna out of here.

When his hand laced around her wrist, she tried pulling free. "Let me go. What about your wife? Will she like you cheating on her?"

"She doesn't care." Licking his lips, he brought her closer.

"But Mrs. Worthington will."

Magic words, for he dropped his hand and sneered. "You're not worth it. I'll ask another ten grand for this stunt. But when it's all over, I'll have us a nice vacation house in the Caribbean and enough money for life."

She stormed out of the living room and retreated back into the bedroom. But this time, Anna wasn't alone.

Evan was with her. And judging from the look in his eyes, he wasn't pleased.

Chapter 22

Belle could be anywhere.

But with this lead, he knew the one person most likely to know her exact location. In his car, he called Clint North.

Voice mail. Again.

"Listen, you son of a bitch, your sister is in trouble and if you don't want her to die, then you'll cooperate. I'm through with you protecting your friends. I'm on my way to your house and if you're not there, I'm sending every available squad car to find you."

Minutes later, sirens blaring and lights flashing on his SUV, he parked in Clint's driveway. Phone in hand, Clint North stood outside, his expression pale beneath the light of the porch lantern.

"I was just returning your call…" he said.

Not wasting words, Kyle rushed out of the SUV and threw an arm up, backing North against the front door, pinning him there.

"Where the hell is Evan Worthington?" he roared.

"I don't know! Why do you want him?" Clint yelled.

"He's got her. I've tried her cell. Nothing. The last location she reported visiting is empty. Her car is missing and the person who took Anna has taken Belle."

Clint's gaze grew wide. "Oh my God. It can't be possible."

He spit out the details and Belle's brother gulped. Kyle eased his grip. "Where would Evan and Mindy Worthington go?"

The man shoved a hand through his hair. "Mindy loves Belle. She wouldn't harm her. Hell, at one point, Evan joked about marrying her."

Kyle fisted his hands in the other man's lapels. "Answer my question! Where would Evan take Belle? Does he have a place that's remote yet close by?"

"He has lots of places. I don't know!"

"Some place where he could hide a child as well as your sister. Think!"

The man sagged in his grip. "The fish camp. Evan has a house on a small patch of island in the middle of the Everglades. You can't get there by road. Only boat. I don't know the GPS location."

A swamp-locked house. Noisy airboats and bass boats with outboards. "If anything happens to her, you're responsible."

Clint sagged. "I know. I should have spoken up earlier."

The man's voice dropped to a painful whisper. "I'd hope that Evan wouldn't do anything to Belle. But he's changed, Agent Anderson. Ever since his cancer diagnosis, he's slid downhill. He's on the edge of a nervous breakdown when he's not roaring drunk."

Kyle phoned his partner to send a search party, praying they weren't too late.

"Belle." Evan's voice sounded strained and high. Arm around Anna in a tight grip, he studied her with a resigned expression.

All the years she'd known this man, she'd never seen him look this tense and fragile. Not even when he was diagnosed with the cancer that would eventually leave him sterile.

"You can't keep me here, Evan," she said in her softest

voice, not wanting to upset him. With that glazed look in his eyes and his nervous twitches, he was hanging on by a thread. No telling what he might do to her, or Anna, if provoked.

"You can't think that my family won't look for me. I'm not invisible."

"Mother already thought of that. She texted your parents from your cell phone that you were taking your family's boat out to think about your future and make a decision."

Removing his cell phone from his pocket, he glanced at the screen. "Two hours after sunset tonight, the boat will meet with a tragic accident, blown up due to a gas explosion. And you will be officially listed as lost at sea. We will be on the yacht bound for the Caribbean soon after and married in another country. Anna is my daughter, and you'll be my wife. One big, happy family."

He didn't sound happy, but angry and bitter.

"Evan, please. We were friends once. Do you really think I'd go along with this?"

For a moment he looked defeated. And then that wildness entered his gaze again. "It doesn't matter, Belle. It's what my mother wants. She wants a grandchild to continue the line and Anna is it. Her only grandchild. What she wants, she gets. It's been like that since my father died. She's always controlled my life."

He didn't want this marriage any more than she did. Kept as a prisoner, never able to escape on her own, Belle saw her future.

Evan had resigned himself to his fate.

She had to try reasoning with him again. "You survived cancer. Chemotherapy. You have a successful career. You have an entire life of your own choosing, Evan. You can break free of your mother and her expectations."

A cynical laugh, so filled with bitterness, rang from his throat. "Like you have done, Belle? You always do whatever your mother insists. Working for that cardiologist when you know you don't want that for your career. Searching for a cardiology residency because it will please your parents. No wonder my mother thought you were malleable. You are."

He hugged Anna tighter and she whimpered. Belle gingerly sat on the bed's edge. Reasoning with him might help. She couldn't reason with Clare. He listened only to money.

"You're right, Evan. I have been too soft when it comes to my future. But that ends here. I'm willing to change and take charge of my life. You can, as well. And give Anna a future where you won't be a fugitive on the run from the law, living in another country. Switzerland year-round? You don't even like the cold!"

For a moment, hope flared in his green eyes. Then it died. "No. It's too late, Belle. I owe my mother everything. My life, my money, everything. This is the only solution."

No. There had to be another one. *Keep him talking—glean as much as you can from him.* She pointed to his cell. "What time is it? I'm so out of it."

Guilt flickered on his expression. "I'm sorry about that. Ted had to knock you out."

The numbers on his cell-phone screen read two o'clock.

Evan kissed Anna's head. "Go outside and tell Mr. and Mrs. Clare you want to play on the swings, honey. We're going to leave here at sunset and then you'll be on a big boat on the ocean. It will be a wonderful adventure."

Anna's lower lip wobbled. Belle nodded at her. "It's okay, Anna. Go play. Be careful."

Evan watched his daughter leave. "She's so pretty. I worry about her out there, so I ordered the Clares to watch her at all times when she's outside."

Belle tried again. "Evan, I'm sorry about the cancer. But you don't have to be a victim anymore. Help me and help Anna. I know you care about her."

"I do," he whispered. "I always wanted a child. She's

my only hope, Belle. I wanted to die after chemo was over and they told me I'd never have a family of my own. They warned me before chemo what might happen and offered to freeze my sperm, but I was too damn arrogant and just laughed. I would be fine."

"Evan." Belle's throat tightened with emotion. "Anna is your daughter from an affair with Mercedes. Did she work for you?"

He nodded. "Her family's from Chile. She was born here while they lived in Florida, but when she turned eighteen, they wanted to return so she could marry this wealthy cattle rancher. They said if she didn't, they'd disinherit her. So she left them and found a job with my family through my mother's company."

"And you slept with her."

"I loved her. Thought I did. But my career meant more to me than anything else, so I returned to Boston and nothing came of it." He snorted. "I didn't even know she was pregnant. My mother never told me. Just paid the hospital bill and let Mercedes remain at the house after Anna was born and paid her to work there, but insisted Mercedes go on birth control pills. Mother told me she would always clean up my 'mistakes.'"

"She's not a mistake, Evan. Anna is a sweet, smart little girl." Belle tried to appeal to the side of him that wanted to keep Anna safe. "But she's scared and grief stricken because she thinks her mother is dead. You have to remedy this."

He didn't seem to hear her. "I was such an arrogant jerk, making money, living the life, not caring about anything or anyone other than myself. And then I got the cancer. I wanted to die. Last year when my mother told me Anna was mine, I found a reason to live again."

Her hand covered his. "Then let her go, Evan. Let her go before your mother returns and something goes wrong. Before someone gets hurt."

"I can't. You've always been the strong one, Belle, the one to find the way home. Not me." He kissed her cheek. "I'm going to lie down and take a nap. I suggest you rest, as well."

Evan walked out of the bedroom, closing the door behind him. Belle rubbed her temple. It was up to her now.

And then she spotted what he'd left on the bedspread.

His cell phone.

The way home.

Hope flared inside. She gazed at it, realized there wasn't a signal. But she remembered her last visit here. Clint had taken her fishing a short distance from the cabin and she'd kept testing her phone for a signal. In the middle of the water, there was a chance she could get a weak signal.

Taking the cell phone, she quietly slipped downstairs out of the bedroom.

Evan's fourteen-foot bass fishing boat was the only boat at the dock. The flat-bottomed skiff wouldn't help her escape, not when she didn't have the ignition key. Belle searched the craft for an emergency transponder. Nothing.

No way in or out. The mosquitoes were horrible, but they wouldn't kill her. The gators would. Or the snakes. She shuddered. The grassy wetlands were filled with danger. During the day, they might be able to wade out because the water was seldom more than three feet deep in places.

But water moccasins and alligators made it too dangerous.

Clutching Evan's phone, Belle went into the living room and peered downward. Outside, a stout woman pushed Anna on a swing as Ted Clare stood guard. The man would never suspect her leaving. He probably thought she was helpless.

Belle crept down the stairs and out the front door, her sneakers making little noise on the grass. The dock was a short distance from the cabin. A well-worn path cut through the thick brush.

Even if Kyle sent up helicopters, they'd have trouble finding this building. It was secluded and private.

At the dock, Evan's flat-bottomed skiff remained tied to a piling. No keys. No way would she leave Anna here along with the Clares and a man who was perilously close to falling to pieces.

She didn't have any hope of finding land. But she didn't need land. She needed a signal. Belle gazed into the murky water. It couldn't be more than waist deep.

If her plan worked, the FBI could find her. If not, at least she'd prevent anyone from leaving.

Belle jumped into the skiff and set down Evan's phone. The battery was running low.

After untying the skiff, she used one of the oars on board to push off. Paddling quietly, she headed through the cypress trees flanking the water until reaching the open trail of water used by boaters. The cell phone registered a weak signal.

Immediately she dialed 911. "Nine-one-one, what is the address of your emergency?" the dispatcher asked in a faint voice.

"I don't know. Operator, my name is Belle North and I'm being held prisoner in Evan Worthington's fish camp in the Everglades, north of I-75. There are two people armed with guns. They're moving us at sunset. You need to call FBI Agent Kyle Anderson and tell him…"

The line went dead.

Frustration bit her. Hopefully the dispatcher had heard her. She glanced at the phone. Chances of anyone picking up the GPS signal were dim, but still…if it meant they'd be found.

Belle placed the phone on one of the boat's benches. She looked around. Water, so much water. The distant croak of an alligator warned she was not alone. Insects hummed in the nearby trees and a great blue heron flew overhead. She envied the bird's freedom.

If she stayed here, used the oars to steer herself south, she might be able to flag someone down. But this waterway was seldom used by boaters during the week, and besides, there was Anna.

I can't leave her alone.

The boat could stay here and get spotted. She could not.

Taking a deep breath, she climbed out and lowered herself into the murky water. It was warm as bath water. In strong, sure strokes, she swam back toward the cabin. To keep herself calm, she mentally recited a list from her anatomy class.

Something splashed into the water from the trees. An S shape, wending its way toward her.

Cervical vertebrae, seven bones. Thoracic vertebrae, twelve bones.

Water moccasin.

Lumbar vertebrae, five bones. Sacral vertebrae, five bones at birth...

Closer now. The snake headed straight for her. Razor-sharp saw grass blocked part of the waterway, but she kept swimming, biting her lip when the grass cut her hand. Now she bled freely, letting every predator in the water know she was injured.

Belle swam faster, kicking with all her might. She spied the dock ahead, a wooden ladder leading to safety.

Ribs, ribs, oh God, the ribs.

Muscles burning, her lungs bellowing air, she pushed harder than ever before. The ladder!

Grabbing it, she hoisted herself up, gasping for breath. Shaken, she lay on the dock, watched the snake swim lazily by.

Too close.

On shaky feet she stood, brushing off her wet clothing when a hand roughly seized her.

"Where the hell did you think you were going?" Ted Clare roared.

Hands went around her neck, squeezing tight. Belle gasped, the edges of her vision growing cloudy.

She was going to die out here.

Chapter 23

Maybe he was a louse in his former marriage, maybe he'd lived his life on the edge, all for the career. Maybe he screwed up a lot. But right now, Kyle would have sold his soul for a break. A big one.

He got it in the form of an emergency dispatcher relaying a call from Belle, out in the middle of the godforsaken swamp.

It was too risky to send up helicopters. The sound would alert Belle's captors.

But it wasn't too risky for his new best friend—a stealth drone. The unmanned aerial drone had optical, zoom and thermal cameras.

It had flown to the spot they'd tracked down via the cell phone's GPS signal. Weak, but traceable. Though the thick canopy of trees made it difficult to see, they could pinpoint the cabin, see the thermal imaging that five people were inside.

Belle and Anna, plus Evan probably. But how heavily armed were the two others?

No way would he risk Belle's and Anna's lives.

About a half mile close to the cabin, they cut the engines on the skiffs and paddled toward the island cabin. An alligator grunted nearby and he saw the sleek black outline of a water moccasin glide through the murky water. A rich, fermented smell permeated his nostrils as sweat trickled down his back.

They were clad all in dark clothing to blend in, bullet-proof vests covering their torsos. As the sun dipped lower into the sky, he stuffed down his fear. Emotions served no purpose on a mission. Kyle shifted his weight, the light-weight Kevlar vest increasing his body heat. Body armor was important on a mission like this.

Suddenly a voice spoke into his earbud. "Pinged the signal. It's coming from a boat drifting in the water."

He and Roarke exchanged glances as the agents and police surrounded the boat. Empty, but for a cell phone. An officer handed it to him. Evan Worthington's iPhone. What the hell was it doing out here?

Someone could have planted it here to guide them. Or lure them into a trap.

Majestic cypress trees flanked the waterway leading to the cabin. He caught a glimpse of gray paint, a roof. Trees on the island shielded the cabin from view, but the dock was straight ahead.

No boat. The skiff must belong to the cabin.

They'd obtained blueprints of the cabin before heading out. Downstairs was storage, the living quarters above.

They pulled up as a detective scanned the island with a thermal-imaging device. No one outside. The dock was a short distance from the cabin, with a path marching through the trees. Fortunately, no one could see it from the cabin.

With the stealth of a big jungle cat, they docked and then headed for the cabin, moving silently down the pathway. Ahead, Roarke used a thermal-imaging scanner to check for body heat inside the cabin.

No way of telling where Belle and Anna were. Adren-aline pumped through his veins. The ground beneath his boots was soft and slightly muddy, so he stuck to the rocks scattered on the path. They moved fast through the pathway. An opening in the trees showed the gray cabin on stilts silhouetted by the setting sun.

Dangerous to move about in the daylight. He preferred waiting for dark, but Belle's message indicated Worthington was moving them out when night fell. Several officers and agents rounded the cabin to the back.

He motioned to approach and they crept up the front stairs. A board creaked under Roarke's weight. Everyone froze.

When no one came outside to investigate, they kept going. Opening the door quietly, they sneaked into the hallway.

A petite figure sat there, crying. Kyle motioned for quiet. Anna.

She gasped, seeing them, but he held a finger to his mouth and lowered his gun. Kyle whispered into her ear.

"I'm with the FBI, here to rescue you, honey. Are you Anna?"

She nodded.

"Where's Belle?" he whispered.

Anna pointed to the room at the end of the hallway.

Kyle hesitated only a minute. Even with the child outside, there was danger of her getting hit if this turned into a gun battle. He quietly removed his Kevlar vest and put it around her. Too big, but it offered some protection at least.

No way was he going to lose this little girl. Not on his watch.

Kyle motioned for two police officers to take her outside.

Once Anna was gone, he moved on. Leading the way, Kyle burst into the living room. "FBI! Throw down your weapons and hands in the air."

Gunfire exploded. He saw a tall woman with a pistol firing at them and a man herding Belle toward the kitchen.

They took cover, firing at the woman. She screamed and dropped the gun as he shot her in the legs.

Weapon in hand, he rushed into the living room, only to see Ted Clare holding Belle, the muzzle against Belle's temple. Bruises ringed her neck.

Someone had tried to strangle her. His temper sailed dangerously out of control. Kyle forced down all emotions.

"Let her go, or I'll blow her brains out."

Belle looked so calm and beautiful.

"I'm getting the hell out of here and she's coming with me. Make a move and I'll blow her brains out." Clare's eyes darted back and forth between him and the other agents.

"Hold your fire," he warned the team. "Easy, Clare. You're surrounded. You're not getting out of here."

"The hell with that! I'm not going to prison," he yelled, the pistol digging deeper into Belle's temple.

Far from looking panicked, Belle looked intense, as if she concentrated on something.

"Did you know the human body has 206 bones?" she asked Clare in a calm voice.

"Shut up," the man snarled, inching toward the door.

Belle was reciting anatomy. Admiration threaded through his intense fear for her. The woman was a rock.

"And the bone easiest to break in the human body is your clavicle, also known as your collarbone?"

No answer. Clare kept dragging her backward in the direction of the dock.

"Of course, if you break a bone, any bone, you would want a nondisplaced fracture, which is far safer since both parts of the broken bone remain in alignment..."

Clare turned his head to look down at her. "Will you shut..."

Belle twisted, ducked, a perfect execution of the move he'd taught her, and then dropped. NOW!

Head shot. Kyle had fired.

A red mist filled the air as the bullet met its mark. Clare dropped to the ground.

Panting, he ran toward Belle.

"You bastard. Trying to steal my bride?" a man asked.

Kyle turned, saw Evan Worthington pointing a gun straight at him. Gunfire cracked through the air and pain exploded in his body.

Damn. "I'm bleeding." He put a hand to his chest and laughed with disbelief as his fingers came back stained red.

And then his legs gave out and he collapsed to the ground.

Chapter 24

As police wrestled Evan to the floor, Belle raced toward Kyle. He lay still, so damn still, on the ground. She felt his pulse. Weak and thready.

"I need a knife, cut off his shirt," she ordered.

Roarke brought out a wicked-looking black knife from a sheath on his belt and sliced through the fabric. He pulled it open to reveal Kyle's tanned chest, the mat of dark hair she'd loved running her fingers through and a round puncture wound.

Single gunshot round to the chest. Gasping, he stared up at her.

Blood, so much damn blood. Red bubbled up from his skin as he gasped. His lungs struggled to fight the increased wound pressure, and Kyle breathed harder.

Her mind shifted into automatic as she listened for breath sounds that came sharper, more wheezing. She couldn't tell if the wound was hissing, the classic sign. *Always assume any penetrating chest wound is sucking.*

If she didn't seal this, Kyle's left lung could collapse in minutes. She had to seal it and still allow air to escape while the lungs inflated.

"Helicopter's on its way. They'll lower a basket for him and rush him to trauma." Roarke knelt beside her. "Jesus, Kyle, hang in there."

They didn't have time. "I need tin foil or plastic wrap from the kitchen, and duct tape. Hurry!"

"Duct tape?" one agent asked.

"For God's sake, everyone has duct tape. Go!"

Kyle's face grew paler and his breathing more ragged.

A police officer rushed over with a length of plastic wrap. Belle tore off a piece, placed it against Kyle's skin, and then cut the duct tape to seal the plastic on three sides. Her mind functioned as she was trained, as if Kyle were an ordinary trauma patient she'd treated in her rounds in the ER during medical school.

As if he were a stranger, not the man she loved. The man who'd made her laugh, taught her to take a hard look at life and what she truly wanted.

Kyle seized her hand. "Belle," he gasped. "Wanna tell you…"

"You're going to be all right, Kyle. Breathe, just breathe," she told him, listening to the chest wound.

Some air escaped, but not as much. She checked for physical signs of a tension pneumothorax, in which a collapsed lung leaked air and pushed the lung to the body's other side. He could die if that happened. Belle glanced at his face. No blue lips yet, but he was too damn pale and still gasping for breath.

With Roarke's help, she elevated his feet, covered him with a blanket to keep Kyle warm. Belle rubbed his hands. "Hang in there, cowboy agent," she whispered. "I'm not going to lose you."

Finally the sounds of a helicopter sounded overhead. Medics came inside with a basket. She followed them outside, telling them his vitals.

They took Anna as well as a precaution, promising to take good care of her.

"Belle," Anna cried out. "Come with us."

Tears formed in her eyes. She hugged her. "You'll be fine, sweetheart. Go!"

Watching the helo fly away, she fisted her hands. "Take good care of him," she whispered.

Then she silently climbed into one of the sleek boats at the dock. Roarke helped her, and sat by her the entire time.

Flashing lights from police and FBI cars lined the parking lot at the marina where they docked. Belle caught sight of a black Mercedes.

"Mom," she whispered, running to meet her parents.

Clint was there as well, hugging her, crying. Between hugs, they told her the entire story, how the FBI had discovered Mindy's plans, and then escorted them to the marina to wait for news.

"I'm so sorry, Belle," Clint sobbed. "I didn't know Evan had lost it like he did."

"It's okay," she murmured, grateful to be in all of their arms.

Lifting her head, she saw a pale Mindy Worthington being led away in handcuffs. Shirley North glared at her. "Excuse me a minute, Belle."

Astonished, she watched her prim, proper mother stride over to Mindy and slap her across the face. "You bitch," she snapped. "How dare you take my daughter away from me!"

The police pulled Mindy away and placed her into the police car. Belle ran over to her mother. "It's okay, Mom. I'm okay."

"Your neck. Oh, honey, what did they do to you?" Shirley touched her, tears in her eyes.

"One of them hurt me, but it's okay. I guess he realized at the last minute it wasn't a good idea to strangle the future wife of Evan Worthington."

She explained quickly what happened.

Hands trembling, her mother touched her face. "I almost lost you once, Belle. I never thought this would happen again."

"Mom? Again?"

Her mother nodded. "We'll talk in the car."

As they headed toward the hospital, her mother and father sitting with her in the backseat, Shirley finally told her. "You were kidnapped as a child, Belle. The FBI saved you."

She clenched and unclenched her hands, trying to grapple with reality.

"When? How?" She gave a brittle laugh. "It's impossible. There would be a record and Harvard would have investigated, done a background check when I entered medical school."

"The records were sealed. You were only three years old." Mrs. North began twisting and untwisting her hands. "It happened when we lived in New York."

She waited, staring at her mother.

"I left you with a second cousin and his girlfriend who lived in Manhattan while your father and I were attending a Broadway play. Bart owned the building, and security was excellent so I was confident you were safe." Shirley gave a humorless laugh. "I don't even recall what play it was. Halfway through, the usher told us there was an emergency. You were missing."

Belle's throat went dry.

"The FBI got involved. The ransom call came two hours later." Mrs. North looked at her hands as if she didn't know what to do with them. "One million dollars. Cash only. Before we even went to the bank, the police found you fast asleep, unharmed, in an apartment two floors below. My cousin's girlfriend took you, kept you there in her place. The FBI found out Bart was nearly broke and living a life of luxury he couldn't afford. They took Bart in for questioning and he broke down."

She felt as if she couldn't breathe. "That's why you moved away from New York."

Her mother nodded. "Bart got twenty years in prison—his girlfriend got only ten. But after that, I didn't feel safe anymore in the city. Not around anyone other than my immediate family."

No wonder her mother seldom visited New York. Shirley always blamed the rapid pace of the city and the cold.

Her mind did rapid calculations. "Twenty years in prison...he's out by now."

Her father offered a grim smile. "His father made sure Bart got a one-way ticket to the Midwest. Got him a job working for an insurance firm. I heard he married, has a family. He tried to contact us a few times to apologize. I told him I'd forgive him when hell had a cold snap. Or two. Every year on the anniversary of your kidnapping, I always send a private investigator to check on Bart and make sure he's far, far away from you."

No wonder her mother always kept an eye on what Belle did. All these years Shirley lived with the terror of something else bad happening to Belle.

"Why didn't you tell me?" she asked gently.

"Because I was terrified you would blame me for being a poor mother." Shirley looked at her, her blue eyes growing moist.

A lump clogged her throat. "Oh, Mom." She held out her arms.

For a long moment, they hugged each other. Shirley North wasn't the hugging type, but she didn't pull back or try to resist. With some effort, Belle swallowed her emotions as Shirley finally did pull away, dabbed at her eyes with a handkerchief in the pocket of her linen pants. Tears had ruined her mascara.

Her mother. Always so perfect, groomed and in control.

The curtain behind all that lifted, showing Belle the real woman behind the mask.

"I would never blame you. Thank you for telling me. It wasn't your fault." Belle smiled at her, wiped her own eyes. "I'm glad you did."

Shirley hugged her again. "Whatever that young FBI agent needs, let us know. Anything. We owe him."

Minutes later, escorted by two police cars screeching their sirens, they pulled up to the hospital. But the doctors and nurses refused to allow her entrance into surgery.

So she waited outside, pacing. A few minutes later, Roarke came into the hallway. Belle ran to him and hugged him tight.

Tears clogged her throat. "He has to be okay," she said fiercely. "He has to be. They wouldn't let me into surgery with him."

Murmuring assurances, Roarke led her over to a bench in the hallway. He greeted her parents and Clint, and vanished for a minute, returning with a box of tissues. Belle wiped her eyes and blew her nose as Roarke joined the other agents and police officers drifting into the hallway to wait for news.

She wiped her eyes again. "Look at me. I'm supposed to be a professional."

"You are a professional, Belle," her father told her. He glanced at her mother. "Your mom and I have talked. We decided…if…when…"

Choking up, he struggled to talk. Her mother gripped his hand and continued. "We decided when you were rescued that it's your life to live. Whatever you wish to do, even if you decide not to be a doctor, we will support you."

Clint nodded. "I'm sorry I let you down, Belle. If you decide against a residency and want a permanent job running the clinic, it's yours."

Unable to speak, she nodded. Now was not the time to think about herself. She was too worried about Kyle.

Finally the surgeon came out of the double doors. She'd been in surgeries before, and knew from the woman's face even before she spoke that Kyle had survived.

"Agent Anderson will be fine. It'll be a rough road for a short time, but he's young and strong," the surgeon assured them.

More tears sprang to her eyes. "Thank you," she whispered.

"Thank you," the surgeon said. "If you didn't act so quickly to seal the chest wound, he would have died… Dr. North."

Belle blushed. The surgeon walked away and Roarke hugged her. "Thanks for saving him, Dr. North."

And then she was once more engulfed in a sea of arms, thanking her as the other FBI agents surrounded her. Through it all Belle could only think of Kyle, and seeing him again.

The man she loved was going to make it.

And what future they had together, she would negotiate later.

Chapter 25

No one told him hospital food could be this bad. If he never saw another cart from Dietary ever again, he'd be a happy man.

Today, after a long week recovering in the hospital, he headed home. Best thing of all was his chauffeur. Instead of her low-slung Corvette, Belle drove her parents' Mercedes.

Grateful he didn't have to stoop down, he climbed into the passenger seat, thanking again the doctors and nurses who came outside to bid him goodbye.

They saved his ass, but Belle, man, she saved his soul. He leaned back, looked at her as she started the car and they drove off. Unable to speak all the emotions churning inside, he rested, damn happy to be leaving the hospital in a luxury car instead of a box.

"We have a stop to make before you go home."

Kyle closed his eyes, resting his head against the window. Felt damn good to be out of that hospital bed. "Thanks for saving my life, Doc."

"Thanks for bringing the cavalry to save me, Agent Cowboy," she quipped back.

When he opened his eyes again, they were pulling into a long, curved driveway. Kyle blinked.

"Family reunion?" This was her brother's house.

Belle parked, mischief dancing in her dark eyes. "Of

a sort. There's someone, actually, two people, you need to see."

Clint greeted them at the door and shook his hand. "Thanks for saving my sister."

He led them inside, and then murmured about going upstairs to give them privacy.

Mercedes and her daughter sat on the sofa. Gone was the hospital gown and the rumbled hair. Mercedes wore her black hair short, and a yellow-and-green floral dress. Annalise was in pigtails and a cute pink outfit.

But it wasn't the clothing or the hairstyles. The look of perpetual fear on their faces had vanished. They looked happy. Normal.

Kyle whistled. "Look at you!"

Anna jumped up from the sofa and hugged him around the waist. He winced, grinned, hugged her back.

This was the best damn gift Belle could have delivered. Not every case ended like this. But for today, he'd revel in knowing she was safe, and with her mother.

"We're going to Chile next week." Anna gave him a shy smile. "My mama says her parents are coming tomorrow and they can't wait to meet me. We're going to live with them for a while in Chile. Do you think they'll like me, Kyle? What if they don't like me?"

With effort, he squatted down so they were eye level. "They'll love you," he assured her.

He reached into his trouser pocket and pulled out the silver dollar. Kyle placed it into her hands. "This is my lucky coin, Annabanana. I'm passing it on to you. Hold on to it, and when you get scared or nervous about your new home, or your grandparents, touch it and remember how strong you are."

Green eyes widening, she shook her head. "No, it's yours. What will you do for luck if you don't have your coin?"

Throat tight, he gazed at Belle. "I have something better than a coin."

Belle's fingers laced around his as he stood.

When they were in the car and headed away, Annalise and her mother waving madly from the driveway, he released a deep breath. "They're going to be okay."

"Yes. Clint told Mercedes's parents they are welcome to stay at his house as long as they wish, but I think they are anxious to get back to Chile and settle Annalise and Mercedes. They already found a private tutor for Annalise and Mercedes is talking about going back to the university. They were so happy to find out she was alive and well, and they have a granddaughter, that they begged Mercedes to come home with them."

He was quiet as she filled him in on details of the case, how Evan pleaded guilty in exchange for his testimony against his mother. Evan was destined for a long stay in a psychiatric institution and his mother had a date with a federal penitentiary.

When they were inside his house, he touched the counters, gazed at the sun shining through the windows. A nice house, yet he never completely felt home here.

"Do you need anything?" Belle opened the refrigerator, peering inside. "I can go shopping."

Kyle strode over, closed the door. "Answers. What about us, Belle? Have you thought about what you want?"

A flush suffused her high cheekbones. "I've thought about nothing else since they hauled you away, Kyle, when I was terrified I'd lose you. My match finally came through. I've been offered a pediatric residency at Mercy Memorial Hospital in DC."

"And?"

"I'm going to turn it down, stay here. With you. If you'll have me." She gave him a sideways glance. "I can always get a job working in a local clinic, get experience…"

"No." He framed her face with his hands. "Your dream is to become a pediatrician and that's what you're going to do."

"But…with you here…"

"I'll get a transfer. Top brass has been asking about me for months transferring to Quantico. I can teach, and go into the field as needed."

The rapt joy on her face assured him he made the right move. Gently, he kissed the corner of her soft, perfect mouth.

"I've been alone a long time, Belle. So very long. I preferred solitude, but up until I met you I didn't realize how lonely I felt. When a man finds the woman who heals him from the inside out, he'd be a fool to let her go. You have dreams, Belle, and I'll help them come true."

"What about your dreams? The FBI, and the field work…"

Giving a rueful glance at his chest, he shook his head. "Roarke has told me to slow down for a long time. I've been charging ahead like a locomotive for years, living to work. I need to work to live for a change."

He pointed to the bandage beneath his shirt. "I've had enough holes in me to last awhile. It doesn't mean I'm giving up, only shifting direction."

"You'll make a wonderful teacher." She leaned into his caress. "I guess this means you no longer despise doctors."

"Far from it." He kissed her, a kiss so deep he wanted to linger in the sensations for a long time. Kyle broke free of her mouth and kissed her nose, her forehead.

Couldn't wait until he got the green light for sex and he could kiss her all over.

"I'll need time off, to fully recuperate." Couldn't help his grin as he added, "Having my own personal physician willing to give me physical therapy in bed will be a great motivator."

A delicate flush suffused her complexion. Belle smiled.

"You okay with this?" he asked.

"Yes. Thank you for believing in me."

"Guess I always did. Just didn't believe in me enough."

Belle's gaze grew distant. "I've been lost, Kyle, catering to my parents' expectations. These past two weeks taught me being a doctor and healing people is more than making a living. It's a calling."

She took his hand, pressed it to her chest. "Not only on the outside, but here, so they can continue with their lives and be what they were meant to be. You taught me that, Kyle. Life is filled with pain and sorrow, but there's also a lot of joy, and you have to grab that joy with both hands and hold on for as long as possible. And remember the good times because they'll get you through the bad ones."

Deeply humbled, he drew her into his arms.

"You're so damn smart. Before I met you, I was moving through life, but not moving ahead with my life. Everything was my career, the job, the job that caused my separation from Caroline, blinded me to what was important. Oh—" he put a finger to her lips as she started to protest "—saving lives is important. You'll do it as a doctor and I'll keep doing it as an agent. But you taught me life is about taking a gamble with happiness, as well. If you don't risk it, you'll never find it."

He kissed her with everything he felt inside, all the longing and love he'd never thought he'd find again. This amazing woman had done more than save his life.

She saved his soul.

When they pulled apart, he stared down into her shining eyes and smoothed back a lock of her blond hair. "I can't promise we'll have an easy time of it. I can be impatient and get lost in the job, but you'll take a chance with me, I'll take a chance with you."

The corners of her mouth tipped upward. "Working at a residency means long hours and working six days a week. We won't get to see much of each other. And DC rent is expensive. We'd be better off sharing a place. Buy furniture, set up house."

"As long as you don't do the cooking," he teased.

Kyle dodged her playful punch. "One thing I have to do before we move. I have a visit to make, a very special little boy who has a very special heart."

Belle blinked, and warmth filled her expression. "You finally answered the parents' email."

He nodded. "I need…to do this. It won't be easy, but it will give me peace, meeting the child who received my daughter's heart. Will you go with me?"

Instead of answering, she flung her arms around him and kissed him again. Kyle closed his eyes, allowing himself to fully feel, to give what she offered with open arms. From now on, it would be different.

He'd been granted a second chance, thanks to a beautiful doctor who taught him love, with all its sorrows and joys, made everything worthwhile.

His life wasn't over.

It had only just begun.

* * * * *